HEIRS OF A BROKEN LAND
BOOK 2

WARRIOR
OF
DARKNESS

MARIE BILODEAU

Cover by Deranged Doctor Design

Editing by Jessica Torrance

Map by Kerri Elizabeth Gerow

To Jessica Torrance,

my sister,

my friend,

my muse.

(Nope, nothing about darkness.)

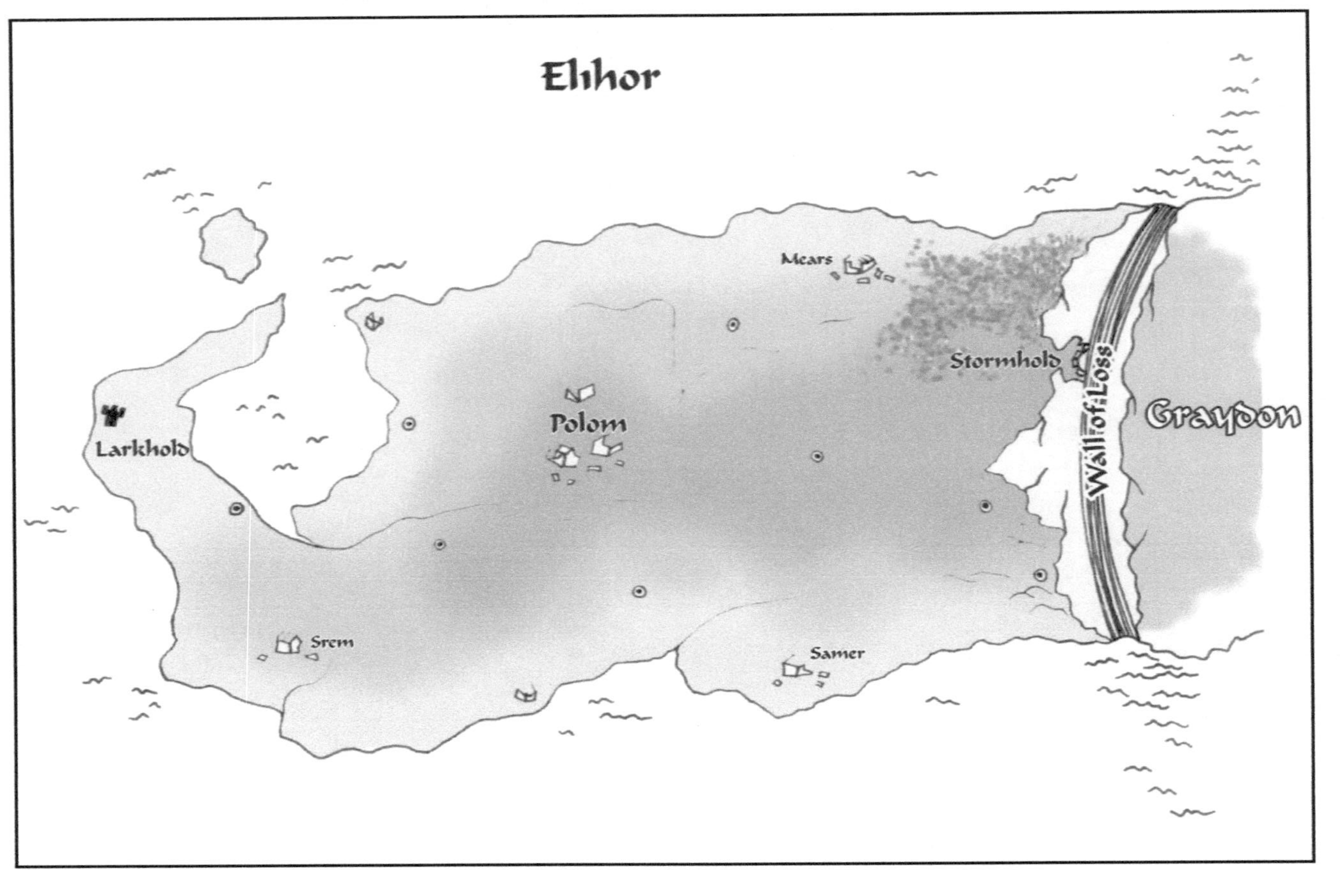
Elhor
Mears
Stormhold
Wall of Loss
Graydon
Polom
Larkhold
Srem
Samer

The world was fire.

Her world had always been fire.

Since she was a child, since her mother's death, since she had first wielded her family's ancestral blade. Graysword's swirling flames danced around her, but she couldn't reach out to grab it, her limbs refusing to move though her hand longed for the familiar weapon.

Nausea twisted her stomach into painful knots as memories sparked to life. She no longer had it. *She had dropped Graysword!*

And now, surrounded by dark red flames, unable to breathe, unable to move, for the first time in her life, Avarielle Grayloft, last daughter of a once-proud family, felt the cold hand of the Fates on her shoulder.

She drifted for some time between consciousness and the void, between light and dark, life and death. Sometimes she wondered where she was, other times she was certain she was in the Afterfate, and her life had proved unworthy of greater halls than this. She wondered where her family was and why she had not been greeted.

Memories softly visited her, first of her father and brothers, of her mentors, Trevon and Eliya, of her childhood and her land. Then her mother came, soothing her with kind words, memories forged from childhood dreams and stories. The words became unintelligible whispers as the madness receded, part of her fighting to break free of it, part of her aching to remain in the warmth of her mother's presence.

Then her father was there, laughing loudly. All three of her brothers surrounded her and their house was no longer empty but brimming with energy. She wasn't alone. Her family was back, no longer buried in unmarked graves. If buried at all.

Coolness washed over her from time to time, soothing her tingling nerve endings, taking some of her memories away. Physical sensation crept back in and the shell that surrounded her began to crumble. Her spirit reconnected with her body, igniting throbbing pain in every single bone and muscle.

"Please wake up," she heard someone plead, the voice tugging at another memory buried too deep for her to grasp. Her limbs were filled with lead and impossible to move.

She heard the voice again but sleep claimed her instead, her dreams broken a few times by the same plea. At one point, she thought she might have cracked open her eyes and seen a blurry face, but she couldn't decide whether that too had only been a dream.

She fought her first battle with Eloms again, only this time she was better prepared and no one had to die. There were no accusing faces, no stench of blood, and no guilt ripping her in half. There was no shame, no fear, no need to leave her beloved land and seek answers she could never find. No need to fight. No need to be hunted by the Circle.

Shirina!

The name jolted her. Her mind and body reeled as the face of the sorceress pierced through the last shreds of her dreams, the dark eyes, high cheekbones, smug look... Avarielle jerked awake, adrenaline and hatred pumping through her aching body. Her muscles felt thin, every joint rusted, and her skin was raw, leaving her gasping.

"Don't move, you're pretty hurt," the youth said. Avarielle gritted her teeth and shifted towards the young man's voice.

Her eyes widened as she saw the face before her— young, bewildered, frightened, and painfully familiar even if she had only met him once.

She swallowed, her throat dry and aching. Somehow, she forced out the syllables of his name.

"Jayden?"

Cassara's brother's eyes lit with suspicion, then with relief as he recognized her from the courtyard of Edoline. Whatever reservations he may have once held about Westlanders, they were quickly forgotten as he hugged her fiercely. Avarielle winced as her muscles screamed with the simple act of hugging the boy back.

Siabala's Rage.

Once formed as a prison to hold the most heinous criminals of magic in Elihor and Graydon, it had been rumored to still exist, somewhere far below the Wall of Loss. It had been created to control, and sometimes destroy, the link to magic of its incarcerated, leaving them little more than broken shells to be used and then killed at Siabala's whim.

Wonderful.

Avarielle ran her right hand over the jagged stones that formed the walls of the room, discovering every crack and irregularity, but still failing to find a door. Her broken lower left arm was secured close to her body with bandages Jayden had helped her fashion from her coat. At least the break was clean and would heal quickly enough. Then she would find Delora and finish her off.

She would have to be careful, she knew. She had broken bones before, but only after particularly impressive displays of danger, not following a single twist of her arm by an older woman. Whatever dark deals Delora had struck with Siabala seemed to have included physical as well as magical strength.

Avarielle still had a few of her knives. Delora had either been too smug or too foolish to remove all of the Westlander's weapons. She intended to put them to good use.

"You say that Delora passes through this wall when she leaves?" she asked Jayden. He nodded from his small bed, looking bored. She shook her head and turned back to study her prison.

The light was definitely magical: constant, unwavering, and tinting everything in a sickly yellow hue. The walls betrayed no seam or break, although Delora somehow had activated a door.

Probably with magic. She sighed and sat down, leaning on a smoother portion of the wall.

"What else did you see?"

Jayden considered her question for a moment, then shrugged.

She snapped. "You've been here this whole time, and you're not more interested in leaving? Don't you want to get out of here and help your sister? She's probably in danger right now!"

Avarielle's blood throbbed in her veins. The last few

moments before being taken prisoner were still a bit fuzzy, the memories struck silent by the magical energies of Delora's teleportation spell. Or by Shirina's little blast that had sent them both through the open portal.

Cassara had held onto Graysword, that much she remembered. To stop Delora from gaining Avarielle's magic, the princess had risked her own life, and then had been left behind with the treacherous sorceress.

Shirina would meet her final moments the next time they met, but if Cassara had been made to suffer at her hands, those last moments would be infinitely more painful.

Jayden's voice sliced through Avarielle's anger. "My sister's still alive?"

Avarielle closed her eyes, feeling like a fool. Of course, Delora had convinced the youth his family was gone to keep him in check. She turned to face him. His eyes were filled with hope and apprehension, and she wished she could see his wonder from the first time they had met. His innocence.

She crouched in front of him.

"Cassara and Altessa both live, as do your sister's old guards and maid. That's all I know. Your father, I'm really sorry to say, is dead."

Jayden swallowed hard. "My sister is in danger?"

Avarielle nodded, wanting to hit herself for snapping at the boy. She was too tired, concerned and in pain to be dealing with her own emotions right now, much less those of a young boy she barely knew.

"Cassara is probably being hunted right now, since she kept my sword safe." She shrugged to make light of the situation. "But she has magic of her own, and she's pretty wily. I'm sure she'll find a way to stay safe."

"Cassara has magic?" His eyes grew wide with excitement.

Avarielle grinned. "Yup! It's in the amulet she keeps, the one your mother gave her."

Jayden turned pale as she spoke, glancing behind her.

Avarielle spun around, jerking her left arm away from her body, the broken bone twisting in agony. She stumbled and fell to one knee, forcing her eyes to see beyond the explosions of light.

"Now now, don't go hurting yourself before I get the pleasure of doing so," Delora said. Avarielle breathed deeply and the pain receded. It would be impossible to fight with the broken limb, at least not until it was properly set and splinted. Ignoring the fatigue that assailed her body, she stood to face Delora.

"You were just telling Jayden about this amulet that would help keep his sister safe?"

Avarielle felt numb as she looked at the amulet that Delora dangled from her hand. *Cassara had no more magic to protect her!*

She forced her legs to remain steady as her head spun.

She didn't utter a word, certain her eyes conveyed the threat.

"I need your sword, Grayloft," Delora hissed, eyes sparkling with malevolence. "I'll make you a deal. You get me Graysword, and in return, I won't kill Cassara."

Jayden sucked in his breath.

"How do I know you'll keep your end of the bargain?" Avarielle asked.

"You don't." Delora knew she had won. Avarielle could see it in her posture, in the flash of her eyes and the slight curl of her lips.

Eli, she hated the woman. She debated attacking her, but her throbbing arm would impede her too much, and she was not immune to Delora's magic. At least it seemed that Cassara had managed to escape Delora, for now. She had to trust that the princess would find a way to keep herself, and Graysword, safe.

Avarielle shrugged. "Then I don't think I can help you."

The instant the words were spoken, it felt as though a thousand daggers pierced Avarielle's body. She gasped and fell to her knees, struggling not to collapse on her broken arm as waves of pain washed over her.

The pain was gone as quickly as it had come, leaving the warrior struggling for breath.

"I was hoping you'd say that," Delora crooned. "The way I see it," she approached Avarielle, her skirt at the edge of her vision, "is that if we force enough pain, agony and dark magic inside of you, Graysword's magic will react, and then I can track it and claim it. Simple, yet effective."

Avarielle took deep breaths and bided her time, part of her aching, part of her numb.

"And then," the insufferable woman continued, "I'll kill Cassara too, for stopping me from getting your sword in the first place."

The warrior reached for her boot and pulled out her long knife. Ignoring the pain in her arm, she leapt and swept the blade up in one clean motion. The blade grazed Delora's face, the sorceress moving faster than Avarielle had anticipated.

The warrior launched herself at her target again, screaming in fury and pain.

She never reached her, Delora's outstretched hand sending her flying back into the wall of stone. The Circle Elder maintained her spell, blood trickling from the fresh cut on her cheek.

Avarielle, crushed between a wall of stone and one of magic, gritted her teeth and fought for breath. Then her arm snapped again and she screamed. The magic wall released her. She crumpled to the floor.

"Bring her," Delora ordered. Avarielle was barely conscious enough to recognize the large obsidian feet that stopped near her face. It was one of those stone monsters that had attacked them, before Delora had taken her prisoner.

Jayden whimpered as the creature reached down,

grabbed her by the waist and tucked her under its arm as though she were a sack of flour. The stony arm pressed against her ribs. She could no longer feel her broken arm, her body growing warmer with each step the creature took.

As Avarielle slipped into darkness, she wished she could make sure Jayden was safe, or at least comfort him by letting him know she had no intention of betraying Cassara's location.

Even if it cost her her life.

2

Cassara ducked to avoid the jagged rocks jutting from the cavern's ceiling, which were barely illuminated by the flickering torchlight. She had never realized so many caves hid beneath Graydon. After two days within them, she hated every single last one of them.

"We should be near the exit, now," Loas whispered near her, his light brown hair gray in the dull light, his tall wiry frame bent in the low cave. She didn't bother nodding, concentrating on keeping her feet moving. The villagers all shuffled along quietly, following Loas, the young archer who had stepped up as leader since Arlos' death. His knowledge of the underground passages had proved invaluable.

He always kept a close eye on Cassara, feeling indebted to her since she had protected him from the fire of the winged monsters. She shivered, remembering the power of the amulet pulsating in her hand, the flames dancing before her, and her unwavering determination to win. Her *certainty* that she would win.

All of the villagers still seemed convinced that she could save them. She looked at Loas, so determined to get them out, so certain that he could make a difference.

Cassara yearned to still believe that about herself.

She also wished she could stand and stretch, but the ceiling was too low. She wished she could lie down and rest, but their fear was too great. And she wished she could hand the awkward Graysword off to someone else, but Avarielle wasn't here, and so it was hers to carry, for now.

She clutched the sword in a tattered blanket, hugging it close to her body. Though the blade was finely crafted and light, it was a still a burden for Cassara to bear. She tripped on the blanket, but Loas caught her arm and held her up. He didn't offer to take Graysword from her, as he had at first. She had quickly made it clear that she would not hand it off. She smiled sideways at him and wondered if she looked as tired as he did, hoping she didn't look worse.

Dayshon will have a wonderful surprise if I don't get to bathe, rest and change before meeting him again. She coughed and swallowed hard, sandpaper coating her throat.

If we make it. She forced the thought from her mind. Of course they would make it. Loas had said they were nearing the exit, and then they would find food, water and fresh air. With their aching lungs and grumbling stomachs, not even the fear of the flying monsters that had driven them into the caves was great enough to keep them here.

She remembered her meeting with Prince Dayshon in the courtyards of her home. The fresh sea air of Edoline brushing her cheeks and stroking her hair, the warm midday sun on her skin, his laughter and warm eyes…she clung to all of it, forcing her tired mind to find strength in the memory. Edoline was gone, but she could find a home, comfort and warmth in Massir. Then she would figure out what to do next. Cassara couldn't fathom leaving those comforts to trudge into the West and return Graysword. She knew she had to, but for now, just the weight of the sword was almost more than she could manage.

The villagers silently shuffled behind them and Cassara briefly wondered in what memories they were finding comfort.

"Wait here," Loas ordered. They halted, most of the villagers collapsing to the ground in exhaustion. Cassara heard a whimper and some crying, and made out that one of the children was dead. The mother clutched him as she rocked back and forth. A few of the villagers gathered to comfort her and take the child from her.

Cassara swallowed hard. She felt a hand on her arm and jumped. "Come with me," Loas whispered, glancing at the unfolding scene.

She followed his dwindling torch into the darkness. They would run out of light soon. He led her to a wall of rocks.

"It must have caved in." Loas shook his head. "I haven't been here since I was a boy. If we were stronger, we might be able to move the rocks, but…"

"We can't tell the others," Cassara whispered. It would be the end of them, she was certain. They would welcome dark sleep and never rise again.

Loas nodded as he stared at the wall, his eyes distant.

"Is there another way?"

He hesitated. "Three days further into the caves."

They both knew they wouldn't make it. The first of the children had died. More would soon follow, and then the adults would start to perish as well.

She put a comforting hand on Loas' arm. "We tell them it's near, and we keep moving. We keep moving until we can't anymore. Some of us might make it."

He nodded. She knew she hadn't fooled him. But none of the other villagers knew how far the exit was and she could convince them it was near. Give them hope to keep their feet moving. She wondered how easily the lie would tumble from her lips, and wished she could convince herself the lie was truth.

They walked back to the villagers, who sat in silence. The dead child was gone and she didn't ask what had happened to him. The mother clutched her knees and stared wide-eyed and unmoving. A few looked at Cassara.

The smile came as easily as the lie. "We're near. We'll be out soon."

A few smiles were returned, and Cassara sat down, laying Graysword to rest beside her. The silence was thick, and sleep evasive, so she pulled out her flute, letting her fingers slip comfortably into place.

She felt rusty. Her hands were tired and her lungs ached for fresh air. The instrument felt small and fragile after carrying Graysword for two straight days. She hadn't played it since they had been in Rockor, when Shirina and Avarielle had been with her.

Bringing the wood to her mouth she blew gently into it, evoking a soft song to exorcise the hopelessness that clung to her weary soul.

She could feel the dark magic slinking inside of her, like a snake wrenching skin from muscle, turning around her broken bone and churning the marrow. The pain blinded her with explosions of light, even through tightly-shut eyelids, robbing her of sight. She bit down hard on her own cheek to bring another pain to the forefront of her mind and distract her from the one she couldn't bear.

The warm trickle of blood on her chin felt reassuring.

Crack! The noise resonated in her skull, and she couldn't tell if her arm had shattered again or if something else had been broken.

Snap! She lost consciousness.

Seconds later the magic forced her awake, keeping her mind alert, not allowing Avarielle the escape into the oblivion she so desperately craved and feared.

The pain ended and she felt light and weightless. She couldn't tell if her limbs were still attached or if she was even breathing, every part of her completely numb. She was slipping into warmth and comfort when a voice commanded her attention.

"Do not push me, woman."

It was deep and growled more than spoken. Avarielle forced her eyes to open, and the mists of sleep slowly lifted. The numbness vanished, leaving a dull ache behind.

She preferred the pain to the void.

She was lying on something hard, either rock or wood, and shackles bit into her ankles and wrist. *Wrist.* Her left arm was also bound, but near her body. The slightest breath threw darts of pain up and down the limb. It was badly broken, several times over, and she doubted it would ever be the same.

She would worry about that later.

She concentrated on her right arm, the dull ache quickly turning into pain. She had struggled hard against the shackles, leaving behind only bloodied skin. But it was a pain she could deal with.

"We must continue, we approach our goal with each new attempt!" Delora implored.

The voice grumbled. "This is my land, woman. Remember that."

Delora mumbled something. Avarielle assumed it was an apology. She squinted to see the newcomer whose back was to her. He was big and bulky, towering over Delora. His flesh was gray and his limbs muscular. Avarielle could see he wore no shirt. His hair was flaming red and long, trickling down his back like a cascade of blood.

"Explain yourself." Avarielle thought she saw Delora flinch.

"I wish to bring down the Wall, as planned, my lord," Delora cooed. "I have the amulet, and is Graysword not what I need next as agreed?"

"Not at the price of one who holds an oath with me." Avarielle struggled to see more, to hear Delora's voice clearly. The large man turned to her, his red eyes piercing her, and she knew he had known she was awake all along. Guttural screams exploded from nearby, but Avarielle forced herself to remain focused on the man.

She couldn't make out his features as her tired eyes began to close, a sleep spell smothering the last flames of consciousness.

"It's time to go, my lady," Loas whispered near her ear, making Cassara start. She blinked a few times to get the cobwebs out of her eyes. She still held her flute loosely in her hand, which rested by her side. She must have fallen asleep while playing, and hadn't even noticed it. Dread formed in the pit of her stomach as she realized how easy it would be to just die in her sleep and never even know until crossing the threshold of the Afterfate.

"How long did I sleep?" she asked as Loas helped her up.

"Not long." He shrugged slightly. She nodded and picked up Graysword, her hands numb yet so tired that the very act of moving stirred the memory of pain. She clutched the sword, her arms cramping. She thought for an instant she could feel some magic course through her, a slight tingle on her skin nearest to the blade.

Pulling down on the cloth covering the sword, she examined the blade. It wasn't dull, and she doubted it could ever be. It caught the poor light of the torch and reflected some of it, but the blade did not shine with magic.

She shook her head and sighed, covering the blade again, wishing she at least had a scabbard to sheathe it in. She was tired and imagining magic. It was silly, she knew, and she couldn't afford fanciful flights of imagination. Even if she had her own magic, truth be told, she wasn't clear on how it would help her. They had encountered no demon since Avarielle and Shirina had left, and her magic couldn't provide them with food and water, which was what they needed most.

Her stomach was so badly cramped she doubted she

could even eat if food were offered to her. She sighed, trying to ignore the pain and fatigue, and turned to the villagers, who were shuffling to their feet.

"Time to go, it's not far." She managed another smile and turned quickly before it vanished. Loas took the lead with his torch, and she stayed close to him. She didn't dare count the villagers that followed. Of the seventy-two they had originally saved, she knew they were now less than sixty, perhaps even less than fifty. She wondered how many fewer they would be by the end of this day.

"What's that?" Loas suddenly asked. Cassara's heart leapt to her throat as she heard banging.

He stopped and handed the torch to her. She tucked Graysword awkwardly under her arm and took it. Loas pulled out his bow and took a step forward. He nocked an arrow, his hands trembling from the simple act of holding the shaft in position. Cassara wasn't convinced he could pull back the taut string.

The noise intensified as they approached the collapsed entrance.

Cassara waved at the villagers to stay back. Some did, others approached with their bows.

"Could that be demons?" Loas whispered to Cassara.

Graysword betrayed nothing, the blade still passive in its cloak. Cassara touched the pommel, but could feel nothing except the cool metal.

"I don't know," she replied, biting her chapped lower lip. *If only I still had my amulet!*

The banging continued and she could hear rocks tumbling away.

"We'd best back up a bit," Cassara said, putting her hand on Loas' shoulder and dragging him back a few steps.

Fresh air infiltrated the cave and the torch flickered and swirled. Another hit, and a stream of sunlight slashed the darkness. She heard gasps and cheers behind her.

She squinted to see through the small opening. It was too bright, but she saw a sledgehammer come down on the rocks above, sending some cascading towards them. Loas quickly stepped in front of Cassara, a few of the larger rocks making him stumble but otherwise leaving him unharmed.

The opening was cleared and the archers held their bows at the ready, even though Cassara doubted they could see any more than she could.

"Lady Avarielle?" The question seemed to bounce off the cavern walls. Cassara took a step forward, and another, her weary legs crossing into streaming sunlight as she stepped in front of Loas.

"Trevon?" Cassara asked, more of a squeak than a question.

"The flutist! I knew I'd heard a flute being played in here!" he exclaimed, taking another step forward, casting a welcome shadow across Cassara's gaze. He was a few feet from her still, looking around with a smile to find

Avarielle, when he spotted Graysword's pommel sticking out from under Cassara's tired arm.

His smile faded to sorrow as he looked Cassara in the eye.

"We're all that's left," she said, keeping her voice steady. "Is it safe to exit?"

He nodded slowly and moved aside to let the villagers through. Loas led them out as they shielded their eyes from the rays of the sun.

Cassara stayed behind, clutching Graysword, the blade still silent in her hands.

When only she and Trevon were left, he spoke, his features hidden as the sun cast dark shadows from behind him. His steely whisper sliced the air.

"Who cut her last breath?"

Cassara took a deep breath. "She may yet live, Trevon, but lies beyond our help in Siabala's Rage."

His hands formed fists at his side. "If that is where she is, then that is where I go." He turned to leave.

Cassara took a step forward. "Wait!" He stopped and turned partway back. "Trevon, I think I can garner help for your people, but I need to reach Massir."

He scoffed. "Even if you could do this, Eastlanders will never help us. Besides, I've sent word. Our people will save themselves, as usual."

"No, they won't, Trevon." He turned to face her slowly and deliberately, glaring at her. He was tall and impressive. Every inch of his body, from armor to scars, spoke of a life of battle, and his steady stance and the steel of his eyes spoke of his lack of fear. Despair trickled cold sweat down her back.

"They can't stop these monsters, not at their increasing rate. You know it, and Avarielle knew it too, which is why she came seeking answers in the East." She stepped closer to him, Graysword the only thing separating them.

"Listen to me, Trevon of the West." She craned her neck up to look him in the eye. "Avarielle was intent on seeing me safely to Massir so that I could help her people, and without her help I stand very little chance of making it. With yours, my chances have increased. And so have your people's."

"Eastlanders can't be trusted. You attack and kill without reason or honor."

"I understand and respect your fears, Trevon." She took a dangerous and perhaps foolish chance. "But not all of us lack honor. Just like not all Westlanders are with honor, or Avarielle's brother would yet live."

He glared down at her, and then at Graysword, and she feared he might take the blade from her and vanish back to the West, leaving her and the villagers at the mercy of Eloms. Or worse.

She needed him to help her. She took another chance. Avarielle Grayloft, like every other member of her family, was bound to protect all descendants of Graydon, which meant Cassara's family. Avarielle might not have risked so much for Cassara if not for that oath. She hoped Trevon, a close friend of Avarielle, would be familiar with it.

"Do you know of the Grayloft oath?"

Trevon's eyes narrowed and then widened slightly. "You?"

Cassara nodded. "Why do you think she wasted her time protecting a princess through infested territory?" She swallowed hard and then whispered, "Why do you think she gave up everything to see me safe? Please Trevon, let me help your people. Before it's too late for all of us."

To save the West was to save the East and save Edoline. To save the West was paying Avarielle back for her kindness, even if saving Avarielle herself was beyond her current means.

"You and all of those people out there?"

Cassara nodded. "I need them."

Trevon sighed and gave a slight smile. "She'll be fine, you know. I taught her everything she knows."

Cassara smiled and hugged Graysword tighter. He glanced once at it, sorrow shadowing his face before he turned around and walked out into the sunlight.

She lingered in the darkness a moment longer before joining him, more determined than ever to do what needed to be done to save the West.

A contingent of guards had followed their prince from the palace, well-armed and riding muscled steeds bred for war.

He had already ridden hard for two days to reach the border. He wasn't sure where exactly he was headed, and his expectations of finding the princess alive were dim. But he had needed the retreat from the gossip and eyes of the court.

The further they went from the palace, the more destruction they saw. It had only been a month since his return from Edoline, and his land had been ravaged. Entire villages, barely a day's ride from Massir, were gone. Dark scorches lined the few remaining walls and the smell of burnt flesh clung to the air.

Dayshon looked away with a scowl at the sight of a small burnt foot jutting out from under a collapsed roof.

He kicked his horse into a trot, knowing they would find no survivors here, that this village would be picked as clean as all the other ones had been. Two days and, so far, five villages.

He knew why he hadn't heard of the destruction of Edoline or of his own land until now. They relied on the Circle for a lot of their diplomatic activities. With the Circle's ability to communicate instantly, it had seemed the logical and sensible thing to do.

Dayshon wondered if his father had ever imagined it would leave them in such a vulnerable position.

Another hour's ride and Dayshon chose a high spot on

an open hill for their camp. The enemy they might fight this night was best spotted early. They had yet to encounter any of the monsters, but he didn't intend on taking chances.

From his vantage point, he looked around the land. They neared Kosel, the large imposing forest a dark stain on the horizon. The rays of the setting sun ignited the forest ablaze with reds, golds and oranges, a sea of fire that frightened him more than the destroyed villages.

"Camp is set up, Your Highness," Jiles said as he joined him. The seasoned warrior still wore his full armor, emblazoned with the purple and silver colors of the royal family.

Dayshon nodded but remained lost in thought. It was too early in the season for the trees to change so drastically. The temperature was already cooler, the crops were failing and the hues of autumn already stained Kosel. Something else was wrong, something his gut told him was worse than the demons themselves.

He noticed Jiles was still standing beside him.

"What is it?" he asked, more roughly than intended. A cool evening breeze picked up and he swore he could hear Kosel rustle and sigh even from here.

"I doubt we'll find the princess alive," Jiles said.

Dayshon doubted it himself. He also knew that Jiles understood his need to get away from the palace. Something else was bothering the guard, and he dared not say it where others might hear. Dayshon played along, wondering who amongst his guards Jiles distrusted.

"I want to review the perimeter, if you'll accompany me, captain." He began walking down the hill without waiting for Jiles' answer, knowing he would follow. The hill was dry, the grass easily kicked up by the two passing men. The earth around them had given up as well.

"The land is dying," Dayshon said in disgust when they were out of hearing range of the camp. "Why did the Circle not warn us?"

Jiles remained silent.

"Out with it, Jiles." After only a few weeks of being back at court, Dayshon had already lost all patience. He wondered what he would do when he became king. Throw half the court out and become a hated king, he imagined.

"I don't think it's a coincidence that Edoline was attacked and that the princess Cassara is missing," he began. Dayshon waited for a few seconds, knowing the captain always chose his words carefully when speaking to him or his father. It was an annoying habit Dayshon had yet to break him of.

"Of late, Delora has been paying particular attention to Princess Malir. According to some of my men, the two would at times spend entire days together, sitting close, sharing whispers no one else can hear."

"So, you worry the Circle is setting up the next queen

of Massir and making sure they have firm control over her and, in turn, me?"

Jiles nodded. "And there's more. Following that logic further, I think the moment you marry Malir, your parents' days are numbered. As long as the Circle has such a strong hold on Massir, anyway."

Dayshon sighed.

"For a second, back at court, when the guard of Edoline collapsed, I thought Malir would make a good queen when she approached. I can't believe I was so easily fooled."

Jiles shrugged. "If Princess Cassara is dead, which is very likely, I fear, then it is expected you will choose her as your bride."

"Well, the courts of Massir don't seem to know me very well yet, do they?"

Jiles chuckled. Then something caught his attention and he whirled around, sword in hand.

A woman stood near them, leaning against a tree. She was haggard looking. Her robes were dirty and in tatters. Her dark hair was half pulled back, half wild, and her skin covered in grime.

"Who are you?" Dayshon asked, his hand on the pommel of his sword. Something about her was not quite right. He suddenly realized her robes and hair did not move in the rising wind.

She did not answer immediately, looking him straight in the eye instead. He gave a slight gasp. Her eyes were almost entirely black, only a slight circle of white remaining on the edge of her irises. He did not think it was a trick of the failing light.

"Give me a horse and some supplies, and I will tell you where you can find Princess Cassara," she said, her sing-song voice raspy.

"You know where she is?" Dayshon asked. He took a step forward, only to have Jiles step in front of him.

"Over her heart," Jiles warned.

Dayshon looked, and his grip tightened on his sword. Barely noticeable under the dirt was the unmistakable emblem of the Circle. He could not make out the color, and so did not know her rank.

"What has the Circle done with Cassara, and my land?" Dayshon demanded to know. She was practically draped on the tree for support, but he had no doubt that, even as tired as she was, she could kill them both with a simple gesture.

"Give me a horse and some supplies, and I will tell you where you can find Princess Cassara," she repeated in the same tones. A shiver crept up Dayshon's spine.

"Jiles?"

"We can spare one of the extra horses, and some food and water."

Dayshon nodded. "Get them. Make sure no one knows why you bring them."

Jiles turned to him and bowed stiffly, a look of warning in his eyes. Dayshon whispered to him, "If she meant to kill us, she would have done so already. Now go. Quickly."

Jiles nodded, cast a long look at the sorceress and jogged back to camp, surprisingly quiet in his heavy armor.

"What has the Circle to do with the demons and the death of the land?" Dayshon asked the sorceress after a few moments of silence. He didn't dare approach her. She stood so still that he thought she hadn't even heard him until she replied.

"Everything," she whispered. "And nothing." Useful little witch. She continued.

"The Circle no longer exists. Ravenhold has fallen." She looked up and held his eyes with her darkness. He gripped his sword tighter, ready to pull it free. He could hear a horse approaching, Jiles having moved faster than Dayshon had believed possible.

The captain brought the horse to a stop by the prince. Dayshon glanced quickly and nodded. He dismounted and was about to walk the horse to the sorceress when she called the steed. It went to her without further guidance.

She let him nuzzle her hand, patted the side of his neck and pulled herself up, with some difficulty. Her robes hiked up to her mid-thigh, revealing damaged boots and scratches on her skin. Dayshon guessed that sorceresses didn't usually ride horses.

"Where is she?" he asked, taking a step forward, which was echoed by Jiles.

"Cassara is in danger and near the border of Solir, one day's ride away. If you choose to save her and stay with her, you will be in danger, as well. Remember that I have helped you on this day, Prince Dayshon. Someday, I shall claim your help in return."

She kicked the steed, which took off faster than Dayshon had ever seen any of his horses manage. Jiles swore as its hooves kicked earth on him, the horse and its rider gone as quickly and effortlessly as the sorceress had appeared.

Dayshon turned to Jiles, who was still swearing under his breath.

"Prepare the men to march early, Captain. I intend to be at the border by next sunset, monsters or not."

3

*A*varielle felt stronger.

Her muscles pulsed with life and her mind was sharp. Her arm was wrapped near her body and no other pain assailed her. She felt alive, satiated and ready to take on the world.

Except she was trapped in a tiny cell, alone. This was different than Jayden's cell and she was grateful he was kept away from here. She was at the edge of what she thought was the ancient prison. She didn't remember the journey, but knew either magic or monster must have brought her here, since her cell exited directly onto the abyss. She could discern no path to see her safely out.

Her prison was high. So high that if she strained to see through the stony bars over the edge, she couldn't see the bottom. A large shaft fell into emptiness, surrounded by more cells than Avarielle could count. Smoke drifted up the mid-section from time to time and screams exploded throughout the prison. Avarielle couldn't tell if they were coming from above or below.

The bars to her prison betrayed neither lock nor hinge and were thin and twisted like an overgrown tree. She assumed they had been created by magic. Smoke billowed up and Avarielle stepped away, her eyes burning from sulfur.

Another scream.

She sighed and slid to the ground, keeping an eye on the entryway.

She didn't know how she would escape, but she was certain she would find a way. She knew that she had only been afforded this respite so that the next pain would be greater, after letting her stew for a while with the screams of the damned ringing around her.

She leaned her head back against the wall and waited, focusing on her breath, on the strength of her muscles and on her certainty that Delora needed her alive. The torture would eventually end.

She was beginning to drift off when another scream echoed through the prison. This one seemed closer. Avarielle stood up and headed for the bars, hoping she could spot something, anything that would eventually help her escape. As she neared them, the bars shuddered. She stopped, her hand instinctively reaching for Graysword, only to meet empty air.

The bars trembled and then shattered into a hundred

pieces. Avarielle crouched and covered her eyes as stone shards sliced her flesh.

She barely had the time to look up when something pushed her from behind. She reached around to grab the intruder, but met only stone.

The wall of her cell was closing in on her! The stone moved without cracking, without making a noise. Avarielle desperately tried to find a ledge, a handle, anything that she could grasp for safety, but the stone wall was polished black and the only thing she could see was her own reflection.

She reached the ledge and turned to find somewhere to leap, but the wall jerked into her. She tumbled over the edge. Avarielle's body was heavy as she fell into the dark smoke below, refusing to scream. She forced herself to analyze the surrounding cells, repeating over and over in her mind: *They need me alive.*

Then she met smoke, the thick sulfur burning a layer of her lungs and stinging her eyes. She forced her breath to stop, tried desperately not to cough, and fought to keep her tearing eyes open. She knew she was losing consciousness, but tried to remain strong regardless, to ignore the pain and the lack of air and just focus on sight.

To see where they would take her, and perhaps spot an escape.

The world stopped. She realized she was no longer falling. She was on stone, on her side, her right arm stretched out before her. She couldn't feel her legs and chanced taking a breath. The air was still riddled with sulfur, making her cough. As the darkness enveloped her sight, she saw the man from earlier, his hair so red it seemed to be made of flames.

Siabala. She knew who he was. His eyes shone red as he watched and waited for her to finally pass out, a smile on his large lips as he rumbled: "Impressive."

Kryde Kolder carefully balanced his feet on the rocks below him, his eyes, used to darkness, adjusting easily to the creeping dusk. He enjoyed the West of Graydon more than he had the East. Granted, he hadn't made it far into the East before being captured, weakened by Graydon's magic. But the West was drier, and even though it could use some more vegetation and life, it felt more like home. He allowed himself a moment of reflection on his home and how much he missed its rolling green hills and the fresh sea air that seemed to drape itself around you no matter how far inland you traveled.

He focused again on the task at hand—to get back home.

He pulled himself up on a small ledge, reaching one of the growing number of fissures that led to Siabala. He wondered how different his people's lives would be, and Graydon's, had they both kept a closer eye on what dwelt below the Wall of Loss.

He could sense the air around him, scorched with the scent of Siabala and his magic, so strong did his dominion grow each day. Above it, if he strained as he glanced up the jagged rocks and peaks, near where the setting sun was turning the clouds pink and purple, he could see the faint shimmer of the ancient magic that separated his land's magic from that of this land.

He hoped either his skill or his luck would see him to the other side before the sun rose again. He took a deep breath of fresh air. He would miss this, if nothing else, of Graydon.

Kryde covered his mouth and nose with a piece of ragged cloth.

He peered into the dark fissure before him, wishing he had managed to save some of his armor from that forsaken village. He had spent days in that chicken coop, with barely any food or water except what the warrior woman had dared provide him. Then the village had been destroyed by Eloms and the magic of Graydon. There had been no time to go back or start searching. At least he had secured some of his weapons.

Pulling his short sword free, favoring its light weight over that of the broadsword strapped to his back, Kryde took a step forward, his eyes burning at the first blast of smoke and sulfur. He took a moment to adjust, his ears pricking for the sound of something, anything.

Siabala was growing bolder. His armies were loose on a divided Graydon, and no guards protected his land.

Good.

Let Siabala think he was invincible, while Kryde and his people concentrated on finding the weakness that would secure his downfall.

The flickering shadows of Siabala were disorienting, but he'd studied the path. He mostly worried about encountering the stone creatures that protected this land and tortured the prisoners. If he had any of those left, by now.

Keeping low, he moved quickly, his hand still firmly gripping the pommel of his short sword. The stone walls of Siabala's Rage were obsidian and silky black. They reflected a fire with no source, as though burning from deep within. The polished metal of his sword reflected no such light.

He paced himself, taking no pause to eat or drink, staying low and fast. The shadows played tricks with his mind, promising monsters or attacks. He concentrated on his path, trying not to get lost in the large hallways, which slithered through the rock with little rhyme or reason.

Even though he had studied the way closely on his first passage crossing from Elihor to Graydon, the maze of light and shadows still proved challenging to navigate. The hallways vibrated with the lazy fiery light as he chased his shadow back towards Elihor.

Hours later, as he peered around a corner before taking it, he heard a scream up ahead, torn deeply from someone's throat. Kryde had heard screams before, especially in this evil place, but he had never heard one so raw. So fresh.

Another scream, and he made out that it was a woman. It was coming from directly before him, right in his path toward home. Unless he tried to find another way. But he could be lost here forever, or worse, discovered and captured.

He crouched near a rugged wall as close as he dared. He could see nothing and so he vanished into the surrounding shadows and waited for the screams to stop and the torturers to leave.

By the time Delora was done, Avarielle was convinced her entire hide had been ripped from her muscles and bones and all that remained of her was a raw bloody lump. She struggled to remain conscious but couldn't force her eyes open.

Sulfur danced around her, and she knew Siabala stood somewhere in this room, where he had brought her. Where Delora had waited.

Delora. Her red Circle robes danced around her feet as she approached. Avarielle tried to lift her head to stare her down, but she could only get partway and glared at the Circle symbol, instead.

The witch extended her hand, and Avarielle's organs felt like they were ballooning and would pop. Too tired to scream, she moaned. Then tiny pinpricks scraped her raw skin, her body feeling overextended and compressed all at once. Her hands were cold and numb where they were tied above her head.

She tried to concentrate on the pain the shackles caused, but even that seemed too much. The broken bones of her left arm, which had just started to heal, were straining. The muscles were ripping and she could feel tremors in the bone as though the marrow had turned to liquid in some places and stone in others.

She pulled back within herself, trying to ignore the pain, to escape into memories or blessed darkness.

But Delora cut off her escape by intensifying the pain. Avarielle's head snapped back and she could taste blood in her mouth, her lungs too extended for her to draw a clean, pure breath. She was convinced she was being torn in two, if not more, pieces.

She spat up blood.

Another wave of magic tore into her.

She gritted her teeth and bit back a scream as more waves smashed into her, forcing the breath from her lungs.

Delora laughed and Avarielle's hatred boiled over. Something snapped within her.

A new, yet familiar fire blazed within her. She knew it as well as she knew the caresses of the dry air of her homeland.

Graysword's magic! The magic was somehow here, deep

within her, and she was activating it without holding the blade.

"I can sense the blade reacting," Delora whispered, and a rumble answered. Avarielle fought against the growing warmth of her magic. She wanted nothing more than to let it coat her, warm her and keep her safe. To use it to free herself and destroy Delora, and deliver the souls trapped here, and return home to her people, to help them before they were destroyed. To use Graysword, her heritage, to stop the pain. To be free again. But part of her still remembered that to do so would mean betraying Cassara and her own oath. Pride and loyalty made her push back on the magic, push it deep, far away, until her pain and hatred remained.

"I think that was enough," Delora whispered near her, and Avarielle's eyes snapped open. The witch was barely a hand's length away from her face. Avarielle's shoulders ached from her hands being tied up, her feet barely touching the ground. She didn't look up or down to make sure she was still in one piece, instead struggled to get as much air as she could in her lungs. Stale, bitter air.

"Thank you," Delora said, passing a finger lightly across Avarielle's throat. Blood surged up right away and she choked on it, spitting as much as she could in Delora's face.

Delora smiled as the blood dripped down her face. She held her palm out towards Avarielle and the warrior felt as though a bull had rammed into her gut.

She fought to quench the rising magic of Graysword before exhaling deeply and waiting for the pain to stop.

If she couldn't fight off Delora, then she would have to find a way to sever her link to her magic. She could only think of one way to do that.

But with Delora keeping a careful eye on her, Avarielle wasn't certain how she could manage to take her own life and deprive the Circle witch of her treasured prize.

He saw a woman leave, and felt Siabala's presence vanish. The scent of sulfur diminished, but Kryde waited in the shadows for a few minutes, listening intently before stepping out into the fiery light and heading carefully towards the room, hoping no one, or nothing, had been left there as guard.

Though he doubted there would be much left to guard after those screams.

He crossed the threshold of the room, examining every shadow carefully before moving forward. The room was circular, with a front and a back entrance, and was obviously used for questioning prisoners. A woman dangled in the center of the room. She wore pants and a short-sleeved shirt, her muscled arms pulled taut by her bound hands. Her skin was crisscrossed with battle scars, some old, some new. Her left arm was black and blue and he guessed badly broken from the odd angle of her elbow.

Her chin rested on her chest. Only her short red hair, which reflected the magical fire that lit the walls, was visible. She seemed familiar.

Annoyed at his own curiosity, Kryde took a step forward. As he drew closer, he could see blood dripping onto the ground, originating from either her neck or face.

Another step forward and her head jerked up and their eyes met. She had been badly beaten, her face covered with bruises. Blood was drying on her chin. But it was her eyes, filled with anger and fury, that commanded his attention.

He knew the woman. She had shown kindness to him, and no fear. The first time they had met, he had been the one dangling, in a chicken coop, weakened by Graydon's magic and the lack of food. She had not been afraid of him, and had allowed him some sustenance.

When he had seen her, he had been reminded of the stories of the warrior women who came to claim the souls of the dead on the fields of Elihor, to train them to become better warriors for the final battles of the world. Now that she was bound, beaten, but certainly not defeated, he knew that no mythical woman could ever be as strong or impressive as her, and that she might in fact be one of them, fallen from the Land of Beyond itself.

"Free me," she commanded, her voice a steely whisper. He examined her closely and recognition flickered in her eyes.

"The man from the chicken coop," she murmured. He

nodded. She had given him food and water, had not shied away from him. But she had not freed him.

"Would you have freed me?" he asked, his eyes trained on her, but his ears listening intently for any strange or unexpected noise.

She pondered for a moment, grimacing slightly as the bonds shifted and pain visibly rippled through her body. Then she answered.

"No."

A slow smile crept onto his features. He reached up and cut her bonds and she fell ungracefully to the floor. She struggled to stand, her movements slow and stiff. She pulled the ropes from the wounds, which had dug into her wrists, tearing flesh and drawing blood. Her left arm hung uselessly at her side. Still, she didn't complain.

"Thank you," she began to walk back into Siabala's Rage.

He reached out and grabbed her good arm. She turned and scowled at him. He could feel her muscles tensing under his grip, and guessed she would give him a challenge in battle, wounded though she was.

"The exit is this way," he indicated with a shake of his head.

"I have a friend that way," she pointed to the way back into Siabala's Rage.

He nodded and released her. He pulled free his short sword, one of his only one-handed weapons, and handed it to her. The broadsword on his back would easily see him back to his home.

"Your land is back that way, but you'll have a better chance of making it to my land. They'll expect you to head back to yours."

She nodded as she tested the weight of the short sword in her hand, turning the blade back and forth with ease, obviously experienced at swordplay.

"I'll come return this then," she said as she indicated the short sword.

He nodded, and without another word she turned around, intent on rescuing whoever was still trapped within the prison. He watched her vanish around the corner, her movements more limber with each step.

For a second he wished he could follow and fight by her side, certain they would make a great team. But he had to report back what he had seen to his people, and prepare them for the biggest battle of all. To claim vengeance, if not salvation.

$\mathcal{A}$varielle moved deeper into Siabala's Rage, the weight of the short sword comforting in her good hand. Only minutes before, she had been planning how to take her own life to ensure Graysword didn't fall into Delora's possession. But now she was free, armed, and with a fairly reliable idea of the floor plan.

She thought she could find Jayden. As long as they hadn't moved him. She had no sense of how long she'd been tortured. It didn't matter. She was free, now.

She didn't bother considering her luck, didn't think about the man who had saved her. She put the aches and pains of her battered body out of her mind. She was alive and had a purpose. That would do for now.

She ran lightly down the hall, her mind clear and alert, pumped with adrenaline. Another right and Jayden would be near. She turned a corner. No one was around.

Breathing heavily, she looked at the walls around her. Beyond one of these was Jayden's cell. She needed to get him out.

She had taken an oath, long ago, that she would protect those of Graydon's bloodline, though at the time she had doubted she would ever meet any of his heirs, as none of her family in recent memory ever had. She took the oath while just a child, as every Grayloft did, in case they were ever called upon to wield the ancestral blade.

But she had taken the oath seriously, regardless of her young age, and she feared she might have doomed Cassara by clutching onto Graysword's magic. She didn't know if Delora had been lying when she had said it had been enough to locate Graysword, but she had to assume it was, and Jayden was now the only one left to save. She felt a pang of regret for Cassara, who had sealed her fate by trying to save Graysword. But the princess was out of her reach now, and the Fates would have to deal her what destiny they felt best.

She stopped. One of the walls didn't flicker with the fire magic. It was black as night, a black that seemed to absorb light instead of casting and reflecting it. Different magic fed this wall.

Avarielle leaned against it, her palms tingling at its touch. It was Circle magic. She hadn't felt it from within the prison, but now she was certain this was Delora's doing. She pushed on the wall. Circle magic had little effect on her, and she might even be able to nullify it.

Avarielle was not affected by Graydon's magic as others would be, a gift to her family by Graydon himself when her family took the oath to protect his descendants. Siabala's magic, however, could kill her with ease.

She pressed her body against the wall, careful to avoid her left arm, pushing back with her feet. The magic was absorbed and neutralized by her body, the tingling sensation amplifying her pain.

One final push and the wall vanished. Avarielle stumbled forward and fell to one knee right in front of a stunned Jayden.

"Time to go," she said, grabbing his arm as she stood and turned, coming face to face with Delora. Without hesitation, Avarielle thrust the short sword, piercing Delora through.

The sorceress had not been expecting either the speed or the weapon. She fell backwards, stunned. With only one good arm, Avarielle sacrificed the sword as she reached for the amulet around Delora's neck, snapping the chain.

Their eyes met as Avarielle stuffed the amulet in her pocket.

Delora smirked despite the firmly embedded blade sticking out of her chest.

"Would you just die!" Avarielle screamed as she reached down and yanked the sword out. She spun around to increase the momentum of her swing, bringing the blade level with the witch's neck, and would have cut her head clean off her body had Delora not vanished.

"Bloody teleportation," Avarielle grumbled. "Come on!" She ran down the hall, Jayden keeping pace beside her.

Then the cave was pierced by a shriek, and echoed by another, and another. The demons of the cave were rising to Delora's call.

She could hear them mobilizing, the stone around her throbbing with angry magic. They needed to get out of there, fast.

Footsteps approached, clanging against the floor. She ducked and pushed Jayden against the wall as large wings beat down the adjacent hall towards the prison and the path to Graydon.

She backtracked. Her rescuer had been right—they wouldn't expect her to make a break for Elihor, especially not after securing Cassara's amulet. They would expect her to run towards Graydon and the safety of light.

She turned into the room where she had been tortured, her blood still slick on the floor.

"Just beyond here," she said to Jayden. He barely nodded, his eyes wide and terrified.

She cautiously walked forward, keeping a grip on the sword as she crossed another few rooms, each empty. In the fourth room they entered, a fissure neatly divided the wall from floor to ceiling. Avarielle approached. She couldn't see much of the land beyond it, illuminated by weak moonlight. She could hear the wind whistling against the rock, fresh air ruffling her hair and cooling her sweaty skin, and she could smell the sea.

"Is that home?" Jayden suddenly asked, the youth's eyes shining in the natural light.

"Let's find out," Avarielle said as she began making her way through the fissure with Jayden, knowing full well where they were, but fearing Jayden's reaction were he to discover they were stepping into the ancient homeland of Elihor.

The land looked the same at first glance. It was dark, so Avarielle couldn't make out many details. She could see rolling hills on the horizon, though she couldn't tell if they were grassy like Edoline, or rocky, like her homeland. The sea was near, or so she thought from the smell on the wind, but she couldn't hear the surf.

She craned her neck and spotted the shimmer of the sea far away to the left. A calm sea, not the choppy waters of the straits that separated Graydon and Elihor.

After being in Siabala's Rage for countless days, maybe even weeks, Avarielle wished she could just jump into the sea and let its salt clean her wounds and body.

Wary of the unknown landscape around them, they traveled in silence for about an hour before Avarielle finally felt they had put enough distance between themselves and the fissure. She wanted to keep going, but her energy dropped quickly. Although Jayden didn't complain, she could tell from his hesitant movements that even if his captivity had not involved torture, it had not been kind, either.

She headed for an outcropping of rocks and they both slid in. The moonlight was strong, but if Siabala sent any of his demons to find them, they would be hidden by the jutting rocks. Regardless, Avarielle maintained her grip on the short sword.

As adrenaline deserted her body and her muscles relaxed, the pain in her left arm throbbed back to life and she took deep breaths to try and control it.

Jayden huddled against her, his breath soon long and quiet. She remained seated, leaning her head back against the rock, wishing she could feel Graysword's comforting magic once again. Instead, she pulled out the amulet from her pocket, the metal dull in the moonlight, as though it had relied on Cassara to feed its light.

Now we're both stuck with items that are useless to us. She allowed herself a grin and then winced as she shifted and pain sparked her body. She settled in and waited to see if dawn would break on the Land of Darkness.

She was jolted awake, squinting to see in the pressing darkness. Jayden's breathing was deep and constant beside her. She pushed herself up slowly so as not to wake him or draw attention to them. The hairs on the back of her neck stood on end.

Something was wrong.

She moved sideways, grabbing the short sword with her right hand as she gritted her teeth against the pain of her left arm. She knelt and took deep breaths.

Movement on the right. She turned, assuming a defensive crouch as she held the weapon before her. Nothing.

Jayden still slept behind her, but over the sound of his breath, she could hear something else. Someone was mumbling or singing very softly.

Standing with her blade at attention, Avarielle took a step towards the sound. It was eerie, and the voice echoed lightly on the air. A chill caught hold of her spine.

She reached the edge of the outcropping of rocks and gazed outside. The half-moon's light shimmered through the Wall, the magic much more visible in Elihor than in Graydon. The clear sky shone with numerous stars. Avarielle hoped the light would prove an advantage to them and not to whomever, or whatever, might be hunting them.

She glanced back at Jayden and decided to investigate further, sweat trickling down her back despite the cool night. Her throat was pasty and sweat dripped into her eyes, her entire body screaming from the pain in her arm. She didn't chance dropping the sword to wipe the sweat from her face, blinking it away as best as she could instead.

She took another tortured step, wishing the enemy would show itself before the pain got the best of her. Another step and she cleared the outcropping. The song stopped for a second, and Avarielle barely had the time to raise her blade before something came at her from the right. She swerved and ducked as a white shadow flew past her head.

She crouched, not trusting herself to be able to get back up if she rolled away. Avarielle turned to face the creature, which now floated just a few meters away. She had never believed in ghosts, chalking them up to fanciful flights of the imagination by those who couldn't let go of their loved ones. But now, facing what could only be a ghost, Avarielle found herself willing to change her mind.

It was a woman, and she had been beautiful, once. Her long hair danced about her body, her robes caught in a wind only she could feel. Her eyes were lit as though from within, so white Avarielle could see no pupils.

She sang in a voice both eerie and enchanting, the cadence never breaking or slowing.

The ghost held up her arm, palm facing Avarielle, and the warrior suddenly noticed the circle over her heart, lit with light.

Circle trickery! The blast came quickly. Avarielle didn't have the time to avoid it, and without Graysword it was impossible to deflect. She felt the magic run through her, absorbed by every fiber of her being. She gasped and collapsed to her knees, the buzz of the magic robbing her of sight and hearing.

Her hands fell to the ground, holding her up as spasms of pain shook her body. Her left arm broke again and again, waves of agony rippling down her spine, from the tips of her toes to the ends of her hair. She was on the ground, she realized, on her side.

All sensation left her body and she could barely tell if she was still breathing.

Jayden! She had promised to keep him safe. He was still sleeping, and she had promised to keep him safe.

She forced her eyes open and pushed herself up, barely able to feel her arms, or the rest of her body for that matter. She blinked a few times to rid her eyes of the cobwebs of magic. The ghost was nowhere to be seen, and the strange chanting had ended. Or so she assumed. She snapped her fingers by her ear to make sure she could still hear. Satisfied her senses were returning, she grabbed the short sword and carefully stood, taking a deep breath.

Something was different. *What did that Circle ghost do to me?* She examined her surroundings, making sure she was alone before examining herself more closely. Her left arm was no longer bent strangely or in pain. She moved the fingers and they obeyed gingerly.

Her body no longer ached, either. She brought up her left hand and touched her face, which had been bruised and bloodied just a few hours ago. It felt smooth to the touch, if dirty.

She had been healed.

Avarielle looked around, searching for the ghost. Why had she done this? Why *would* she do this?

Rejuvenated, Avarielle returned to the sleeping Jayden and sat by him, keeping watch for the rest of the night. She wondered if all the demons of Elihor would prove this useful, or if this was just a sprinkling of sunlight before a terrible winter storm.

Jayden woke her by shifting against her. The sun was rising. "Your arm's better?" Jayden asked as she stretched it out before her.

Avarielle grinned. "Looks that way!" Not wanting to scare him with talk of apparitions, Avarielle didn't elaborate as she pulled herself out of their hiding place.

"Stay here until I call you," she told Jayden.

They hid near the base of the mountain but she saw neither monster nor human. The land around them stood quiet and still, as though it held its breath before being struck.

Except it seemed to have already been struck. The land had been scorched, the disaster old enough that the scent of death wasn't immediately apparent on the wind, but recent enough that ashes still clung below. It was like looking at a sea of shifting darkness, despite the sun shining down on it.

"Come on," Avarielle whispered as she helped Jayden up. He looked around for a bit, shielding his eyes against the sun.

"This isn't your home, is it?" he suddenly asked.

"No, it's not. And I don't know how safe it is." She hesitated for a moment, but decided the young prince would find out sooner or later anyway. "I'm pretty sure we're in Elihor, Jayden."

The words felt funny on Avarielle's tongue, but Jayden simply nodded. Avarielle guessed that after spending more than a month in Siabala's Rage, this might not seem so bad after all.

"Where do we go?"

Avarielle shrugged. "Forward, I guess. I have a…friend, here, somewhere." She hoped he would prove to be a friend, anyway, if she could even find him.

Jayden didn't question her as the two resumed their descent of the mountain. They reached the base and stepped out onto the burnt land. It had been full of life once, but now the strands of grass were scorched or covered in ashes. Some trees were fallen over while others still stood, their bark black, their leaves shriveled. It was as though a fire had flashed through and not burned long enough to eradicate all signs of life, but rather just to smother and scar it.

Avarielle wondered if the ghost had come from those

incinerated in the blast. She kept a sharp eye out, not trusting that every creature here would prove as useful as last night's Circle witch.

Jayden stayed close, and Avarielle made sure to keep her pace reasonable for the boy. He was sturdier than she had expected, but then again, she hadn't expected Cassara to be able to keep up with her either, much less prove useful in battle.

She felt a pang of regret, knowing the princess was probably doomed now, by Avarielle's own lack of control over her magic. She hoped she would find Cassara and Graysword first, but knew that it was a foolish hope. Cassara's amulet rubbed against the fabric of her pocket. There was nothing she could do for the princess now—the amulet's magic as useless to Avarielle as Graysword would be to Cassara. Hopefully stabbing the Circle witch through had bought her some time.

They had just scaled a hill when they heard a noise coming from up ahead. Hoof beats. Jayden stopped in his tracks, and Avarielle stayed near him as she looked around. There was nowhere to hide, and no good fighting spot.

Incoming riders kicked up ashes as they head straight for them. The men riding the horses seemed human enough.

"Let's see who they are," she told Jayden, smiling at him with a confidence she didn't feel. Depending on how armed they were, she might be able to fight off a few of them, but not without endangering Jayden. All that she had was a short sword, which was plenty in her hands, but Jayden had no weapons.

She thought of giving him the amulet, but wasn't certain it would work for him. Also, remembering the story of how Cassara's mother had perished at the hands of her frightened daughter, she feared the consequences of Jayden's first usage of the magic. Especially since she didn't have Graysword to protect her.

The riders approached and surrounded them. They were heavily armored, their faces hidden beneath face plates. They did not draw their swords or bows. Avarielle kept the short sword lowered and waited for them to make the first move.

One of the men jumped off his horse and came forward. He lifted his visor, and Avarielle was careful to hide her surprise as she peered into full dark eyes. She wondered if all the inhabitants of Elihor had eyes pooled with inky blackness.

He was an older man of strong build, and Avarielle wondered how difficult he would be to take down, the battle lust throbbing through her blood.

"We've been expecting you, people of Graydon." He spoke with the same loose accent as the man from Siabala. "I am Pack Nacker. Leader Kolder sent us to retrieve you."

"Leader Kolder?" Avarielle asked, keeping her tone as neutral as possible.

She had no idea what might prove offensive to the

residents of Elihor. "You have his short sword." He nodded towards her sword.

"Ah. Then I owe him twice the thanks." She lowered her head in acknowledgment, a gesture he returned.

"We'd best go. This place is not safe, even in daylight."

Pack Nacker held his hand back and another horseman brought a horse for them. Jayden looked up at her, curiosity in his eyes. She grinned at him and he smiled back.

"Come, let's get you up there." But Pack Nacker brought his horse closer and addressed them.

"Women generally ride alone in Elihor. The boy can ride with one of my men."

Avarielle stiffened but tried to keep a pleasant smile on her face. Let them try and separate her from Jayden, and they would find out just how quick she could be.

"We are from Graydon, where women ride with whomever they choose. And," she added, an edge to her voice, "it is my duty to protect this boy, so you'll forgive me if I don't immediately trust you with his safety."

The large man looked down at her with narrowed eyes. Jayden held his breath beside her, and she let her stiff muscles relax and loosen, preparing for battle.

Then he broke into laughter. "Kryde said you'd be a handful! Very well, you two ride together. I personally don't care, truth be told, but you should know that here only married couples ride together on horseback."

Avarielle gave him a skeptical look. "He's twelve.

Unless you wed at a much younger age, I doubt that should be a problem."

"Only twelve?" Pack asked slowly as he nodded. "You're right, that's not a problem."

Avarielle was about to say something when he pulled his horse away. She shrugged and turned to Jayden. His eyes met hers, and she suddenly understood Pack's confusion. Gone was the laughing twelve-year-old boy. His eyes were grave and lined with sorrow. His lips didn't automatically furl into a grin like they used to. His skin was pale and taut, his hair was dull and he just didn't look like the kid she had met in Edoline anymore.

He looked ageless, as though the wisdom and fears of a much older man had been implanted into a young man's body. She doubted he would ever be a kid again, after dwelling in Siabala's Rage for so long.

"Well," she said, swallowing hard and forcing a grin. "If you don't mind being married to an old woman like me, shall we ride together?"

Jayden cocked his head. "I could do worse than you."

He smiled, and for a second she could see the boy again. The horse wore a bareback pad, which meant no stirrups. Avarielle cupped her hands and the prince settled his foot into it and she boosted him up. He settled near the shoulders of the horse, obviously used to riding. Pack held the reins firmly to keep the animal from shifting.

She patted the neck of the horse before heading to its

side, hoisting herself up behind Jayden and swinging her legs into position.

Pack Nacker set off and they all followed, the horse so accustomed to the group that he followed without urging. Avarielle and Jayden were surrounded by horsemen, and she hoped that she had not made a mistake by trusting this Kryde Kolder.

5

varielle gritted her teeth as the horsemen from Elihor set a merciless pace. She had ridden before, though she preferred to walk, and she was unaccustomed to the movements of the steed. Her arms ached and were turning to jelly as she clutched the horse's reins. Jayden was huddled in front of her, his small frame safely tucked between her arms. He was crouching forward to hold on to the edge of the bareback pad, and she was impressed that he hadn't uttered a complaint.

She could tell from his posture that he was exhausted. His frame was lean and almost skeletal from lack of movement while imprisoned. Delora had kept her nephew fed, but that was about all she had done. She could feel his head nodding down. How he could fall asleep while riding a horse was beyond her.

Avarielle stretched, trying to accustom her body to the horse's movements. She relaxed her stance, clutching the reins with one hand and wrapping her other arm around Jayden's waist. Her arms were beginning to tire, but she still felt no pain, only stiffness. The Circle ghost seemed to have healed all of her wounds.

She felt a shiver and concentrated on her comfort instead. The horse's legs hit the ground in a predictable rhythm, sending her bouncing up and down. She gripped the horse's sides with her knees while adjusting her body to the beast's. Like a dance, she allowed herself to follow her partner's movements, mimicking its motions so closely that soon her entire body was timed to them and wasn't just jostling on the beast's back. Jayden nodded forward, the young prince of Edoline's breathing slow and steady.

Avarielle smiled and held him close. She hoped sleep would bring him much needed peace.

The steed breathed heavily as he followed Pack Nacker's and trampled the ashes, the kicked-up debris clinging to Avarielle's boots and pants. She sighed. She seemed cursed to be forever dirty. She wondered what being clean and wearing fresh clothing again would feel like. It had been so long she could barely recall.

After a few hours' hard ride, just as Avarielle was wondering if either her horse or her muscles would give out, they crossed a charred hill and before them lay a settlement. Pack kept their speed steady for a while longer, before slowing as they neared it. The settlement was scattered with makeshift houses, still-thriving gardens growing around and under the badly erected shelters. At the center of it was a large fenced-in building, two stories in height, made of stone.

Nothing in the settlement looked like it had been touched by the fire that had consumed the rest of Elihor. Silent stone guardians stood around the village in formations, rocks piled together to form a pattern. Each formation stood about two meters apart, forming a large circle around the entire settlement.

They were all different, but they did have one thing in common: their outward-facing sides were charred and covered in soot, while their other halves were perfectly intact and clean, without sign of fire.

As they crossed between two stone formations, Avarielle felt the hairs on her arms tingle.

She was convinced that if she had Graysword, its magic would react to the magic that bound these stones and protected this settlement.

Jayden woke up, shifted in front of her and craned his neck to get a better look at their surroundings. From within the makeshift houses, mostly made of old pieces of wood and tarps, people started to emerge. Curious eyes peered from behind walls of worn fabric. Some of the occupants came to cautiously greet them. Pack Nacker didn't utter a word, his mood more somber since they had entered the settlement.

"Leader Kolder is waiting in the outpost," he announced as he slowed to allow them to catch up. He grabbed the reins from Avarielle as the horse came to a halt.

She jumped off and helped Jayden down, his eyes flickering towards her. She winked at him. He raised an eyebrow slightly, not convinced by her show of carelessness, which made her smile. His blue eyes, speckled with yellow, looked inquisitively around him, and his fair hair, light brown unlike his sister's golden locks, gathered in unruly waves near his face. His skin was pale from not having seen the sun in weeks.

"You need a healer?" Pack suddenly asked as he leapt off his horse. Avarielle shook her head and looked at Jayden. He shook his head as well. She heard his stomach grumble and grinned.

"We could use some food, but we'd like to speak with this Kryde Kolder first."

Pack nodded. "He's expecting you. This way." He walked towards the central structure.

Avarielle kept Jayden close as the darkness-filled eyes of the residents of Elihor followed them. She hoped trusting him was not a mistake, remembering Kryde Kolder's strained muscles as he sat bound in a small, airless chicken coop in Rockor.

She wondered if her instincts not to fear him then

would bear out today when he was freed, armed, and surrounded by allies.

Pack Nacker led them through the central building. The stone tower was built high to keep an eye out for incomers, with several storerooms and bedrooms lining the second floor. Avarielle wondered how close they were to a fortified city for a guard tower to silently stand watch in the middle of this desolate land. She wondered if the city still stood from the fires, and why this fortification had survived the destruction.

She wasn't certain and didn't trust anyone enough to ask, so she simply followed and kept Jayden close. As though sensing her unease, Jayden remained near.

They crossed the length of the building in a few short minutes before exiting out the back. A fenced-in yard with yellowing grass and half-blooming gardens sprawled before them, the smell of ashes still on the air despite the greenery. Avarielle spotted the man named Kryde Kolder immediately, sitting on a rock near the wall, sharpening a broadsword that made Graysword look insignificant. He heard them coming and stood, a slow smile spreading across his face.

"Well met, woman of Graydon." He nodded towards Jayden. "I see your mission went well."

Avarielle couldn't help but return the smile. He had a

warrior's ease about him that she found comforting after traveling either alone or with Shirina and Cassara for so long. Her instincts told her she could trust him, but still she stayed close to the young prince. If they planned on attacking them, she would have to move fast to save both of their skins. She was tired, but also eager to test her recently healed body.

"I'm Kryde Kolder. Welcome to the land of Elihor."

He extended his hand and Avarielle took it, matching his firm grip. His eyes creased in amusement. He also extended his hand to Jayden.

"My name is Avarielle Grayloft, and this is Jayden Edoline."

He nodded in acknowledgment. "We don't have much to offer, but what we have we'll gladly share. In exchange for information, of course."

"What kind of information?"

"Whatever you know that might help save our people. Stories, rumors, whatever you think will be useful. We'll share ours freely, as well. Whatever plagues the Land of Graydon also plagues the Land of Elihor, and unless we find a way to unite our forces, I doubt any of us will live much longer."

Avarielle nodded and was about to ask the thousands of questions running through her mind, when a man bearing a broadsword and dark blue armor, obviously some sort of soldier, approached Kryde.

"We need your help reviewing some defenses, Leader."

Kryde nodded. "Excuse me. We'll speak shortly." He walked away, instructing that they be shown to their room inside the settlement. Avarielle watched him go, not one bit tired, and not intending to sleep until she at least had some answers from the Leader of Elihor.

Kryde now understood that 'reviewing the defenses' simply meant that something else had failed, usually some form of Circle magic. Today it was one of the stone formations. It had taken a hit last night from a falling winged monster of Siabala, which his people now referred to as srocks. The stones were no longer able to effectively conduct magic, leaving a weak spot in their protective shield.

His people expected him to have answers he simply didn't have. How was he supposed to protect them when he had no magic? He had been raised as a warrior, so he at least had that knowledge, but the enemies they fought used weapons much stronger than bows and swords.

"Can we replace the broken rock?" he asked a Crimson Circle adept, one of the few still awake at this time.

"We're working on it. It's taking time, though."

"Time is a luxury we don't have. Tell the Circle to concentrate their efforts here, and I'll gather some men to help them. If we're lucky, we won't have to worry too much about being attacked tonight."

The Circle adept nodded and walked off with the uncertain steps of a body devoured by overuse of magic. Kryde sighed.

"It looks like you could use some help." He turned around to see the woman from Graydon walking towards him, eyeing the broken rock structure.

"We can handle it," he answered, not sure he wanted to trust her with their safety. She walked with the assurance of a seasoned warrior, her body already free of the wounds of Siabala's Rage. He wondered if she had magic, and would not be surprised to learn she did.

She looked around at the charred land surrounding the outpost. Then her eyes came to rest on his.

"Did the Circle do this to your land?"

"The Circle? Surely you jest, woman. Of course it wasn't their doing."

She shrugged, unconvinced. "Are you sure you can trust them?"

He pierced her with his stare. How dare a stranger question his strongest allies? "Yes. I'm more certain of them than I am of you."

She ignored him.

"What happened here?" Her eyes focused unwaveringly on his, and he noticed that between the white and the black was a layer of dark brown. He focused on that as he answered her, fascinated by the specks of green he could also spot in her eyes, as though an entire forest lay hidden there.

"Siabala tried to destroy us and, unless we figure out a way to fight back soon, he just might win." It sounded so simple when he said it like that. He didn't go into the gory details—the smell of burnt flesh, their inability to help the fallen, the search for food and survivors, for water and a shred of their humanity, the children eating the dead in an effort to survive, and the missing, stolen by Siabala for his twisted experiments.

He didn't bother describing the fear that intensified as the Circle outposts failed along with its sorcerers and sorceresses, and he didn't bother mentioning to her that there was no way to win. None that he knew of, anyhow, and he had looked. Having elected him leader when he had saved so many after the Great Fire, and for his bloodline, his people expected him to win. But he had no answers.

He didn't bother telling her that, either.

Yet when he looked in her eyes, he thought that she understood, anyway.

Avarielle was pacing the room, trying to remain quiet to let Jayden get some much-needed rest. She couldn't sleep, energized by the mysteries and dangers of this new land, and by their need to return to Graydon. Her people and Cassara still needed her, and she was trapped here in Elihor.

She looked at the sleeping figure of Jayden and sighed. She had to keep him safe. If she had been alone, she would have set off through Siabala to reach them. Eli, she'd have just headed to Graydon in the first place, monsters or not!

But she wasn't alone. She had to keep herself in check.

The stillness of the night was suddenly shattered by a scream. Avarielle crossed the room in two large steps and reached the window, keeping to the side of it in case of projectile weapons. The night exploded with lightning flashes, forcing her to squint.

Then she realized they weren't lightning flashes. They were flashes of magic around the outpost. Avarielle leaned forward against the window frame, curious to see what was taking place. Undoubtedly one of the attacks Kryde had alluded to.

"What's going on?" Jayden whispered from behind her.

"I don't think we have anything to worry about," Avarielle replied without turning around. "But stay there just in case." She heard him shift in the bed and he was quiet after that.

The troops gathered below and the settlers moved closer to the tower, where she and Jayden had been given a room. She spotted Kryde, who shouted orders without hesitation, deploying his men around the perimeter. They seemed well trained, but they were too few to stop any real attack.

The sky flashed again with light and Avarielle spotted the first line of defense of the outpost. The few Circle witches that remained were spread thin around the perimeter, wearing dark robes instead of white, their hands held up, their chants soft in the night air.

Avarielle heard the scream of a srock seconds before the sky burst with light as it hurled itself against the magical shield. One of the Circle witches stumbled forward and fell outside of the magical barrier.

"Cover!" Kryde shouted, but it was too late, a srock landing near her. She screamed, and then all was silent.

The world held its breath for a moment, and then a strange chant filled the air. Avarielle had heard it before, on the mountainside. Ghostly figures hovered near the magical shield, towards where the Circle witch had fallen. It was too dark for Avarielle to see what they were doing.

Then an old witch screamed from within the compound, white cloak against her black robes, running towards the fallen adept. Kryde was faster, tackling the woman to the ground before she could cross the magical barrier. She shrieked and then sobbed, holding her knees to her chest as Kryde stayed near her. Avarielle watched the scene unfold, taken aback when the witch threw her head back, silver hair dancing in the windless night, cackling madly.

"Take the Elder Tan to her room," Kryde ordered and two soldiers quickly obeyed.

The attacks seemed to have stopped. Avarielle clutched the side of the window, her body pumped full of adrenaline.

Kryde looked up and nodded at her as their gazes locked. She nodded back and left the window, part of her wishing the battle would continue so she could partake, part of her knowing she couldn't afford the risk of falling.

Not as long as Jayden's safety relied solely on her.

6

———————

*A*s shadows stretched into dusk, the villagers' whispers ceased and their tired eyes darted from sky to ground. There was no telling where the attack would come from, assuming one would come.

We can't afford to think any other way. Cassara pulled the remaining tatters of her coat closer. At least with Trevon's appearance and their exit from the caves, the villagers had regained hope and energy. The fresh air alone was worth more than all of Massir's and Edoline's combined riches. Not that Edoline had much to contribute.

Cassara's heart ached. She missed her homeland and her family. She missed her father's stoic presence, Kaden's and Carsyn's dry humor, Emala's fussing, Jayden's laughter. She missed the blooms, and the sound of the surf, and the smell of the sea. Everything was so quiet here, a grassland turning yellow before high summer. The wind bore no promise of storm or rain, and no fresh sea air.

She wondered what was happening to Edoline and how Bestian was changing her beloved home. She hoped Altessa would manage to stop him or at least stay his hand for a little while longer.

For what? For my return. She realized she still believed that, somehow, this nightmare would end. That none of it was actually real. None of the battles, none of the losses, the fears, the death…she still believed that she would wake up one day and Edoline would be as it had always been.

Except for you, mother.

She reached into her small bag and held the flute, the wood dry and starting to crack. She swallowed hard, remembering the rearing horse and her mother's fall, the feel of the amulet in her hand as she unleashed its untested power.

She forced herself to focus on Trevon's strong back and Loas' steady presence beside her. The silent villagers scuffled behind her, a small army that relied on her to make a difference.

She wondered how many knew she no longer had her magic.

The sun set and Trevon paused. Cassara held her breath, knowing her nightmare would not end this night as she forced a deep gulp into her lungs.

It tasted of blood and corpses.

The Eloms had already found them.

"Loas," she whispered, her grip on Graysword so tight it cut into her flesh.

She wished she could sense its magic.

The archer looked at her, his features pale and drawn, yet determined as he nocked an arrow. She nodded to him and then turned to address the villagers in her calmest and most authoritative voice.

"Archers surround the villagers. Those without weapons, stay in the middle!"

She heard a few whispers about her magic, and how it would save them again. Her heart pounded in her chest as she placed Graysword on the ground and fetched her first arrow.

Someone shouted behind them: "Elom!"

Cassara barely had the time to fire an arrow as one ran straight for her. It fell, the wooden shaft sticking out of its head. Another leapt out from behind the trees, and a few crossed the shallow stream near them. Cassara could hear the sounds of battle and screams echoing in the night.

She fired arrow after arrow, hitting her mark each time. Still more came.

There are too many! She pulled another arrow out, and felt that it was her last. The hollow pit growing in her stomach intensified as she closed the gap between her and Loas, seeing he too was out of arrows.

She chanced a glance around, and only Trevon still

held his ground, wielding a broadsword in one hand and the sledgehammer in the other with a speed that defied the weight of the weapons.

"Fall back behind Trevon!" she ordered, her voice ringing in the night. She moved to follow her own order when an Elom charged at her. She raised the bow and hit it, sending it reeling for a second before it whirled back around and slashed out with its claws. Throwing herself on the ground to avoid the blow, Cassara tried to scurry away, but the creature was on top of her in an instant.

She screamed and felt the earth tremble beneath her, wondering for an instant if her magic was reacting.

Then the Elom was jerked off of her and Cassara was pulled up by a strong arm.

"Are you all right?"

Cassara expected to see Trevon, but was greeted instead by the face of Prince Dayshon. She was so surprised that she couldn't answer him.

An Elom jumped out from behind him, to be downed by another soldier on a horse. They were surrounded, no longer by Eloms, but rather by the cavalry of Massir, banners flapping in the darkening night as they slaughtered the remaining monsters.

"This field is clear, your Highness," a soldier reported, casting a curious glance at Cassara.

Dayshon nodded and turned his attention back to the princess. "Are you all right, Cassara?"

She felt herself blush and curtsied in her tattered clothes to hide her face, regardless of the growing darkness.

"I am. Thank you for rescuing us, Prince Dayshon." He nodded and examined her quizzically.

She straightened her shoulders and looked at him fully. "I didn't expect your company today, or I would have surely donned something more appropriate."

Dayshon grinned, and when she looked into his eyes, she could imagine they were back in the Courtyard of Stars, meeting again for the first time.

"I'm glad to see you," she whispered.

"I'm glad I found you," he replied as he held out his hand. She took it without hesitation, her hand trembling as the adrenaline flowed from her body.

"Your Highness?" The question came from beside him, snapping Cassara back to reality. He grinned and squeezed her hand in comfort.

"Captain, I'd like you to meet Princess Cassara Edoline. Cassara, this is my most trusted of guards, Captain Jiles Ionas."

"My Lady," Jiles said, bowing deeply.

"A pleasure to meet you, captain," she said as she gently squeezed Dayshon's hand. He smiled at her. She found her composure again as she battled the encroaching fatigue.

"These are villagers from Solir, fleeing from the Eloms," Cassara said, letting go of Dayshon's hand to wave towards them. Trevon and Loas stood near and kept a close eye on the encounter.

"They have had no food or water in many days, and some are very ill and weakened." She coughed slightly.

"Jiles, set up camp and make sure provisions are distributed amongst the villagers." The captain was barking orders as he walked away. Dayshon handed his water skin to Cassara. She hesitated and then took it, but didn't take a sip until she was satisfied every last child and adult had eaten and drunk.

And then, as they laid down to sleep, exhausted, Cassara bid Dayshon good night and joined the villagers, sleeping near Graysword, Trevon sitting near her as though he intended to stand watch. Cassara briefly wondered what fortune had brought Dayshon her way, but the question was quickly lost from her mind as she drifted into a dreamless sleep.

Cassara woke up feeling as though cotton had been stuffed in her head. Her stomach leapt to her throat and she knew she was about to throw up. Trevon sat near her, asleep as he held his weapons.

She stood and passed near him silently, feeling dizzy as she cleared the villagers and reached some bushes, bending forward to throw up quietly. Flushed from fever and embarrassment, she stood up to look around and ensure no one had seen her.

The sky was brimming with stars, so bright they seemed to sing from far above. She allowed herself a smile and took a deep breath of fresh air, her stomach settling.

Too much excitement and food today, Cassara thought as she took a step back towards the settlement. Or tried to, bouncing off an invisible wall instead. Wide-eyed, Cassara reached out to touch the wall, which shimmered and tingled at her fingertips. She could see the camp, but she was blocked from it.

A trap!

She felt nauseous and lightheaded.

"If there's one thing I must give you, it's that you are too proud to stay amidst commoners and let them see you retch."

Cassara turned around slowly, her limbs numb with fear, but intent on not showing it as she faced her aunt.

"What have you done with Avarielle?" Cassara demanded, knowing full well her aunt had no intention of answering.

Delora's face twisted in a grotesque smile. "You can help her, if you'd like."

Graysword. Cassara knew Delora would ask for the sword, which she had thankfully left by Trevon. But still, Cassara didn't want to perish at the hands of her own aunt. Sweat trickled down the small of her back as she kept her poise.

"What may I do for you?" she sweetly asked, cocking her head slightly sideways.

Annoyance and amusement flickered in Delora's eyes. Buying time would only get her so far. How could she fight an Elder of the Circle, especially when she had no magic of her own?

"I need Graysword," Delora said. "Bring it to me now, and I'll let you and these pathetic humans live."

Cassara nodded and swallowed hard. Delora wasn't going to get the sword herself, which meant she was low on Eloms, or power, or perhaps even both. There had been fewer Eloms of late …perhaps they were finally running out? Perhaps whatever magic had created them was gone, or extinguished?

Think! Cassara could go back and get Graysword, but Delora would probably break her word and kill them all regardless, once she had secured the blade. The woman had proven she was without honor and mercy by attacking her own family.

Cassara trembled with fear and anger. "I can't believe I'm related to you."

Delora smirked. "That makes two of us."

In that instant, Cassara noticed something she had not seen before. Red light flickering in her aunt's eyes, on her skin, even all around her, as though she was lit by a magical fire from within.

Red and unlike any other magic she had ever seen while still in possession of the amulet.

The amulet. She could see the magic, like she used to be able to…did she still possess some powers? Could she still make a difference?

Cassara would not go get Graysword quietly and doom the villagers, herself, and all of Graydon. Maybe she could save them all yet. Or die trying.

"I'm not giving you Graysword," she said, bracing herself for the attack, seeing Delora smirk and the red energies grow wild around her as she prepared to attack her niece. Cassara could feel the heat of the magic even before it had incarnated.

She concentrated on grasping or extinguishing, but nothing happened. Delora gathered her powers as she cast her spell, the red flames exploding around Cassara as she gasped, red magic dancing around her, ready to engulf her at its mistress' command.

Cassara remembered the throbbing power of the magic of the amulet. She placed her hand below her neck, where it should be, and she could feel its ghost, warm and soft and soothing. But she couldn't conjure it, no more than she could reach out and soothe Delora's angry flames.

Please! she implored, remembering the first night she had met Eloms, when the amulet had flared to life based on her fear alone.

"One last chance to get me Graysword," Delora said, twisting her hand as the flames came closer, encircling and threatening to smother Cassara. Or to burn her alive as their heat increased.

Save me! Cassara pleaded with her magic, its shadow just below the surface, but unwilling or unable to come to her rescue. She felt its power boil down, as though accepting her fate.

"Your warrior friend has been suffering these fires without pause," Delora said. "Will you not save her from Siabala's torture?"

Avarielle! Hot tears ran down her cheeks, imagining her friend suffering at the hands of this wretched woman.

"To be honest," Delora said, as though chatting over tea, "I think he's fond of her. Might keep her as one of his pets. Unless you give me Graysword, of course."

Cassara gritted her teeth and closed her eyes. It didn't matter—she would not give her Graysword. Avarielle wouldn't want her to, and she had to believe her friend would understand.

Still, the thought of her trapped in that place...*I'm sorry, Avarielle.* A sob escaped her throat as the pain increased.

Then she heard a shriek and felt the magic around her dissipate. She opened her eyes and saw Trevon standing where Delora had been just seconds earlier, wiping blood from his broadsword. Delora was nowhere to be seen, but Cassara doubted she was dead.

Trevon sheathed his sword and walked up to her, his

voice dripping with an equal amount of annoyance and concern.

"Next time you can't wait until morning, you make sure I'm with you."

Cassara blushed and nodded. A question lingered in his eyes, and she wasn't sure how much he'd heard. She didn't offer details, and he let the matter rest. She let him escort her back to camp, still feeling the warmth of Delora's magic on her skin and the cold emptiness of her own magic in her heart.

Avarielle bit back a scream of frustration as the sword slapped her hand hard. She was so slow, her body healed but still weakened by the recent wounds. Dodging to the left, she reached up and almost hit him, but he jumped sideways and knocked the practice blade out of her hand.

He was handsome, there was no doubt about it. And as annoying as a swarm of mosquitoes.

Even his dark eyes didn't bother her anymore, after three days of being surrounded by nothing but Elihor, except for Jayden, who sat bored on a nearby fence. For a young boy, he certainly wasn't very interested in swordplay.

"You push yourself too hard still. But you almost had me there!" Kryde smiled as he took both of their practice swords and leaned them against the wall of the outpost.

They were in the back, one of the only private places in the entire settlement, for which Avarielle was grateful. Now that the settlers had decided she wasn't a threat, they'd apparently decided it would be fine to gawk openly at her and Jayden. Jayden didn't seem to mind and was already making some friends, but after months of being gawked at for being a Westlander in eastern lands, she was growing increasingly impatient with it.

"It's just frustrating. I'm not exactly maiden-in-distress material," Avarielle grumbled.

"You don't strike me that way, no," Kryde responded as he walked back to her.

She shook her head, frustrated with being trapped, not having Graysword, not knowing what was happening in Graydon, not having her strength, and not being able to do anything about it, not with Jayden relying on her to keep him safe.

"But you'll need help fighting at some point, and I want to make sure I'm ready," she said, frustrated. "You can't tell me even with all those weapons and fortifications that you have this place secured! Not to mention it's crawling with Circle witches."

Kryde looked questioningly at her. "Why do you hate the Circle so?"

She couldn't believe what he had just asked her. "Well, for starters, you remember the whole trying to 'bring down the Wall of Loss' bit, right? On top of that, I have personal issues with an organization that tries to steal from me and tortures me. I can't help it. I'm difficult like that."

He shook his head. "It just doesn't make sense. The Circle is there to protect and maintain the Wall, on both sides of it. Why would they be trying to tear it down?"

She shrugged. "I suggest you find out, but with caution." He shook his head again, as though unwilling to believe what she said, but unwilling to dismiss it, either.

"Anyway, don't you have anything better to do than practice sword with me?"

He grinned. "I have to find out everything that I can from you while you're here. I've already found out more than I had during my entire stay in Graydon!"

She smiled at him and shook her head. "You're not good at the whole scouting thing, you know that, right?"

He winced. "Apparently not. I've proven more skilled in my own land, where I know the rules and the people."

"Right. I completely believe you. Don't you, Jayden?"

A few moments passed before Avarielle's grin vanished and she turned to see why Jayden was silent. He was still sitting on the fence, looking towards the distance, as though lost in thought.

"Jayden?" Avarielle repeated as she walked towards him, Kryde not far behind her. Her heart leapt and bounced in her throat. He had been quiet and tired, but that was normal after everything he had been through.

"Jayden?" she asked again as she reached him, gasping

as she looked at his face and saw her reflection in his entirely black eyes.

"What did you do to him?" Avarielle spat at the Circle Elder, who had come at Kryde's bidding. The Elder's robes were black, with a white circle over her heart, mimicking her white cloak. A complete reverse from an Elder of Ravenhold.

"Calm down, this isn't helping anything," Kryde said, putting a hand on her arm as though to hold her back.

She whipped around to face him. "Jayden is my responsibility, and I'll not let him die at the hands of the Circle, whether in Graydon or in Elihor!"

"But the Elder Tan is the only one who can tell us how we can help him." He grabbed her other arm as well and forced her to look at him. She couldn't remember a time such eyes had been unfamiliar to her.

Avarielle couldn't shake the sight of the Elder, head thrown back, laughing madly into the night. "Kryde, can I trust her? She seemed kind of insane during the attack."

Kryde sighed and looked tired. "I swear to you I will do everything in my power to help him and you. But we need the Elder's help." She conceded and nodded, but glared at the Elder Tan as she approached Jayden.

The Elder either didn't notice or didn't care.

Jayden still sat motionless. The sun was just setting in

the Westland sky, the horizon free from the shimmers of the Wall of Loss, the sunset stunning with its vibrant shades of orange, pink and purple. The Elder put a hand on Jayden just as the wind picked up ashes and scattered them all over the settlement. She wasn't growing any fonder of the smell of charred remains.

"There," the Elder said, and Jayden, as though obeying a silent order, closed his eyes and tumbled forward. Avarielle quickly bridged the gap between them and caught him before he hit the ground.

"What did you do to him?" Avarielle demanded. His face was drawn and pale, and he looked stricken. His lungs rattled with each labored breath.

"He's dying," Tan said, her silver hair covered in ashes, her dark eyes unblinking.

Kryde asked before Avarielle blew up. "How? Of what? Can you help him?"

The Elder looked at Kryde as though seeing him for the first time, and then asked incredulously, "Help him how?"

Avarielle got up, stepped over Jayden and would have slapped the woman had Kryde not stepped in her way. "You will not hit an ally on my watch, woman," he threatened. Avarielle closed the gap between them, leaned in and bit every word she spoke.

"And Jayden does not die on mine. So, what are we going to do about it?"

Kryde was the first to step back, turning to the Elder

after giving Avarielle a look of warning. Her muscles pumped with adrenaline, her senses heightened and alert at the imminent threat.

"What ails him?" Kryde asked the Elder.

She looked quizzically at him. Eli, Avarielle hated every last member of the Circle, whether on this side of the Wall or the next. They were all useless, idiotic fools with too much power and too few brains.

"He's from Graydon," she stated, as though it were the most obvious answer in the world.

"Kryde, I'm going to have to hit her if she keeps this up," Avarielle warned.

"What do you mean, Tan?" She could hear the impatience in his words, and wondered briefly if it was aimed at her or the Elder. Then again, at that moment, she didn't really care.

"He's from Graydon, and we're in Elihor."

"I'm hitting her."

"Could you just calm down a second? Please? Tan, what do you mean? Can he not live in Elihor?"

Tan snapped to attention for a second and began lecturing. Avarielle really disliked the woman.

"The Wall has been up so long, my dear boy, that the magics are no longer compatible. Just like you felt ill the further you strayed from our land, just like your strength dwindled to the point where you allowed yourself to be captured." Kryde's arm twitched at that. "So does this boy suffer, except he is younger, and has very little power against Elihor, apparently."

Avarielle swallowed hard. "He's a relative of Graydon," she whispered, and Kryde looked with surprise at Jayden, still unconscious on the ground.

"This is unexpected," Tan said. "But Elihor's magic must want him dead." The adrenaline that had clutched Avarielle's muscles dissipated in seconds, and she felt drained. And helpless. Then an idea struck her.

"What about those ghost-things?" Avarielle suddenly said, remembering the healing of her own wounds.

"What ghost-things?" Kryde asked. "You mean kealers?"

"Whatever you call them—the ghosts with the Circle emblem. They came the night the srocks attacked. One of them healed me in the mountains. I was in bad shape too, so surely they could help Jayden."

"They healed you?" Kryde asked incredulously. "Those things don't heal, Avarielle. They find and kill the unprotected wounded. They're a plague on this land, dwindling only as they kill."

"It is possible," Tan intoned. The old woman grabbed hold of Avarielle's left wrist with a speed the warrior did not expect. Avarielle clenched her jaw and fought the urge to yank her arm back.

"Yes, it is possible," the Elder said, looking intently at Avarielle's hand. Kryde moved closer, as though to stop

Avarielle from hitting the witch. "You must be careful though. Not to summon your sword."

"What?"

"Graysword. They need it, you know. It's one of the two keys. The sword and the fully activated amulet, and those with the power to wield it, can bring down the Wall of Loss. It's what Siabala will want from you, and undoubtedly why you still live."

Avarielle growled her reply. "I have no intention of giving them what they want, and no intention of blindly following your advice either, witch."

Tan continued speaking as though she had never mentioned Graysword. "The kealers, we can only assume, are members of Graydon's Circle, turned to monsters by Siabala. It seems they still connect to Graydon's magic and attempt to use it for good, but in this world, their magic kills, and does not heal."

Avarielle jerked her hand out of the old woman's grasp. "Well, regardless of what they are or where they come from, they're still our best bet, I think. Not that I'm inclined to trust the Circle, but in this case, I'm willing to chance it."

"Don't you even care about what the Elder Tan just told you?" Kryde asked.

She turned to face him. "That the Circle finally got what it deserved and met an enemy stronger than itself and wound up getting themselves slaughtered? No, not really. And, if you were from my world, I think you'd understand a bit more."

"I doubt that."

"Look, I'm trying very hard to understand your care for witches, and considering you're completely dependent on them for your survival right now, I get it. But in my world, I don't count on them for anything more than grief. So how about we just make peace with that—you like your Circle, and I won't beat on them. I hate my Circle, and I'll beat on them as much as I want to. Understood?"

He looked annoyed with her but nodded nonetheless. "So, how do I find those kealers?"

Tan answered her. "Wait for nighttime. They're drawn to the suffering of the people, so they'll come. The more you suffer, the more your chances of encountering one. You'll just have to bring the boy outside the protective barrier."

"We won't be able to protect you out there, should anything happen," Kryde added. "We have no weapon that works against them, and I can't justify sacrificing my men for the boy." He paused, looked her straight in the eye. "But if you think you need me, I'm willing to come."

Avarielle grinned. It was the best offer she'd had in a long time. "I appreciate that, but stay here. If we're right, their magic can't hurt us since we're from Graydon." She shrugged. "If we're wrong, we're dead anyway, and there's nothing you can do to save us."

"We'll give you a proper burial then, should that happen."

"That's wonderful, thanks."

"Least we can do."

She grinned at him and looked back towards Jayden, his pale features drawn. She had brought him to Elihor to save him, but had only succeeded in prolonging his suffering.

7

―――――――

Avarielle walked around the settlement, desperate for answers, for action, for the comforting feel of Graysword in her hand, but she didn't know where to find any of those things. She would have gladly beaten up the Circle Elder, but Tan seemed more lost and confused than evil, and Kryde was protective of her.

She had to trust that her plan of using the Circle ghosts to heal Jayden would work, wishing she had some sort of assurance, or at least a method of defending herself.

She walked past one of the stone formations that served as protection to the settlement, a Circle teleportation outpost, like the many that existed in Graydon. Except this one had served as refuge to the people of Elihor, and when attacks came at night in the form of kealers or the great srocks, the Circle protected them.

Which was why Tan was half-mad from overuse of her magic, and useless in helping Jayden. Most of the other sorceresses here were Circle sproutlings, barely initiated in its magics. Apparently, in Elihor, joining the Circle was an honor and not a blatant act of kidnapping. She wondered how differently everyone would feel about the Circle in Graydon if even just that simple fact was changed. Choice, instead of duty.

She saw a young girl donning the dress of the Circle, black here where it was white in Graydon, a green circle above her heart—green like a new sprout, a novice—and wondered if she would ever be anything more. The girl concentrated on a stone formation, as though trying to feed magic into it.

"Our defenses are failing," Kryde's whisper made her jump. She hadn't heard him walk up beside her.

"They're failing?" she asked, and he took her by the elbow and led her away from the beleaguered settlers, towards the gardens and storehouses that now fed so many.

When they were far enough that no one could hear them, Kryde continued speaking. "You've seen it yourself. The Circle doesn't have the strength to keep up the defenses. The srocks are too strong for us to defeat with sword and arrow."

Avarielle nodded. She remembered fighting them, and

knew that even Graysword would have little effect on them. Only Shirina had been able to defeat them, but that hardly made Avarielle wish for the sorceress' presence.

"I have to save Jayden," she said as though in apology. She wanted to help them, as they had been kind to her, but Jayden had to be her first priority. "I really do want to stay and help, but I have to make it back to Graydon. One way or the other."

Kryde nodded. A moment passed before he spoke. "It used to be beautiful, this land. I wish you could have seen it then."

He stopped, and Avarielle stopped with him. He glanced around, beyond the gardens, which looked so much like Graydon's, and into the charred landscape. Avarielle imagined what he was seeing, how beautiful it must have been, with its soft hills, and she imagined the rivers that might have run near, the sunlight glistening off their waters. When the wind was strong enough, she could smell a trace of the sea, reminding her of the crispness of Edoline.

She turned to look at him, his strong chiseled profile and proud nose, his dark shoulder-length hair and his eyes that absorbed the light and fostered it within.

"I wish I could have seen it too," she whispered, seeing nothing but fire in his eyes.

She found comfort in those flames.

Delora grew increasingly impatient. She should have all the pieces by now. This should have proved an easier task. Whatever success she had achieved by retrieving the amulet, hers by right, had been lost because of that Grayloft.

And then that other Westlander, who had cost her Graysword with his sneak attack. She had been careless, but it didn't matter. She would see that all of the West would be made to pay, the wretched land holding a much more important one hostage.

Delora stood on a mountain overlooking Elihor, enjoying the fresh air after spending so much time in Siabala's realm. The scent of sulfur clung to her like a second layer of skin. She doubted she would ever get it all off.

No matter. Siabala was her greatest ally, the sulfur but a mere inconvenience.

Her true problem lay in securing what she needed. The amulet, the Grayloft and Graysword. Triggering the two items by its wielders from Stormhold would bring down the Wall, according to Siabala.

And considering he had helped to create it, he was well aware of its flaws. The hairs on her arms prickled to life, and she knew he was near. She didn't bother turning around.

"To what do I owe this honor, Siabala?"

He grunted, a sound she now knew meant he was laughing.

"Are you going to go retrieve the items you so easily lost, witch?"

Delora nodded, knowing she didn't even need to. By accepting Siabala's powers, she had also given away more of her freedoms than anticipated, including full privacy of thought. At least Siabala didn't bother monitoring her unless he was close, but it was still an annoying and disconcerting invasion.

"Get the boy tonight." Siabala's voice hissed in the night.

"Why would I get the boy?" Delora was not so simple as to think that Siabala wanted to please her, knowing Delora had tried to save her nephew at least once from the Eloms. Jayden was too young to be involved in this, and he couldn't wield the powers of the amulet. He was useless, but innocent.

To think Siabala would be humanistic in his approach was foolish. "I want the Grayloft to come after him. I wish to see her fighting skills. Never before have I had the chance to see the bloodline tested firsthand."

Delora fought hard to hide her impatience. "I can just go in and get her and the amulet. Those are the pieces we need."

She felt him near her, the scent of him so strong it overpowered her stomach. She fought not to retch. When he spoke, it was in her mind alone.

You do not have the power to take her. And you belong to me. Do as I say.

And he was gone.

Delora closed her eyes, her body wooden and foreign to her, infused with Siabala's magic, making her stronger, but turning her into a monster as well. And it was too late to stop it.

She wondered how she could save Jayden and get what she needed at the same time, knowing that her will wasn't strong enough to overcome Siabala's orders, knowing that the time to break away had long come and gone.

It was Siabala's bidding, and therefore her will.

The day was drawing to a close when Jayden finally awakened. The youth was pale and drawn, but some white had returned to his eyes. He grinned weakly when Avarielle entered.

"How are you feeling?" she asked as she sat beside him on the bed.

"Tired, but alright." He shrugged. She guessed he was feeling much worse, but didn't want to admit it.

"I'll find a way to get you home, Jayden," Avarielle said, the words spoken more for herself than for him.

"I know," he said simply, so trusting in her abilities that it made her heart ache. "You did get us out of Siabala's Rage. This seems much easier."

Avarielle gave a short laugh. That much was true,

except she wouldn't have been able to escape without Kryde's help.

"I have a plan for tonight, Jayden. It's going to be scary, but it might buy us time to get back to Graydon."

He tilted his head sideways. "If you'll be there, I'm sure we'll be okay."

Avarielle stood up and grinned at him. He didn't ask for details and she didn't give any. He looked terrible, and she knew he was putting on a brave face for her, so she let him rest and went to find Kryde. He had made it to Graydon once. If she could find out how, then maybe she could get Jayden across before it was too late. The Circle ghosts would probably not be enough to keep Jayden alive for long. Not if Elihor's magic was intent on killing him, as Elder Tan suspected.

The air outside was heavy as the sun set, filled with ashes stirred by a growing wind. Avarielle could barely see ahead of her as she covered her mouth and nose with her sleeve, squinting to find her way. She could see some of the cloth walls of the makeshift houses blowing wildly. Settlers were being ushered to the outpost, the one stone building that could withstand the onslaught of wind. She was glad Jayden was already safe in there.

She saw Pack Nacker, shouting orders as men dragged the terrified horses towards the outpost. It was going to be crowded in there very soon. Spotting her, Pack walked towards her.

"The Circle sorceresses don't think this is a normal

wind!" he screamed at her as he approached, his hair, skin and armor covered in ashes, his cloak billowing madly behind him.

"What do they think it is?" Avarielle asked the obvious question.

"An attack! It could come soon! We're gathering everyone in the outpost and preparing for battle!"

"Who's attacking?" she asked, worried for Jayden and Kryde.

"Who else? Siabala, probably, come to finish his handiwork!"

Avarielle nodded. "Where can I get weapons?"

He indicated a garden shed that was buckling in the wind. "Take what you want, but it's hardly first class!"

She nodded and ran towards the shed, almost knocked over by the door as it blew off its hinges.

Pack had been right, there were very few quality weapons left. Still, Avarielle managed to find a well-balanced broadsword that was to her liking, and it fit in Graysword's empty scabbard. She considered taking a bow, but in these winds, decided the weapon would be useless. She grabbed a long knife for her waist, and two shorter ones which she stashed in her boots. She also found some throwing knives and stashed them in her gauntlets.

Her strength had been returning quickly thanks to her practice, and it felt good to bear weapons again and to head into combat. Everything seemed so much simpler when the enemy was obvious and the course of action clear. She had missed that most of all.

"Are you fit to fight?" Kryde screamed from the entryway, and she turned around and grinned.

"Want to test me?"

His eyes glowed with mischief. "Another time, perhaps. We should get to the outpost! We'll make our stand there, where we can actually see and breathe!"

She nodded and followed him into the rising winds, shelters blowing past them as they were torn free and dragged away. Avarielle kept her mouth covered as the winds relentlessly tried to steal her breath and fill her lungs with ashes.

They entered the keep and her ears rang.

"I have to give Jayden something," Avarielle said as she left Kryde, who was organizing guards near the main entrance. Avarielle passed frightened villagers and huddled families, each so gray from the ashes it was hard to tell anyone apart. She found Jayden sitting near his room, now filled with people. He looked up when he saw her, his eyes dull with fatigue, the strange darkness still clinging to the sides of his irises.

She knelt beside him. "I'm going to give you something, but you have to promise me to be careful with it." Avarielle pulled out Cassara's amulet. The metal was dull, empty of magic. She hesitated for a moment, hoping she was doing the right thing, before handing it to Jayden.

"That's Cassara's necklace," he said as he took it.

"It has magic, Jayden. It's what your sister used to fight Eloms. I'm not sure it'll work for you, but there's a better chance of that than there is of it working for anyone else here. But," she looked at him sternly, making sure she had his full attention, "it's very powerful and dangerous, Jayden. Don't ever use it unless you absolutely have to."

He nodded and kept it in his hand, clutching it tightly. The amulet gave no hint of glow or magic. But Jayden seemed stronger for holding a piece of his home.

"I'm going to help them with whatever's coming, but be careful. Stay clear of windows and stay low. If anything happens, I'll come find you."

He nodded. Avarielle ruffled his hair and stood up, and he gave her an annoyed look. She took a moment to examine her surroundings. The windows were all well-barricaded, and everyone seemed fairly certain the attack would come from downstairs. Avarielle wasn't so convinced, and was glad to see some soldiers posted at the windows. At least Kryde had a good head on his shoulders, so she didn't have to worry about following some idiot into battle.

She left Jayden and headed back downstairs, reaching the front as the first hit came on the door. At first everyone hesitated, uncertain if it was just the wind, but then another, stronger blow shook the doors. And another. And another. The thick wood shook under each blow and trembled at the might of the attacker.

As she pulled her broadsword free from her scabbard,

Avarielle wished for the hundredth time that she still had Graysword with her.

Jayden wasn't terrified. After the first few nights in Siabala's Rage, he hadn't been that scared anymore. Mostly just numb. And now he had Avarielle with him, and he knew she could put up a serious fight.

He held Cassara's amulet and wished he knew if his sister was in pain, or lost, or maybe even dead. Avarielle didn't talk much about her, but he knew enough to see that the warrior thought that if she wasn't dead by now, she soon would be. Jayden examined the amulet closely, hoping to glean some answers in its flawless surface, but none came to him. He could only see his own reflection.

He clutched it, ignoring the murmurs of the settlers around him, but he could feel them stare. A boy from Graydon was strange to them, and now that his eyes were gaining some more of their traits, it somehow made him even more of an oddity.

He was huddled in a corner, having left his room to families seeking refuge. The walls and floor were all stone, and they were getting cooler as the wind kept pounding on the building. He could make out some of the whispers around him, about how the Circle might not be able to save them. How their leader was strong, but not strong enough to beat back an army.

He closed his eyes as the pounding on the doors began. Fear was starting to win him over now, but he fought against it, clutching the amulet until it bit into his skin.

"Hello Jayden," someone whispered beside him. His eyes snapped open and he stared directly into the eyes of Delora, too frightened even to scream.

The pounding increased and the doors buckled, but still, they did not fall.

"What's taking them so bloody long?" Pack whispered, and Avarielle grinned. Kryde put a hand on Pack's shoulder, as though to calm him.

"Do we even know what's trying to come in?" Avarielle asked, tense but growing bored with the wait.

"Srocks, I assume," Kryde said.

"But none have broken through our defenses yet," Tan said as she appeared beside Avarielle, making the warrior jump.

"Eli! You want me to cut you in half, woman?" Avarielle cursed.

"The only magic that broke in," the Elder said, ignoring the warrior, "is magic from Graydon, which we are powerless against."

"Graydon?" Kryde asked, but Avarielle understood. The windstorm which blinded them, and then an illusion spell to make them think they were under attack...*Delora!*

Avarielle pushed past Tan and ran up the stairs, taking them three at a time, barreling through anyone who had the misfortune of getting in her way. She heard Kryde call her name but she ignored him, intent on her goal.

She turned down the hallway towards the spot where Jayden had been just instants earlier. It stood empty.

"Where is he?" she demanded, scaring the settlers into silence.

"Answer her!" Kryde ordered, and one quickly obeyed.

"A woman came for him, from Graydon, and took him in there." He pointed to a small storage room. Avarielle kicked the door open and charged in, only to find it empty and smelling of sulfur.

"He's gone," she announced as Kryde joined her. Her stomach fell into her heels. She was going to be sick.

Kryde put his hand on her shoulder. *First Cassara, now Jayden...*

"Could she have made it back to Siabala in one jump?" she asked Kryde.

"I'm not the one to ask that," he answered. As though on cue, Tan appeared behind Kryde.

"Could she have teleported all the way back?" Avarielle asked, before adding, "She was run through with a short sword just a few days ago."

Tan looked pensive for a moment. "If she summoned the windstorm outside, plus the illusion out there, while still casting or having recently finished a healing spell, then probably not. Did she teleport in?"

Avarielle shook her head. "She must have walked in amongst all the confusion and waited for me to give Jayden the amulet before grabbing him." She could have hit herself right then. Everything she did to help Jayden just seemed to make things worse for him.

"Amulet?" Tan asked. Avarielle hesitated for a moment, but chose to answer. Keeping secrets wasn't going to help her at this point.

"It was Graydon's, I believe, or at least it belongs to Graydon's family. How do we find them, Elder?" she pushed, annoyed at having to depend on a Circle witch.

"Was it an amulet made of a gold disk and a silver quarter moon?" Tan demanded, eyes focused.

Avarielle nodded.

"That is Elihor's amulet. All of this time, it was kept in Graydon. Smart."

"What? It's Elihor's?" Avarielle shook her head. "Look, this is all very fascinating, but the fact remains that Jayden is missing and I intend to find him before they make it back to Siabala. Now, where do I go?"

Kryde stepped in. "If she couldn't teleport all the way back to Siabala, how far would she have gone?"

Tan pondered it for a moment, and Avarielle feared the woman had just forgotten what they were discussing when she finally answered. "There are two Circle outposts within distance. One is still occupied by two Elders, who could easily stop her teleportation spell. The other was deserted during the Great Fire, its defenses too weak to withstand the attack that close to the Wall."

"That's where they must be. How do we get there?"

"It's half a day's ride to the Tash Outpost," Kryde answered.

"How long before she can leave again?" Avarielle asked Elder Tan.

"If she keeps the boy with her, I'd say about a day. If she decides to kill the boy or leave him at the outpost, then she could teleport after a half-day's sleep," Tan answered. "If you follow the valley right to the south of here, it'll lead straight to it."

Avarielle nodded and turned to Kryde. "I need a horse. Now."

"You'll never make it in this storm. There's too much wind, and there's too much ash in the air. If you don't die of suffocation, then the horse will."

"I'll take my chances. Give me your poorest horse if you don't want to lose a good one. Or I'll just walk."

"I'm not worried about losing a horse!" He took a step forward and placed his hands on her shoulders. "I'm worried about losing you."

Avarielle shook his hands free. "I already lost one heir of Graydon, Kryde, I can't stand to lose another." Then she added with a grin, "Besides, who says I won't come back?"

He stood silently, not budging. She pleaded with him. "Please, Kryde. He needs me."

"I must be insane," he sighed, "but all right. I'll give you a horse. But the second this storm ends and I'm satisfied these people are safe, I'm coming after you."

Tan stepped out of the small room, as though disinterested with the proceedings. The room suddenly seemed much smaller.

"I should come with you, but I can't," Kryde said in a whisper. Avarielle took a step forward and pushed back a strand of his hair. He closed his eyes as her hand strayed down the contour of his face.

"You're needed here, Kryde," she said softly. "And I do mean it. I *will* come back."

She forced herself to take a step back and remove her hand. He opened his eyes again. She found comfort in their darkness, now.

"I'll come for you as soon as I can."

"I know."

She turned and walked back down the stairs, knowing full well that if the opportunity to get Jayden back to Graydon arose, she would take it in a heartbeat.

Avarielle had been in sandstorms before, and she found them much less disturbing than this storm of ashes. Sandstorms hurt. They whip at you and throw grit into your eyes, they steal breath from you and can even draw blood.

But ash was a silent killer. It didn't hurt, unless rocks

or branches were loosened with it, but it would cut off your air supply much faster and more efficiently. She could barely keep her eyes open and the horse stumbled beneath her. She jumped off and pulled the horse by its reins, forcing it to remain standing as she struggled for breath.

She needed speed to reach Jayden.

Her strength was being sapped by the storm, her eyes watering from the ashes, and she was reminded of Siabala's Rage, and the sulfur that had robbed her of breath. Anger ignited within her, giving her the strength to pull the stumbling beast, ignoring her aching lungs.

She closed her eyes to protect them from the ash. They were useless now, anyway. She felt her way forward, letting her feet guide her on the terrain, one step at a time, not loosening her grip on the reins for one second. She wished she could at least hear her own breath, but all sounds were sucked into the vortex of the storm.

Another step, and the ash abruptly stopped assailing her. The horse stomped its hooves, the beast celebrating their freedom from the storm.

Behind them stood a wall of wind and ash that rose into the sky as high as she could see, so thick it blocked the world beyond it.

"Guess they don't make storms like they used to in the Circle," Avarielle mumbled as she removed the rag covering the horse's mouth and gave it some water. The mare whinnied gratefully. "No time to rest yet!" Avarielle said as she got back on the horse, kicking her into a trot.

The valley was burned like the rest of Elihor, although some spots, nestled in crevasses, had been missed by the fires. A few trees still bore fruit and some flowers bloomed. It was a welcome sight after all of the ashes that still clung to her.

A gentle breeze blew in, and Avarielle could smell the sea. The horse galloped faster, also excited by the fresh air. A few minutes later, they cleared the valley. To their right the sea glimmered with the first rays of dawn, and the Wall of Loss shimmered beyond the mountains. If Elihor's sunsets were more magnificent, Graydon's sunrises were much superior.

She wondered for a second how bad it would really be for the Wall to be lowered. Elihor wasn't full of possessed creatures of darkness, as they had all been made to believe.

And the people reminded her of her own, making the bond with Kryde so much easier to forge. *A warrior who'd lost his home. Like me.*

After a few hours, she spotted the outpost—a burnt building, barely standing, near the base of the mountains. It was close to Siabala's Rage, she guessed, not certain where exactly in the mountains his reign began and ended.

Avarielle suspected she was heading into a trap. Delora needed her for Graysword, that much she knew. Delora knew Avarielle would come for Jayden. And Avarielle had no protection against Delora's magic, and no magic with which to fight.

"I should have chopped her head off," Avarielle mumbled as she moved the horse into the shadows, in case someone was on the lookout for her.

It was dawn, and so she had no doubt Kryde would soon come, if the storm had abated and he felt his people were safe enough. But she could hardly sit here like a lump and wait for him to show up, knowing full well that Delora would probably be gone by then.

She sighed and dismounted, leaving her horse in the shadows to graze on some unburnt grass.

A little walk wouldn't kill her.

The doors ceased trembling, the pounding ended and the winds no longer raged outside by the time the first streaks of dawn crossed the Wall of Loss and struck the outpost. Kryde smiled at Pack, hitting him on the shoulder as he helped open the door.

Pack looked too tired for his age. He and Kryde had been friends for a long time, growing up together, and when Kryde was named leader of this outpost, it had only been natural that Pack became his first officer. Of course, it had been sheer luck that they had both wound up here, with Pack's men still armed.

The doors swung open, revealing settling ash glinting in the sunlight, and Kryde wondered if he believed in luck at all. It had all fallen into place almost too neatly.

The outposts, the Circle's call for Pack's troops, Kryde being near an outpost himself…he had thought nothing of it until Avarielle's accusations. *Could the Circle have orchestrated this too? To keep me alive for whatever purpose they may harbor?*

Kryde hated thinking that way, as the Circle had proved his greatest ally. But he couldn't help feeling as though he had been manipulated, and worse yet, that someone else still pulled his strings. Sneaking off to Graydon had been the only thing he had done of his own accord, and now it was time to do another.

"You're in charge until my return, Pack," Kryde said as he walked outside, ash still falling from the sky like dirty snow.

Pack caught up with him quickly.

"Are you mad, Kryde? You're going after the woman from Graydon? What about the outpost?"

Kryde stopped and faced his friend. "Pack, what am I doing here?"

Pack seemed taken aback by the question. "You're leading these people, and protecting them, of course!"

Kryde smiled and shook his head. He liked Pack in part for his blind loyalty, but sometimes his head was so thick it rivaled the strongest metals.

"Pack, I'm doing nothing here. I'm a leader in name,

through my bloodline, and nothing more. The defenses are failing and you know it as well as I do. I really believe the answers lie in the people of Graydon. I need to find out, Pack. Before it's too late."

Pack nodded grudgingly. "The fact that you and that warrior woman seem destined to ride a horse together has nothing to do with it, I suppose?"

Kryde looked at his friend, stunned. *Maybe not that thick.* Then he burst out laughing.

"Pack, I underestimated you, my friend."

Pack's expression turned serious. "Be careful, Kryde. No matter how useless you might feel without magic, the people here need you for more than that."

Kryde nodded.

"I promise I'll come back."

Tan could feel the wind dissipating around the outpost, once a great stronghold of the Circle. As dawn broke, so did the witch's spell, falling like ashes from the sky and lying just as dead on the ground. Her students were exhausted, and she feared some might soon crack under the weight of their own magic.

What was supposed to have been a simple training exercise in teleportation, one sunny day long ago, had turned out to be the fight of their lives. She wondered how her other sisters in Larkhold fared. She hoped dearly that the Covenant still held, and that none had fallen prey to Siabala's powers, as the Covenant from Graydon obviously had.

Tan remembered being powerful. She remembered the air crackling with possibility and magic, and how it sparked at her fingertips when she stroked its potential. But the Great Fire had burned much of that potential away, as though it had used the very fabric that held Elihor together to set her ablaze.

She had come to rely on her own reserves of strength to cast her magic instead of drawing it from the land around her. But those reserves were almost empty, and she knew it. She drifted too often, finding herself in places she had not meant to go, not even recalling walking there. She held entire conversations she couldn't recall but a few minutes later. She was losing control of her faculties.

But she still knew the scent of an attack when she smelled it. And she did now, despite the growing daylight.

She passed by Pack, who seemed annoyed that Kryde had left. She caught his attention and nodded towards the defenses. He seemed confused for a moment and was probably questioning her sanity when he heard it too.

The song of the kealers on the morning breeze.

Siabala had sent his monsters to finish them off, or more likely to gather them to grow his army and attack Graydon.

Pack held her eyes for a moment and nodded. It was a

battle they would lose, but he still held his shoulders proudly as he assembled his soldiers.

Tan watched him go, letting the sound of the settlers wash over her, watching her students fighting to restore defenses that no longer mattered, feeling the fear grow with the song, and hearing the whimpers.

Then she blocked it all out, knowing today would see her death, no matter which battle she chose.

Carrying a lantern, she headed downstairs, to the basement of the keep, where no one else was allowed. Only Circle Elders had access, and she had strictly enforced the rule regardless of the changes in circumstance. She did not tell anyone where she was going, nor did she expect them to look until the attack had begun and her powers were needed. If they even had the time to come looking for her.

Kryde rode towards the Graydon witch now, and she knew he could not win. Although Graydon's Circle had forgotten its way, Elihor's Circle had not, and she still understood the reason for the Wall of Loss, and the need for Kryde to survive well beyond this day.

She needed to reach the Graydon witch before Kryde, and stop her from robbing Elihor of her sole descendant. Kryde knew he had to survive, but his heart was too embroiled and clouded to see clearly. That was why she was here.

To do the things he could not do.

She stood in the center of the basement, arcane

symbols of the Circle surrounding her, drawn on the walls so long ago even she could not interpret some of them. A simple circle, reflecting the silver one above her left breast, was painted on the floor, and she stood within it.

She didn't have the power to teleport to the outpost and fight. Teleportation would leave her drained and helpless. But she did have enough power to teleport and harness the energies of her spell before they vanished and re-absorb them, killing herself and destroying everything around her.

It would take care of the Graydon witch and save Kryde in the process, though it meant dooming every settler here, and her students who had fought so hard to save them. She hardened her heart and clung to the bigger picture.

Graydon had to be stopped, and Elihor had to retain her final heir, in case the Wall should fail.

It was the Circle's bidding, and therefore her will.

he day was dry and sunny, like every day had been for the past week, and Shirina's skin felt cracked and burned where her cloak and robes no longer covered her. She was a disgrace to her rank, and she knew it. An Elite of the Circle, dressed like a beggar and clinging to the back of a horse for dear life. She still managed to care, wishing her pride was the most wounded part of her.

She had cast a spell on the horse telling it where to go. It was strong and needed little food or rest, for which Shirina was grateful. The horse trotted, which was as fast as it could go without Shirina falling off. No Eloms seemed to be in the area anymore, which made for another blessing.

The land was deserted. In almost a week's travel, she hadn't encountered a single human. She had crossed several destroyed villages, but that was it. No sign of survivors, and Shirina hadn't lingered to search for any.

She had to get help, and Ravenhold, should it still stand, was not an option. Not now that she had disobeyed direct orders by not collecting the amulet. And especially not after casting a spell on Delora, an Elder of Ravenhold. Should Delora still be part of the Circle, death would be welcome by the time it was inflicted on her.

Drifting in and out of sleep, she could tell she was muttering. She knew she was running a fever, and she understood that the magic she had absorbed from the two large obsidian creatures had been from Siabala itself, or from Elihor, and it devoured her from the inside.

As day turned to night again, she could taste blood in her mouth, the bitter taste of defeat. She drifted and dreamed. Of her life before the Circle. Of her mother, her father, her older brother, her cousins…she dreamed of them but she couldn't remember their names. Or her name.

The name she bore before Shirina, which her parents had chosen for her at birth.

She cried, she thought, but she wasn't certain. The absorbed dark magic played evil tricks on her mind, fighting off the defenses the Circle had taught her to create.

To create and maintain.

Defenses against future and past assailants, whether enemy or memory.

The Circle. Her family. No, it was gone. Tangia was long dead by now, and with her the last of her connection to the failed Covenant.

She was alone.

Without family or friends. And she was surprised to realize that she cared. She tried to wipe her face, to remove the sign of passage of her tears.

Night turned to day. She didn't know where she was, and the horse couldn't help her. Though she knew they were headed where she had demanded, she didn't recall where that was.

Where am I going? Where am I from? She was lost inside and out.

"I need help," she mumbled, clinging to the horse as it came to an abrupt stop outside the gates of a heavily barricaded village. The guards had heard the approach of the horse and rider, and though they only opened the gates a crack, the animal pushed its way through, heedless of their protests. Shirina didn't have the strength to tell them it was alright, she meant them no harm, and she certainly wasn't part of the Elom armies.

The horse moved forward without guidance. She didn't want to be seen like this, broken and beaten, without allies and hope.

The horse stopped. She cracked her eyes open and she could see a picket fence and a garden flowering beyond it. It was beautiful.

Then a man stood near her, and he looked closely at her face. She opened her eyes wider.

She knew him.

"Marguerite?" he asked, and all of the remaining defenses the Circle had so carefully taught her to create and maintain crashed around her at hearing her birth name.

She was a child again. At home and warm in bed. The house smelled of roses and lilies, just like it always had. She could hear her mother humming in the kitchen as she cooked, although the sound vanished the closer she clawed her way to the surface.

And there was no scent of cooking. Only the scent of dusty furniture and pipe smoke.

She opened her eyes. It was light outside, the sun beaming in despite the curtains on the window. She sat up, her body still drained and feeling strange to her, as though her limbs were not truly her limbs and her thirst not truly hers.

She leaned back against the pillows and drank deeply from the glass of water that had been left by her bedside, grateful for the gesture. She was in her old room, although much had changed. It was smaller, for one, though she suspected that was simply because she was bigger. The walls had been stripped bare of all memories and the dressers cleared of old mementos.

She remembered being happy here. She had loved her family, which is why it had hurt so much to be taken from them, why it had been in her best interest to forget them. And despite all that Tangia had done to her, to help her forget, she had come to love Tangia as family, too. The ache in her heart deepened for the two families she had lost.

A knock sounded at the door.

"Come in." Her voice cracked. She wished she didn't feel so weak and helpless. She hated it.

A man entered, and she recognized him immediately. He was taller, much older. His frame had grown considerably, and he had filled it well. His eyes were green and his hair light brown, and she would know him anywhere, even if he were a hundred years older. It was her cousin, Marx.

He, her older brother and she had always gotten in trouble together, although as the youngest she usually got away with the most. He had laughed a lot when they were children. They all had, running through the hills of Solir, near the border of Kosel. How could she have forgotten where she came from?

"Little Margie," he said, his voice choked with emotion. "You've been asleep for two straight days. What did they do to you, Margie?"

Shirina wanted to tell him to stop calling her that, that

her name was Shirina, that no one had done anything to her except herself. That she had been the one stupid enough to absorb a magic she shouldn't have, and then had betrayed the only allies she had left. She wanted to tell him she wasn't even Margie, that he was mistaken, and that she was simply passing through, tired and exhausted, and that she should be in the Lisal Gardens as she had planned. But she'd told the horse where to bring her, and had pictured the wrong flowers, the wrong home, her mind clouded by fatigue and pain.

She wanted most of all for him to stop looking at her with such kindness and pity. It made her feel like a ridiculous five-year-old again, a child who had tumbled down a hill because she was too stupid to just stay where she was supposed to stay, because she felt the need to break rules she knew existed for a very good reason.

But she couldn't say any of those things, nor could she answer his question. It was all that she could do not to cry and become that child again.

"I need a bath," she said, not meeting his eyes, looking down and examining her dirty clothes. She would need to clean the sheets, too.

Marx answered in a whisper. "The tub's where it always was. My wife laid some clothes out for you. We'll be outside doing some chores."

He paused and then spoke the same words he had when she'd last see him, almost twenty years ago.

"Come find us when you're ready."

Except that she never had.

Shirina examined her body closely in the old mirror. She was covered with bruises from the horse ride. But those weren't what she focused on. She was examining her neck, now clean from the grime and sweat of well over a month's travel and battles. Despite all of her attempts to clean it, a shadow clung there, where it formed its crevasse, just above her breastbone. It wasn't black per se, but it was definitely some form of shadow.

She knew the dark magic she had absorbed still slithered within her. She could feel it coursing through her veins. But she hadn't expected it to leave physical signs, if that was what this was.

Marx's wife had left her a practical outfit: pants, a shirt, a small coat and some boots. Shirina had not worn pants since she had been a child, and she found them uncomfortable and restricting, but did not want to insult her cousin's wife. Especially since she had not even met her yet. She took a scarf that was in the bathroom and tied it around her neck, letting it dangle where it could hide the growing shadow.

She was more dressed than she had ever been, and yet she had never felt more naked and vulnerable. No one could now tell she was from the Circle. Her Circle dress was so tattered she would be surprised if it could be saved, although she left it to soak in the washing basin, in case it could be.

The kitchen was different too. Decorations had been changed and moved around, the table much smaller than when she had been a child, and she could easily tell only the two of them lived here. Two sets of silverware in the sink. Two plates on the counter. Two chairs pulled up to the table.

When she had been a child, they had always run out of room at the table and had to squeeze in children wherever there was a spot. Her parents had always been taking in family, and they were so closely knit that it hadn't mattered. Aunts and uncles were second parents, and cousins other siblings.

Now, there were only two.

Shirina needed to clear her head. Now that her body was cleansed, she needed to do something about her mind. She still needed to reach the Lisal Gardens, that much was obvious, but what would she do afterward? Say that Grasky was willing to help her after all, and she found something there that could help her cleanse the dark magic from her own, then what? Would she go off and fight Eloms? Return to Ravenhold, just in case something remained for her to do? Go see if Cassara had survived and wanted her help?

Not likely.

Or should she head to Siabala's Rage on a suicide mission to save her mentor, who was probably already dead? Or maybe rescue Avarielle, who would then undoubtedly turn around and kill her?

Or maybe she should just stay here with her cousin, and tend the land with him. She was good with plants, and her magic, once cleansed, would help these people rebuild.

She gave a bitter laugh. The world would heal itself from whatever disease had been inflicted on it, and the Circle would come and seek out its traitors. She would only be putting her cousin in danger.

She stepped outside and took a long, deep breath. She needed to walk a bit before talking to Marx. She didn't want to see him yet, or meet his wife, or figure out what to do. She just needed to walk.

Her horse was tethered beside the house, munching on some oats. The mare had been washed and brushed and seemed generally content. She grunted in greeting and returned to her oats. Shirina patted her side and walked away from the house, up the small road and past the tree that was still very tall even though she was much taller herself now. She had climbed it and fallen out of it, once. She had broken her ankle and her uncle, a healer, had nursed her back to health. It still bothered her once in a while, in dampness. She always seemed to lose her footing because of it.

Little Margie, falling out of a tree...

She had completely forgotten about that too. Had thought it was a weakness she would learn to overcome.

As the Circle taught her to do.

She passed the tree, brushing its old bark with her hand, and went up the little road beside it, made of patches of grass and rocks. The palisades surrounding the village stood near, the shadows they cast already deep. They had not been there when she had been a child, but they seemed old enough that she knew they had been erected before the Eloms' invasion. She wondered if they had been put up to keep the Circle out, after she had been taken. If that was the case, then her being harvested had saved all of their lives.

She turned right and veered off the path, knowing full well where she was going, where she had often headed as a child to be frightened by silly stories and child's play. The cemetery was quaint and well kept. It had grown much bigger than she last remembered. Memories flooded her mind as she passed the old section, where her grandparents were buried and where the ghost stories had been told. Her gramps had loved a good ghost story, and would no doubt have haunted them all, were such things possible.

She went to his grave first, then her gram's grave. Shirina stood awkwardly before them for a while before moving down the row to where the rest of her family, the Monlies, were buried. One by one they lined the path, the graves of her uncles, her aunts, other cousins, and then, her parents. They had died not too long ago, only three years ago, probably during one of the epidemics. This region had seen the most death.

She had thought nothing of it at the time, safe in Ravenhold.

There was another grave beside theirs, and she had to force herself to read the name. *Stuard Monlie.* He had joked as a child, puffing out his chest. "Stuard Manly to you!" When she laughed or mocked him, he simply laughed in turn and puffed his chest out more.

Her mother would shake her head and say that their father still made that bad joke, and the day any man in this family developed any type of original joke would be a fine one indeed. Shirina had laughed at that, too.

Her brother had died young, before their parents. They had been left without children. She closed her eyes and pulled her coat closer. She suddenly wished that she had bothered remembering who she had been before now, and the promise she had made to come back when she could. Even if that might have been impossible. To have tried, or at least simply to have thought of it.

She wished her parents could have seen her, and known they had one living child that they could still hold. Shirina remembered her mother holding her, singing her fears away. Holding her so tightly when the Circle came to claim her that she thought her skin would rip and break. And the screams, the fear, the tears...

She looked at the tombstone beside her brother's.

Marguerite Monlie.

Dated to the day the Circle had taken her. They had

buried her too, just like she had buried them deep in her mind.

"We put that one up after your parents died," Marx said as he walked up behind her. "We figured that the whole family should be together."

He came to stand beside her, his hands in his pockets. She looked at the graves of her family and knew she couldn't stay here. The time to come back and belong had come and gone, long ago.

"You did the right thing, Marx," Shirina whispered. "Marguerite Monlie died on that day."

She left the next morning with a few supplies in hand, including what remained of her Circle robe. She intended never to return. She didn't even tell them what her new name was, in case her cousin ever chose to come looking for her.

Somehow, having made peace with her death long ago, she doubted he ever would.

$\mathcal{A}$varielle crouched as she approached the outpost, staying in the shadows of an outcropping of rocks. She intended to reach it before the sun crept up too high in the sky and betrayed everything below, including herself. The air smelled of fresh sea air, blowing a lot of the ashes away, leaving behind a dead and scarred land. Avarielle slowed her breath and was careful to conserve energy, knowing a battle was soon to come.

She didn't have a plan, driven simply by the need to save Jayden. She had failed at too much lately, unable to save anyone, not even herself, and she needed to grab at least one victory, or die trying. Besides, when she had taken up Graysword, it had deepened her oath to protect the descendants of Graydon. Even though the two families had not crossed paths in ages, Avarielle couldn't help but think she was meant to help the Edolines, which is why they had a nasty habit of showing up in her path.

She jumped over some rocks and landed right beside the easternmost wall of the outpost. It was charred black. The rock formations were very close to the outpost and, unlike those surrounding Kryde's stronghold, were all broken and destroyed, having failed to stop the onslaught. Avarielle skirted the wall. The outpost offered no nooks or shadows to hide in, and so she hurried around it. She found the entrance where the burnt door hung on its hinges, and she slipped inside.

She crouched and hid in a corner, allowing her eyes precious seconds to adjust to the darkness within. There was no one in this room with her, but there was no way for her to tell what traps Delora might have in wait. Then again, the sorceress might not expect her to have left while the storm still raged, and so might not expect her so soon. That would be a mistake Avarielle would not allow her to repeat.

She pulled a long knife free, not wanting the bulky sword in her hands just yet. She could be faster with the short blade.

The keep offered two directions: up or down. A stone stairwell clearly outlined the choices. Avarielle hesitated for a second before choosing to go down. There once were windows on the upper floor, and Delora would have been waiting for her, she was certain, had she seen her coming. She guessed they were downstairs.

She crouched low on the stairs as she took them slowly, worried about traps. This would be a great spot for one. None of her senses or instincts detected anything out of the ordinary. She reached the bottom, emerging into a cramped hallway flanked by dark stone walls. It led to a small enclosure which was probably the opening of a room. She peered carefully around the corner. There was light, which was a good sign. It was a lantern, flickering from the center. Odd symbols were generously painted on the walls. Avarielle spotted Delora, seated in the center of the room, in the middle of a circle.

Her head was lowered on her chest, her breathing regular. Avarielle guessed the witch was sleeping to recuperate her strength.

She took a slight step inside to examine her surroundings. On the other side of Delora lay Jayden. She suspected the witch had cast a sleeping spell on him.

She took another careful step into the cramped room. The ceilings were low and Avarielle could barely stand. The drawings on the walls danced eerily in the light.

She had almost reached Delora when she felt a strange sensation around her midsection. It took her only a second to recognize Delora's magic. The magic clamp closed around her waist and tossed her hard against the wall. Avarielle threw the knife at the same time, embedding it in Delora's face. Delora stood, her head lowered, blood trickling from where the blade was lodged.

Avarielle stood up and pulled her broadsword free,

screaming as she leapt for her enemy. The sorceress held up her hand and shoved back with a spell, but Avarielle managed to hold her ground. Delora was still weak.

Time to die. The warrior ran forward to deliver the final blow.

Then Delora looked up and Avarielle gasped as she gripped the pommel of her sword tighter. The right half of Delora's face, the one without the knife sticking out of it, seemed to be made of stone. Her right eye glowed red. The other half of her of looked just as lifeless, even if still human.

"I will be more powerful than you have ever believed possible," she whispered, a raspy sound that bore no resemblance to the voice Avarielle had grown to hate.

The Westlander didn't wait to hear anything else, leaping up as she screamed, bringing the sword down with full force. The sword cleaved through the sorceress' shoulder, but stayed stuck halfway down her breastbone. Something rammed into Avarielle, sending her flying through the air. She rolled as she landed and crashed into the wall.

She scurried back up, but Delora was already chanting, weaving strands of dark magic to cast a spell. Avarielle quickly pulled another throwing knife free and let it fly, hitting Delora in the face again.

How do I kill this monster? Avarielle wondered as she moved, trying to think of another tactic.

Delora held out her hands and chanted a quick,

strange word. Avarielle threw two more knives at the sorceress' stone half now, just to see, and they bounced off uselessly. Delora's spell struck brutally, wrenching Avarielle's gut, tearing her apart from the inside. She gasped and collapsed to her knees, gritting her teeth as she pulled a long hunting knife from her boot.

Avarielle screamed again as she lunged with the knife, ready to cut Delora's heart out if necessary, when a light flashed beside her. The sorceress took a step back, shock evident in her eyes.

Black mists clouded the center of the room, and Avarielle recognized the teleportation spell. She stood up and rushed to Jayden, who was shaking himself awake.

The mists dissipated for an instant, and she saw Delora struggling against the Elder Tan, who held her firmly with a strength Avarielle would have never guessed the woman possessed.

Tan looked her square in the eyes and screamed: "Go!"

Avarielle grabbed Jayden, half-dragging and half-carrying him towards the stairs. Jayden was waking up faster now, moving quickly to keep up as they raced up the stairs and ran through the door of the outpost. As they ran past the burnt stones, the ground shook and the air rang of thunder as the entire outpost exploded in flames and shards of rock.

Avarielle threw herself on top of Jayden. A large chunk of rock landed beside them, and then it was over as quickly as it had begun.

The warrior stood and brushed herself off.

"Eli, I hope she's dead!"

"She still had the amulet," Jayden said as he stood up, looking towards the fiery keep.

Avarielle placed a hand on his shoulder. "Might be for the best. They needed it to bring down the Wall of Loss, so we can only hope it's destroyed and we'll never have to worry about that again."

"Thanks for coming for me." He looked embarrassed and grateful all at once.

Avarielle grinned. "It's what I do, Jayden."

Jayden grinned and stared at the remains of the outpost. "That was a pretty big explosion."

Avarielle nodded. "Let's just hope it was big enough."

By the time Kryde thundered towards them on horseback, Jayden was throwing up blood. Avarielle held his shaking body, cradling him like an infant.

Kryde jumped off his horse and knelt beside her.

"What happened?" he asked.

"I don't know," Avarielle said, voice trembling, "he was fine and he just started throwing up a few minutes ago. He's losing whatever battle he's fighting against Elihor's magic, Kryde!"

"I'll send someone back for Tan. Maybe the Circle can think of something else."

Avarielle shook her head. "I'm sorry Kryde, but Tan is dead. She took out the outpost and Delora with her."

Kryde turned as pale as Jayden.

A cry pierced the sky and they looked up to see srocks unfurling their great wings and leaping from their mountain perch, stirring up ash from far below.

"Cover!" Kryde ordered, and they scurried to the nearest shadows. Kryde covered Avarielle and Jayden with his dark cloak, breathing near her as she held the moaning Jayden.

A few cries from above, and they were gone.

But unless they changed direction mid-flight, which Avarielle doubted they would, they were headed straight for the outpost.

"Tan is dead? Then who will protect the outpost?" Kryde's voice shook with worry and anger.

"You'll never reach them in time," Avarielle whispered as Kryde removed the cloak from over them. "And even if you did, what would you succeed in doing except losing your life as well?"

Kryde gave her a bitter smile. "If loss of life was the only thing I was worried about, I wouldn't be nearly as concerned."

"What do you mean?" Avarielle asked as Jayden seemed to calm with the passing of the srocks. She wondered if Siabala using his magic caused him more pain.

Kryde looked at her incredulously. "You mean you don't know?"

"Don't know what?"

He sighed. "I was convinced you knew. The creatures in your world, what do you call them, Eloms?" Avarielle nodded. She hadn't seen any since their arrival in Elihor. "They're us, Avarielle. They're citizens of Elihor, turned into monsters by Siabala."

The full horror of that statement took a moment for Avarielle to register. "You mean they're all from Elihor?"

Kryde nodded. "Yes, they're our people, stolen from us, those that survived the Great Fire. I had hoped to save some while in Graydon, but they have been driven mad by a magic I could not stop." Kryde paused at the sight of the horror on Avarielle's face.

"I have killed so many of your people, Kryde!" She clutched Jayden tighter. "I have hunted your people and killed them quickly and without mercy. Never once did I think…" She stopped and took a deep breath, knowing she was being irrational. There had been no choice. Still, she added in a whisper, "I could have killed you, or someone you once loved."

Kryde gently brushed the side of her face with the back of his hand, speaking softly. "I've seen what has become of my kin, and I too would have killed them, had they been invading Elihor as well as Graydon. You did what you had to do."

Avarielle nodded, feeling numb. She had done what had been needed, but she wondered if that was why the

Circle had been gathering the Eloms. Maybe, just maybe, they had been trying to help.

No. The Circle had betrayed them all. *The Circle of Graydon,* she corrected herself, remembering Tan's sacrifice in saving Jayden and herself.

She suddenly thought of something. "I think some of your people are regaining their senses, although I doubt they're acting of their will alone." She told him of Edoline, and of the Eloms that seemed cunning, as opposed to the ones that simply craved blood.

He nodded pensively. "I think we'll need another journey to Graydon to figure that out. And I think sooner rather than later would be best." He looked at Jayden, who seemed asleep, blood drying on his lips.

"Why is he so much worse now?" Avarielle despaired. He had been fine a few moments ago. He shook in her arms as a fever flared. What he battled was not an enemy she could help him fight, which infuriated her.

"Does he still hold the amulet?" Kryde asked. Avarielle shook her head.

"Then it must have helped to protect him, to shield him from the effects of Elihor's magic. Perhaps even its proximity was enough as you held it. Without it, Elihor really is trying to kill him."

"But he's just a boy. He has nothing to do with any of this!"

Kryde sighed. "It's Graydon's bloodline, Avarielle. That's all the magic knows, now."

Jayden stopped shivering, his face flushed. She placed her lips on his forehead, feeling only a slight fever. At least Jayden seemed to be putting up a good fight.

"Hang in there, Jayden," she whispered in his ear, still cradling him.

She shook her head and mumbled. "Elihor must have been really mad at Graydon to want him dead like this."

Kryde shrugged. "Women in general are dangerous, or at least the best ones are," he winked at her. "Now come on, we'd best get moving before the sun sets." He picked up Jayden from her arms and carried him to his horse. Avarielle looked back to where she had left her horse. There was no time to go back for it now. Not with Jayden so sick. She turned to Kryde.

"To Siabala's Rage?" she asked as she took count of her weapons. Thanks to Kryde, she possessed one long knife, two short blades and two throwing knives. Hardly enough to storm Siabala, although the last time she hadn't done too badly with only a short sword.

But Kryde shook his head. "He'd probably expect us, and I don't think we have the skills to take him."

Avarielle remembered the large ash-colored man. He had been imposing, but she would like to try her hand battling him. Rested and with Graysword, she even thought she might stand a chance. But she was tired, and her blade was far away.

Kryde continued. "There is another way, although it's risky."

She shrugged. "If it wasn't risky, then I wouldn't know what to do about it."

"We cross the Straits of Tears."

"All right, that's not just risky, that's completely insane."

Kryde grinned again. Avarielle shook her head. The Wall ended on two choppy waterways, the Straits of Tears and the Straits of Grief. They were both such treacherous waters, rumored to be riddled with monsters, that no one dared try them. Except for Kryde, apparently.

"It's not that bad," he explained as he leapt on his horse behind Jayden, propping the prince up. "The straits run towards Graydon, so it's just really rough sailing. But it's doable, as long as you don't run aground on the rocks."

"You've done it before?" she asked incredulously.

"No, but I've heard stories."

"Oh good. Reliable sources, I assume?"

"Grandfather."

"Good enough for me." Avarielle sighed. "I would pay good money right about now for a quiet day sleeping under a tree somewhere."

Kryde laughed. "Well, let me know when and where."

"She must have been really angry," Avarielle suddenly said.

"What, who? Elihor?"

"The straits are blocking Graydon's inhabitants from entering Elihor. Her magic is tearing Jayden to pieces. I mean, really angry."

Kryde shrugged. "Graydon is known here as The Great Betrayer. He set off the chain of events that led to Elihor's death."

Avarielle shook her head. "That's not how it's told in Graydon. In Graydon, Elihor's armies betrayed her, and both lovers perished longing for each other."

"I like your version better. But who knows who holds the truth. It's all stories, and all we have to work with is what we see before our eyes and our instincts. All I know right now is that Jayden is dying, and you care about him a lot, and therefore so do I. We can make it, Avarielle. I'm sure we can make it through the Straits of Tears."

Avarielle hesitated. Jayden didn't have long. It was either try the water, or watch him die.

"I'm not a good swimmer, Kryde." she whispered. "I've lived in a desert all my life."

"I'll make sure you don't fall in," he told her.

"Comforting."

He grinned. "Hop behind me. My horse can carry all three of us for such a short journey."

Avarielle raised an eyebrow. "Isn't that a sign of union in your land?"

Kryde laughed. "Well, come on, woman! I'll be insulted now if you turn me down!" She laughed and hopped behind him, slipping her arms around his waist.

He brought his horse around and looked back towards the outpost, where the srocks must now be. Avarielle felt her heart lurch as she heard him whisper, "Safe journeys, my friends."

She leaned her head on his back and held him a bit tighter. He squeezed her hand in his before kicking his horse into a trot.

They were finally heading back to Graydon, yet Avarielle's heart ached for Elihor and her people.

I O

assara felt clean again. It was a strange feeling, after so many weeks of looking like a patch of dirt. But she could definitely get used to it.

She fixed her hair and dressed by herself, having refused the aid of the maid Massir had to offer. Her new home was big and imposing, and it frightened her. She had heard the whispers as Dayshon had brought her back, nothing short of a royal mess. It had pleased quite a few ladies of the court who seemed to be waiting for her to fail.

She had chosen a blue dress from her brimming closet, thinking Emala would approve. The thought of her maid made her feel nostalgic and homesick for the quiet, intrigue-less land of Edoline. She feared for her sister, and hoped her maid and guards fared well in Kosel, despite reports of increasing Elom activity in that area. She missed them, but still had no intention of calling on them. She would just have to get used to doing things alone.

She knew her one guard from Edoline, Gragor, waited by the door. He had told her of Altessa, trapped with her dying husband, having sent her only loyal guard to rally help. The very thought twisted Cassara's stomach.

Loas had stayed with her as well, despite her attempts to encourage him to follow the rest of the villagers of Rockor into their new homes in Massir. Trevon wasn't far and had promised he would visit soon to help her garner help for the West, but he felt too distrusting of the people of Massir to stay in plain sight.

Cassara took a moment longer to examine her reflection in the glass. She was pretty, some might say beautiful, although it wasn't the innocent beauty she had once had in Edoline. There was a certainty and calmness about her features that hadn't been there before, and she found that she didn't quite know the woman who stared back at her from the glass.

I suppose that's what too much fighting will do to you. She sighed and braided some of her hair back, so that it didn't fall in her face quite as much. She left most of it loose, the waves cascading over her shoulders and down her front and back. She mostly did it because she was fairly certain it would annoy the ladies of the court. And that seemed like a good reason right now.

She didn't bother putting any fine jewelry around her

neck, although much had been made available to her. She had never worn any other necklace but her mother's amulet and, until she could find it again, she would wear no other.

Standing, she took one last look at herself, not liking how much weight she had lost. Although it had mostly been replaced by muscle, she could use a few more of her old curves. On the upside, she was certain she would now easily fit into her old blue dress.

Cassara was as ready as she would ever be. She opened the door, Gragor's eyes shining when he saw her. He bowed deeply. "You make Edoline proud, Princess Cassara."

"Thank you, Gragor. But please, reserve judgment until after today." He nodded, confused, but she didn't elaborate. She hated being cryptic with him, but she couldn't bring herself to voice the request she was about to make of the King of Rashim.

If only you knew, Gragor. He had survived the attack on Edoline and traveled through Elom-infested territory to garner help for her sister. He would never understand what she chose to do this day.

She stepped out onto the fine carpet, her feet quiet on the thick fabric, the smell of lemons and flowers on the air making her long for home more than ever. Gragor and Loas followed closely. Her two new guards, who trusted her to do what was right, one for Solir, the other for Edoline.

And she knew on this day she would disappoint them both.

The court of Massir was as elaborate and intimidating as the rest of the royal palace. Large columns jutted along the sides of the room, casting frightening shadows despite the sunlight filtering through the high windows. It was decked in silvers and purples, the colors of its royal family. Everything seemed so vibrant and bright that Cassara found it quite dizzying at first. She paused at the threshold.

She heard her name announced, and the court grew silent.

"Princess Cassara Edoline, fiancée of Prince Dayshon." All eyes turned to her and she was certain she was blushing, but she met their looks nonetheless.

"It's not that bad, Princess," Gragor whispered, which made her smile.

"From what I hear, Gragor, you passed out at the front of the court."

"That was Circle magic!" he protested, which made her smile even more.

"Thank you," she whispered back before taking her first step, stately and timed, each step firm. She was not about to give the court of Massir any reason to doubt her royal status. Especially not her new father, whom she would meet for the first time as he waited seated upon his throne.

She walked confidently, the two guards flanking her, and she was certain they bore the greens and blues of Edoline with pride underneath their leather armor. Even Loas, who had never seen the sea.

She neared the throne when Dayshon appeared beside her. She paused and he bowed to her formally. She curtsied in return. He offered her his arm, which she gratefully took. For all the air of confidence she was trying to portray, she still felt extremely intimidated by all the jewels and gowns of the court. Not to mention the piercing eyes from most of the ladies, and the gossip flying from lips to ears.

"Is it always this charming?" she asked him casually, low enough that no one else could hear.

"Oh yes, we try to keep things consistently charming around here." Dayshon gave her a quick grin. "Don't worry, you'll do fine. I'll be right here if you need me."

She squeezed his arm a bit in thanks and he smiled at her.

Then they reached the end of the carpet. Dayshon bowed deeply, and Cassara performed her best curtsy.

"Approach, Princess Cassara," the king ordered.

Cassara stood and walked forward without hesitation. Her two guards and Dayshon stayed back, as they had not been invited to join her.

King Darmir was an intimidating man. His eyes were

piercing where Dayshon's were warm, and she found him extremely difficult to read. Beside him stood the queen, who looked more like Dayshon. She smiled warmly, but it was the king Cassara concentrated on. She didn't dare let him see how much he intimidated her.

He examined her briefly before speaking in a soft voice, taking Cassara by surprise. "I was sorry to hear of your father's passing, Princess Cassara. King Alexavier made many enemies in his time, but I always respected his courage. Graydon is poorer for his loss."

Cassara had expected many things from the king, but a show of sympathy had not been one of them. Caught unaware, she curtsied again to buy herself time to take a deep breath and control her rising grief. That wound was still too fresh to discuss.

She stood again and met his gaze. "Thank you, Your Majesty."

He waited to see if she would continue before speaking again. "I suppose you want to recommend that we send troops out to Edoline and free it from the Circle's grasp, or so we've heard?" She heard some shuffling behind her and assumed it was Gragor.

Cassara swallowed hard. She wanted to scream yes. She wanted to beg him to save her sister and her beloved kingdom. But instead, she said: "That is a generous offer, Your Majesty, but I fear my recommendations do not include Edoline at this time."

She heard some intakes of breath and knew Gragor was reliving the death of Edoline in his mind.

I'm so sorry, Altessa. I'm so sorry, father.

The king was obviously interested now and he leaned forward in his throne. "Oh? Then what do you recommend, princess?"

She took a deep breath. She had practiced this moment in her mind, over and over again since Avarielle had vanished to Siabala's Rage. She had rehearsed and prepared, and even made peace with Edoline, but it made the words no less difficult to utter.

"All that stands to the East of us is now lost, Your Majesty. I have witnessed it, and so have many others who come from there. We cannot waste manpower trying to save what no longer exists." Her words stabbed her own heart. She paused and swallowed hard, forcing her voice to remain steady.

"The armies of darkness come from the West, my Lord. They attack from Elihor itself, and will increase in strength and number unless we find a way to stop them. We must go to the West and save what we can of it and, with the Westlanders' help, stop the invading hordes."

"How do you suggest we stop them?" King Darmir leaned forward, fully engaged. If he ever thought Cassara was but a weak princess, that concept was now gone.

"I have some magic at my disposal that I believe will help." It was only half a lie. She had Graysword, and the West needed her help. "And I believe that there are some from the Circle who would be willing to join our cause. Those who did not follow the Elder Delora."

More intakes of breath and murmurs.

"Silence!" the king shouted, making Cassara jump. The room grew so quiet that Cassara could only hear her own breath.

"Delora betrayed Edoline and is capable of betraying us all," the king said in a lower voice. "Those who still hold allegiance with her will be made to pay." She heard some gasps behind her. Though he was intimidating, Cassara was starting to enjoy the straightforward dealings of her father-to-be. "Do you know any of those left in the Circle?"

Cassara nodded, hoping she was not being foolish. Dayshon had told her of the strange woman that had led him to her, and Cassara knew he spoke of Shirina. Whether she agreed with Shirina's actions or not, right now they needed her connections as an Elite to gather what remained of the Circle and help them fight.

If the Circle's duty was to maintain the Wall of Loss, then the sorceress certainly had a stake in this.

"And in the meantime, you want us to head West?" the king asked.

Cassara nodded again and fought back the urge to bite her lip. "They are more knowledgeable on how to fight the monsters than we are, Your Majesty. And they need help. If we offer it, they could instruct us on ways to fight the monsters together, and contain them before worse attacks come." She remembered the flying monsters who had been her party's downfall, and wondered how even an army would contain them.

The king raised an eyebrow. "And you know some of these Westlanders that could help us?"

"I do. I know some of the best among them."

The king looked towards his son. "And you say everything she's revealed about Delora, the Circle and the monsters, is truth?"

Dayshon stepped forward to stand beside Cassara. "We've verified closely, father. Ravenhold is gone, the Circle is broken, and the East," he put his hand on her lower back, a gentle gesture that almost made Cassara cry. "The East is lost, father."

The king nodded. "Very well, then, organize the armies and report to me what has to happen. You will go with them, but remember, the defenses of Massir must stand strong." He paused. "You are certain you want to bring your future wife with you?"

Cassara blushed. She hadn't thought for one second she would be left behind, like a useless maiden, to knit until her husband's return from the front lines.

"She has knowledge and experience that is necessary on this journey. And I've seen her fight, father. She can take care of herself." Cassara felt herself grow even redder, but she didn't lower her gaze, looking defiantly at the king.

"I believe it," the king said, a half-smile on his lips.

"One thing before you head off though. If you are to ride with my army, Princess Cassara, you must first marry my son."

Cassara stood in her room, in front of the glass, feeling numb. Gragor had not spoken a single word to her, not even as he had opened the door for her to step through to her chambers. Loas had offered her a tentative smile, but he also had said nothing. Then again, she had not felt like talking.

She had betrayed them. Her father, Altessa, Jayden, Edoline, and herself. She had betrayed everything she'd ever known and loved. She clutched the back of the vanity's chair and fought the rising nausea. How could she have done this?

But she knew even as she thought it that it had been necessary. Regardless of her feelings of guilt towards Avarielle's predicament, it wasn't even for the warrior that she did this. She knew the West was falling and, without it, they had no other line of defense. She took deep breaths and tried to soothe her stomach and her head, which ached.

She had done the right thing. She had to believe that. To save Graydon. Not just Edoline, but *all* of Graydon. So much had been lost already, while the people of Graydon had slumbered, not realizing their communication relied too heavily on a Circle that no longer cared for them. So that when one of them had fallen, the others had not known until the same monsters clawed at their door.

She looked at her bed, knowing Graysword lay underneath, the blade cold and useless without its wielder. If Avarielle were here, she could make such a difference, but the warrior was still in Siabala's Rage, either dead or insane from torture.

She swallowed hard and closed her eyes, taking deep breaths. Avarielle had tried to save her. To find Jayden. To help her find her way. And she was giving up on her just as easily as she had Edoline.

A knock at the window caught her attention. Cassara looked over to see Dayshon standing on her balcony, waving to her. She walked over and opened the glass door.

"I'm sorry, I didn't mean to startle you," he said as he walked in.

"You didn't." Cassara was grateful she hadn't just run in here and changed right away. The gowns of the court were pretty to look at, but she missed her soft, comfortable clothing, no matter how in tatters it had been towards the end of her journey. She doubted she would ever see them again after the maid had taken them away with a look of disgust.

"Our balconies are beside each other, if you're willing to climb some vines," Dayshon said as he sat in one of Cassara's chairs. She took one facing him.

"I'll let you do the scaling, if that's all right with you. I've had quite enough of it for one lifetime."

Dayshon gave her a weak grin. "That was a brave thing you did, Cassara." Cassara couldn't stand to be seated and called brave for betraying Edoline.

She stood and walked towards the window.

"I did what was necessary, Dayshon," she said softly. "But it doesn't make it any easier."

"I understand." Dayshon also stood but he stayed near the chair.

"We can wait longer, if you'd like," he suddenly said. "I mean, for the marriage. My father has odd concepts of marriage, but I'm sure I can get you out of it for now. I promised you a year, Cassara, and I meant it."

Cassara looked outside, her balcony facing the heart of the palace. Colorful blossoms from all over Graydon filled the garden at its center, some of which Cassara had never seen. A cherry tree swayed in a corner the garden, almost forgotten where it stood. But it would grow strong, if they could help Graydon thrive again. *Just like Edoline.*

She wondered if Massir would come to feel like home, in time.

She turned to him. "No Dayshon, we must obey your father's wishes. He stated it in front of the entire court, and I do not want his credibility to be questioned. We need to head West, Dayshon, and nothing must stop us."

Cassara raised an eyebrow. "Unless you're the one having second thoughts, your Highness."

A slow smile spread across his lips. "I never doubted it, Cassara, and now I never will."

He walked forward and took her hand in his, kissing it gently before stepping back out on the balcony and closing the door.

He was gone, but Cassara no longer felt so alone.

"Are you sure this is a good idea?" Avarielle asked again as she stood by a small wooden skiff. She hated to admit it, but she was nervous. She hated and distrusted water, and had been glad to leave Edoline for that reason alone.

"Well, it'll take some doing," Kryde said as he pulled on one of the lines that secured the skiff, "but trust me, it's doable."

She grunted. The waters here were clear and calm, but she could hear the lapping water just around the bend, angrily beating on the shore further down. There must have been a fishing village in this area, with the number of boats tied near the pier, all shielded from the Great Fire by either the rocks near the coast or the water. It was difficult to tell which, but thankfully they had been spared.

Kryde had examined a few of them before choosing the skiff.

"Did your grandfather fish around here?" Avarielle asked, intent on concentrating on something other than the water.

"He lived on this coast most of his life. Made it to Graydon a couple of times, although it was never clear to me how he came back. Who knows, he might have even crossed through Siabala, or maybe used magic."

"Your grandfather had magic?" Avarielle asked, surprised.

Kryde hesitated for a moment. "He had magic, yes, in this land, at least. He wasn't with the Circle, if that's what you're thinking, but he was a direct descendant of Elihor."

Avarielle stared at him, stunned. "You're a descendant of Elihor?"

He shrugged. "Yes, but I don't seem to have any of the powers my grandfather had."

"But won't Graydon's magic affect you like it does Jayden?" She took a step toward him, concerned. "I can get us across otherwise, and you can stay here," she said with more confidence than she felt. She had never actually even been on a ship.

He laughed. "That will get you far underneath the sea. Don't worry, the magic of Graydon weakens me, but it doesn't try to kill me."

He glanced towards Jayden, who was breathing heavily on shore, eyes squeezed shut in pain. Avarielle wondered what Cassara would think now, to see her brother suffer so. And then she wondered how Cassara would react, knowing she had killed so many people of Elihor with her magic.

"All right, but we stay in the West, closer to the Wall. It's my homeland, so we'll be safe there."

Kryde nodded. "We're ready to go."

He gently picked up Jayden and placed him in the skiff, securing him with ropes to hold him in place at the bottom of the skiff. Avarielle hesitated on the shore.

Then Kryde extended his hand without questioning or mocking her, and she gratefully took it, wondering how much further her family's oath would push her before she might consider giving it up.

It took the better part of an hour to reach the turbulent waters, even though they had seemed very close to the pier. Avarielle was just getting used to the movements of the boat and rowing when Kryde told her to hang on.

"To what?" she asked before the boat fell into the first set of rapids. It pulled them down fast, Kryde using his oar to push them away from the rocks. Following the instructions she had been given earlier, Avarielle did the same, using the oar more like a sword. They managed to make it through the first set well enough. Jayden was still secured tightly.

She couldn't see the shore anymore, only the rocky mountain jutting up near them, a few trees clinging to the rock face. The air sizzled with the crack of magic.

"Are we near the Wall?"

"Next rapids—look up!" Kryde screamed over the sound of the rushing water.

Avarielle had been concentrating so hard on the water that she drew in her breath as she looked up, amazed she had missed this sight. Although she had lived near the Wall her entire life, she had never seen it from so close. They were almost beneath it. It grazed the rocks below and reached upwards without pause and with no apparent end. She could see from here that the Wall was thicker than it seemed, and the shimmers refracted and danced with the light. It seemed more opaque than transparent, a strange purple hue unlike any other Avarielle had ever seen.

She swore she could hear it sing. Not peacefully, but rather like a swarm of angry bees. The sound made her heart accelerate, as though she should expect battle or something big at any given moment.

"It's beautiful," she whispered, and she meant it. It was strange too, and frightening. But also breathtaking.

"Stories say the worst rapids are just beside the Wall. Be careful of rocks, and everything else!" Kryde took up his oar as though preparing for battle. Avarielle did the same after checking that Jayden was well-secured.

"Hang in there, Jayden, we're almost through," she whispered in his ear.

She thought she heard him grunt.

She turned to face the water just as they hit the next rapids, dragging forward at such speed that Avarielle leaned back and almost toppled over. Kryde pushed them off a rock, and they were covered with salty spray. Avarielle was soaked, making her movements more difficult, the wet sleeves of her coat and the cool air turning her limbs to ice. Still, she clung to the oar and fought off the rocks and tried to keep them as straight as possible in the choppy waters.

"We're almost through!" Kryde called, and Avarielle could see they were just beside the Wall. The air crackled and sizzled, and Jayden began to cough. Avarielle hoped that was a good sign.

Then a large purple tentacle leapt out of the water, grazing Avarielle as she threw herself down. It came back up quickly, Kryde barely avoiding a rock as another tentacle flew up and struck the boat, jostling them as the wood splintered.

"We have to move!" Kryde screamed. The boat lurched sideways.

Avarielle held her breath, waiting for the enemy to strike. The boat stopped flowing down the rapids. Kryde looked towards her and then down at the water in horror. Avarielle looked as well, the water purple just below the surface, where a giant creature held them fast.

The world stood still for a moment and then the boat flew up, clearing the waters, sending Kryde overboard and making Avarielle lose her balance. She frantically grasped for a handhold, anything to keep her onboard, seeing Jayden's eyes flutter open as he lay secured under the ropes.

But Avarielle found nothing to hold onto and she struck the water hard, immediately sucked down by the waves and pulled back towards Elihor, spotting a glimmer of the giant purple monster in the distance.

Her body was so heavy, and she didn't know which way was up or down anymore. She was being thrown around like a rag doll when she struck a sand bar. She kicked hard against it, pushing herself up with all of her strength in an attempt to reach the surface. But the current was relentless, dragging her back under and throwing her against a rock, knocking what breath she still had out of her.

She swallowed water and knew she was done. She convulsed, struggled for air, pain lacing across her chest. Her body would no longer move. Time slowed, she floated in the water, the sunlight so near yet so far, and the waters so turbulent yet so pure and clear.

Someone swam towards her, and she wondered who amongst her family would greet her in the Afterfate. Dark eyes met hers, and Kryde grabbed her and pulled her up, tugging at her as though she were a mere doll. Avarielle didn't fight, didn't move, forgetting how to cross the border that separated her mind from her body.

Her chest hurt. Kryde called her name. She coughed, violently and painfully. Then she felt air again, and rock underneath her. The air was fresh and whipped at her skin, and she could feel the cold as she coughed up sea water.

Her body hurt. And it was good to feel again.

"Are you all right?" Kryde asked between labored breaths.

She nodded, wiping water from her mouth with a trembling hand.

"Where's Jayden?" she demanded, sitting up too quickly, her head spinning.

Kryde put a steadying hand on her shoulder. "I don't know. I didn't see him after I was thrown from the boat."

Avarielle stood up and looked towards the choppy water, leaning against a rock to steady herself. She could see nothing in the white foam. No broken boat, no oar, no Jayden.

As though reading her mind, Kryde spoke up behind her. "If he made it just a bit further, the currents would have taken him to Graydon. He'll more than likely end up there."

If he still lives, the treacherous words danced in her thoughts. She looked up towards the Wall of Loss, shimmering in the East. She and Kryde were still trapped in Elihor.

"I'm not taking that chance!" Her limbs grew cold and numb, but not nearly as numb as her mind had felt of late, as though every battle led to some form of defeat. She was coming to terms with the numbness, afraid of feeling too much lest she come face to face with the truth of her situation. Her sword was probably lost, her people destroyed by now. She was trapped in a land with no chance of escape, and she had probably just let the last heir of Graydon perish.

Can I not claim one victory? She was angry and grief-stricken all at once, her fists clenched as tightly as her heart.

"I'm just not taking that chance!" she repeated, taking a deep breath as she jumped in the water, or at least tried to. Kryde grabbed her by the shirt and yanked her back, throwing her hard on the rock face.

"Are you insane?" Kryde screamed over the rapids. "You can't swim, and you'll never make it without a boat!"

Avarielle stood up and threw a punch at Kryde's jaw, intent on getting him out of her way. Expecting the move, he easily dodged it and grabbed her arm, twisting it to get her to her knees.

She kicked his legs hard and he fell, but he brought her down with him, turning her on her stomach and pinning her arm behind her back, immobilizing her.

"Listen, you fool woman. You can't save him now. He's beyond your help. And he might have made it. You'll just have to trust that he made it."

"In case you hadn't noticed," Avarielle said as she struggled against him, managing to wrench her arm free and push herself up enough to strike. One uppercut and he was off of her, groaning as he flew back. "I don't trust easily!"

She jumped to her feet.

He might have made it. She didn't know. She didn't think he could have made it, with those creatures lurking in the waters. And it had been her job to protect him, to keep him safe. *Just like Cassara.*

She looked towards the rapids, Kryde scrambling up to stand in her way.

She wanted to scream, to rip her own skin, to slam her fists down on the rocks around her, to tear down the mountains and claw Siabala to pieces.

Instead she just stood there, trapped by her own inability to change things.

To save one boy, that was all she had set out to do. *Just one boy!*

Kryde was right. Even if she jumped in, what could she do except bounce off some rocks and get herself killed by the current? Who would that help, then?

"Are you all right?" Kryde asked, concern in his deep dark eyes. "I'm sure he made it. He's survived much more than we thought possible, and he was so close to shore…"

"How do you know?" Avarielle snapped. "We were thrown off the boat, and we're bigger and stronger, you might not have noticed."

"He's resourceful."

"You don't know that," she spat. "I swear, continue trying to lessen the blow, and I'll hit you again, Kryde Kolder. He was *my* responsibility and mine alone, and no happy wishing will bring him back."

I killed him, she stopped herself short of saying, but the unspoken words echoed in the air between them.

Kryde walked to her and gently pushed some of the wet strands of hair from her face. The water was lapping near. The song of the Wall seemed quieter now, as though night brought it peace. The air was fresh and didn't smell of death, ashes, or Eloms. It even smelled a bit like moss, of growth and life.

She hated it. It was wrong. Right now, all that she wanted to smell was death. She craved a battle to fight, to kill demons before her instead of having to face the demons in her own heart. She felt the tears rise in her eyes. Kryde reached up to her face and she hit his hand away.

"Get away from me!"

"You're being foolish," he said. Avarielle closed the gap between them and hit him, but he moved fast and grabbed her, dragging her down with him. "Are you going to fight everything and everyone?" he whispered in her ear.

"If I have to," she answered, turning around to face him, his eyes dark and promising the oblivion she desperately craved.

She grabbed his head and kissed him deeply, as eager

to discover his body as he was hers, intent on losing herself in him as darkness fell, and taking the only escape she could find.

When Avarielle awoke the next day, it was as though the world had fallen asleep with the rising sun. The Wall glittered above them with the rays from Graydon, the sky was crisp and the air fresh. It was cool for summer, the fall encroaching on Elihor as quickly as the spring had deserted Graydon.

No birds filled the air with their song, not even the great eagles that graced the mountainside, their survival defying the Great Fire.

"The others...they're all gone, now," Kryde said as he stood beside her, his features drawn and his jaw set in determination.

"I'm sorry," she whispered, leaning into him. "Can we do anything? I can't help Jayden," she swallowed hard, "but maybe we can help others?"

He chuckled. "Still looking for a fight?"

"Aren't you?" she asked, and he grunted. She waited, following his gaze towards the middle of the mountain range.

"If the weather holds up," he said slowly, mulling over his plan as he spoke, "and our feet are fast enough, we should be able to reach Stormhold within a month. The mountain path can be treacherous, so we'll have to be careful, and make sure we don't attract any unwanted attention."

"Stormhold?"

Kryde nodded. "It's the central Circle keep, created before Graydon and Elihor's time. Legend has it that the Wall now splits it in two. It's also infested, and we've managed to scout enough of it to know that that's where Siabala changes our people." He paused. "Into your monsters."

Avarielle nodded as her throat grew dry. Her heart felt heavy and tired again. Just like it had since she had left her homeland.

"It takes a while to turn them. We may be able to save some people from the outpost."

"Then let's go," Avarielle said.

"You don't have to come, Avarielle. You can try to head home, if you will. This is my battle."

Avarielle gave a bitter laugh. "Just like saving Jayden was my battle Kryde. Don't fool yourself. We're in this together."

She held his eyes with hers. "Until the end." She shrugged to make light of the situation as he studied her with his dark eyes. "Besides, what else am I supposed to do? Wander endlessly in these mountains, alone? A bit of fighting seems more fun to me."

Kryde gave her a slight smile, kissed her deeply, and they set out.

~

They trekked for days, scaling the mountain as best they could before they could come down again. Kryde set a quick pace, which Avarielle easily matched.

A week later, they were scaling a small rock face, maybe fifteen feet in height. Avarielle didn't hesitate to follow him up, easily securing hand and footholds and pulling herself up with grace.

Once they had cleared that peak, a few days later, they climbed another mountain, at least twice the height, and this one proved to be more challenging but just as conquerable.

At the top, Avarielle smiled for the first time since losing Jayden. Elihor spread below them, farther than her eyes could see. She could still see the Straits of Tears, and she could look out onto the vast sea that stretched to eternity below them. But she could no longer hear and smell the surf. To the north, far in the distance, spread another vast expanse of water, where the Straits of Grief fell, and the sea beyond it. The surreal shimmer of the world in that direction, not unlike the Wall of Loss, led her to imagine the cry of gulls.

But the path led them into the mountains, and she could feel the sturdy land below her, ancient and solid, constant and not ever-shifting like the waves of the sea. This was something she understood and loved, like the mountains and deserts of her homeland, which didn't shift and change with the mood of the weather or its people. Which defied even the Wall of Loss with its eternity that far outdated it and that would, she deeply hoped, long outlast it.

They found a semblance of a path, and Avarielle was careful to stick to it. It was narrow and broken. On one side was a rock face too steep and smooth to climb, and on the other side was a treacherous drop, too deep to survive.

She followed Kryde, mimicking his steps in the difficult portions and admiring the ease and confidence with which he traveled. They were both sure-footed and cleared the path quickly, coming out on a ridge overlooking the mountains, the land spreading below, a dark mass broken by some emerging clumps of yellow.

She took a deep breath of fresh mountain air.

She felt like herself again, more so than she had in a very long time. In a way, she no longer had responsibilities. The Edolines were gone. Graysword was possibly lost, so she had no magical weapon which made her feel obligated to fight. And she had no people to fight for, no one expecting her to rescue or lead them into possible death.

She felt free. As free as when she lost herself to the dance, letting her feet choose their own path, not worrying about the consequences of her actions or the expectations of her family, all long dead. There was no next step. No mystery to solve. No escape from this land.

She was trapped.

Yet she had never felt more free.

After almost two weeks of travel, Kryde pointed towards the largest mountain in the middle of the range, easy to spot now that they had reached this altitude. "There's Siabala's Rage. As far as we can tell, the center is there, but it spreads into the other mountains, too. We don't know how far. It's proven impossible to chart safely and efficiently."

"How many fissures give way to your land?" Avarielle asked, squinting her eyes and shading them from the sun to see if she could spot any.

"We're not sure," Kryde said. "But there are quite a few near Stormhold. That's where the main activities take place."

"Yet Siabala never leaves his Rage?"

He shrugged. "The Circle said that something holds him there, still. Let's hope that proves accurate."

They stopped for a quick dry meal before heading off again, not speaking another word for the duration of the hard day's travel. In the fading light of dusk, they found a shallow cave to sleep in for the night, too exhausted to do much more than hold onto each other in comfortable silence. Avarielle felt the rise and fall of Kryde's deep breaths well into the long, quiet night, wondering if they were the last two souls alive and still human in all of Elihor.

As the sun started to rise, Avarielle woke suddenly, taking two steps before she bent over and threw up, the nausea rolling over her like the current of the straits. Kryde stopped and looked back, concern flickering in his dark eyes.

"Are you alright?" he asked. Avarielle tried to nod, but the simple motion made her retch again. There was no blood, but it was obvious that the sickness that had attacked Jayden had finally taken hold of her.

She closed her eyes for a few moments and took slow, steady breaths. She wasn't of Graydon's blood like Jayden, but still Elihor's magic attacked her.

How long did she have until she could no longer function, or was even killed by the magic? And what could she do about it? She was too far from the straits to try crossing them again, too weak to cross Siabala's Rage alone, and she couldn't desert Kryde now. She had to help put an end to his people's suffering.

She opened her eyes.

"We should get moving," Avarielle said as she stood back up, not meeting his eyes. He examined her for a moment before nodding, and the two continued towards their goal as Avarielle wondered how much time she had left.

Kaden struck down on the log. Each strike of the axe reverberated through every muscle and joint. He picked up the two pieces of wood, now good sized, and slowly straightened, his back so stiff he had to lean against a nearby tree to push himself up the rest of the way.

It seemed that for every day since Cassara had left, he gained a year. Carsyn ambled by with a pot of water, grumbling under his breath. Kaden hid a smile and shook his head. He was getting older, but Carsyn was just getting more difficult, so much so that Emala had instituted a "no grumbling at the table" rule, which made for very quiet meals.

Kaden leaned against the tree and looked around. The forest leaned heavy around them, and he barely remembered the smell of the sea, so potent was the sweet and sour scent of pine. Brown needles covered the soft ground. Even the needles on the trees were starting to turn brown, as though the trees were dying or inflicted with a disease.

The maples and oaks were all barren, and it wasn't even high summer yet. Fall had ripped through Kosel quickly and now claimed the evergreens as well. Kaden touched the dry trunk of the tree. It made for easy lumber, but concern was growing over food and water. The streams trickled instead of poured, and gardens wilted. Game was scarce with the Eloms in the area, and even the population of Kosel dwindled.

Kaden had been surprised by how welcoming the citizens of the hidden country had been. Their nights were spent with them, in underground safety enclosures the Eloms had yet to find. And during the day they all returned to their homes and undertook the chores necessary for their survival.

Kaden sighed. *Survival.*

That was the big word of late. Even during the Westland War they hadn't been so worried about survival. There had been more worry about accomplishing goals and plans. Survival had been a possible and desirable outcome, of course, but not the most important one. Success had been more important.

He threw the two pieces of wood onto the pile and looked west. He couldn't see the sunset through the trees, but the sky was changing color and the shadows stretched into darkness. The Eloms would be out within the hour. It was time to head to the underground shelter.

He placed the axe on his shoulder and walked towards the small hut they had claimed as their home. It was small but cozy. The shelter beside it was a bit bigger, where they housed the carriage and the two horses. Thankfully Eloms didn't seem attracted to horse flesh. Only human flesh tantalized them. He wondered how Cassara fared. She had been driven by success and not just survival, which made him both proud and terrified. He had watched her turn from girl to woman in the span of a few weeks, and he feared it would get her killed before long.

And he had not been able to follow. He would have given anything to be young and fast again, but he had nothing to give that would gain him that. Even his old magic proved almost more than he could handle.

He dropped the axe near the hut, frustrated. Never before had he felt so useless and without a purpose. He had loved being Cassara's guard for that very reason—she kept things interesting. He'd always had to think fast and try to predict the wild schemes of the princess. But she was gone, and with her, almost seventeen years of purposeful watch.

Emala hummed outside, a lullaby she had sung to Cassara as a child. The maid was young, but she seemed to have put her life on hold a long time ago. He shook his head. They had all become dependent on Edoline to provide them with a purpose. Now that Edoline was gone, did that mean they had no life of their own?

"This is stupid," he heard Carsyn grumble as he walked up, his arm still aching from their last battle, his skin having assumed a grayish color that worried Kaden and Emala. Kaden wondered how much of it was due to the wound, and how much was due to lack of purpose.

"Time to go, Emala," Kaden said through an open window. The singing stopped and she stepped outside within seconds, throwing on a shawl and carrying extra blankets for Carsyn and Kaden, as well as a basket filled with food and water. It was the best they had to eat, even though chewing the dried meats and vegetables left Kaden's jaw sore and aching.

He took the blankets from her and handed one to Carsyn.

Carsyn took it and thanked Emala. She told him he was welcome.

In that second, Kaden realized that what he missed the most was the jesting camaraderie that Cassara had somehow taken with her when she left. Along with, Kaden hated to admit, their reason for being.

Jayden was trapped in a waking nightmare and he didn't know if an escape was even possible. The skiff was still intact, though the waters around him threatened to tear it apart. He had awakened just in time to see great tentacles knock Kryde and Avarielle overboard, snapping the bonds that had kept him firmly in place and almost throwing him over as well.

He had been clinging to the edge of the boat ever since. He wasn't even certain this was real.

His life had turned into a nightmare, and he just wanted to wake up safe in his bed, with cherry blossoms blowing in through his open window and his sister's escapes to the village as the greatest adventure of all.

He was soaking wet as the skiff spun out of control and all he could do was cling and hope, his arms so frozen by the water and wind that he wasn't even sure his grip was firm at all.

Then the waters calmed. Jayden chanced looking around, and the air above him sizzled with sparks of light.

The Wall of Loss! Jayden's mouth opened in a silent scream as he hit it, a thousand lights exploding in his mind, his heart banging his chest apart.

He could feel the magic course through him like a thousand fireflies, buzzing in him and igniting his senses. Light burst before his eyes. Screams echoed within his skull and he could taste sorrow, defeat and pain. He wanted to scream, to hear his own voice, to move his arms and ensure he was still whole, but he was frozen with fear and magic.

Please help me! he shouted in his mind, for someone, anyone to come to his rescue, pleading for the guards of

Edoline to answer his call, no matter that most were dead and scattered.

He wished he could close his eyes, frozen as open as his mouth, the magic like a wildfire that would consume him.

Then he cleared the Wall of Loss and fell forward, still clinging to his wish for Edoline, but now understanding he had gone too far and seen too much to ever truly go home again.

Another day, another chore.

Kaden brought down his axe and chopped another piece of wood, Carsyn piling more logs at his feet. They were cutting enough for the entire village and had shared spoils with nearby families already. They were just keeping busy, they both knew. Emala was as well, sewing every piece of cloth she could find, turning rags into respectable clothing again and helping neighbors with cleaning chores.

Carsyn stood up and offered Kaden a slight grin. "It's amazing how much we get done in one day when we're not busy following the whims of the princess."

Kaden chuckled. "I miss her too, Carsyn. Now get back to work."

Carsyn grumbled and Kaden smiled. He considered Carsyn his closest friend, a chain of command and duty keeping them at once firmly tied and apart. Yet Carsyn was his oldest companion and they had witnessed enough horrors and survived enough heartaches together to have formed a sense of kinship Kaden would never find elsewhere, he was certain. And he found himself content with that.

He took a deep breath and felt a pain in the thumping of his heart. Kaden dropped the axe and collapsed against a tree, clutching his chest. Carsyn was beside him in an instant, pain lining his gray-tinged skin.

As though sensing something wrong, Emala came out of the house, skirts flying as she ran to them and knelt down.

"What's wrong? I'll get a healer!" she exclaimed. She was about to stand up again but Kaden took firm hold of her arm and kept her kneeling. Carsyn sat cross-legged beside him and grinned.

"That's a kick I haven't felt in a long time," he said with a chuckle. "Ah, and here I was, hoping for the good old days, fool that I am."

"What are you talking about? You both look terrible," she glanced from one smile to the other. "What's wrong with you?"

Kaden felt the ache in his chest dull. But it was still there. And he understood what it meant, as surely as he knew his own name.

"Jayden is back," Kaden said to Emala, whose eyes grew wide with shock and lack of understanding. He couldn't blame her. She didn't even know Kaden and Carsyn had magic at their disposal. Though how the young prince had discovered it and managed to send a flare to them was beyond him, he knew the magic well enough to recognize it for what it was. It had been a necessary and basic spell during the Westland War.

It seemed the young prince had powers of his own, just like his sister. Or at least he'd figured out how to tap into some of Graydon's magic. "Emala," Kaden implored as he took her hand. "You have been a wonderful companion and friend, and I need you to trust me now when I tell you we have to go. You stay here and wait for us."

Emala turned from concerned to annoyed. "What are you talking about, you crazy old coot?"

Carsyn chuckled again. Kaden sighed. "Jayden has returned. We must go find him. Trust me when I tell you this, we know he has returned."

She glanced from Kaden to Carsyn, making it clear she thought they had both gone mad. She broke free from Kaden's grasp and stood up, then helped the two men up.

"That had a heck of a kick! I almost feel alive again!" Kaden looked at Carsyn, whose skin was less ashen. He wondered if the activated magic had also healed him in some way. He wondered if they would be able to use their magic in battle now, or if their age would prove their downfall. Could Jayden even rely on them to protect him? Why would he call them and not someone more powerful? Or did he not have any other options? Did he even realize what he had done, or was he just so hurt and terrified that he had acted out of instinct? Kaden set his jaw. He did not intend on letting his call go unheeded, hoping they would make it in time.

"Say the prince has returned and you two can somehow tell, which, after everything that's happened, I'm quite willing to accept," Emala said, brushing pine needles from her skirt. "What makes you believe I would let you two leave me behind?"

"Emala," Kaden said. "We don't know what we're heading into. The young prince will need allies, and I fear we may be all he has, until we can get a message to Cassara." No one mentioned that they had no idea where Cassara was, nor did anyone voice the fear that their princess had not survived the wrath of the Eloms, despite the promised protection from the Westland warrior.

"I'll pack our things," Emala said as she walked with determination towards the hut.

"Stubborn woman," Carsyn said, but Kaden heard admiration in his voice.

"Carsyn," Kaden said, an old edge back in his voice. "We vowed we would never use our magic again. Cassara has her own magic and can protect herself, but I doubt Jayden has that luxury. That vow no longer applies as long as Jayden's protection is in our hands, understood?"

Carsyn nodded, slow determination creeping over his features, made stronger by the wrinkles time had stamped on his skin. Kaden hoped their magic could make a difference now. He hoped that the fire rekindled by Jayden's magical call could be harnessed and used in battle. And he hoped their bodies could follow. He knew, without a doubt, that they would try no matter the uncertainties and danger.

They had been called back to battle. And this time, they would not fail Edoline.

The sun hung low in the sky, orange hues dancing on the lapping water. Gulls flew in lazy circles and dragonflies danced on the water. Fireflies flickered amongst the reeds on the distant shore. It was still too light for the stars to be appearing.

He looked back, and in the distance he could see the Wall of Loss. He had traveled far, and he guessed he neared the Southern Coalition, an unstable land his father had warned him would someday come for Edoline.

Jayden stared at the shore, reaching down and sticking his arm in the water, using it as an oar to turn the boat towards an upcoming sandy beach. The oars had been thrown overboard, just like Avarielle and Kryde. He remembered some things, foggy images of his aunt, of Avarielle telling him it would be all right, of her holding him, keeping him safe. Of Kryde screaming her name.

It felt surreal to him, being here, now. The pain that had been so strong just this morning clung to his bones and muscles like a memory, and he could still taste blood every time he swallowed.

The air of the sea and Graydon soothed him and drained him of what little energy he had left.

The boat hit the sandy bank, and he pulled off his boots and rolled up his pants before jumping out and pulling it to shore. He fell on the sand, which retained some heat from the day's sun and warmed his aching muscles.

He gathered his boots and the few supplies Kryde had left in the skiff, and began walking up the beach. With no oar, navigating the boat closer to Edoline would prove too difficult, and he was just as likely to be swept out to sea.

Behind him, the Wall of Loss shimmered, just as impenetrable as before. Except he had been to Elihor now, and had left a friend there. He refused to even consider the possibility that Avarielle hadn't survived. After all of the battles she had seen, he thought it would be an absurd death for her to drown.

He walked for a while as the sun continued its descent. He followed the sea, knowing he would hit either a fishing village or the town of Sharrow, if he was interpreting the land around him correctly. He had never traveled this far from Edoline, but his lessons in geography and history were emblazoned on his mind. Sharrow was not the biggest city of the Southern Coalition, but it was one of its founding cities. His father had warned him often of the Coalition, but had named possible friends as well, some of which inhabited the old city.

At the thought of his father, Jayden felt tears well up in his eyes and fought the urge to cry. He had never had the chance to say goodbye. He didn't remember his mother, really. He knew his sisters missed her a lot, and so did he, by extension. But he had always thought of Altessa a bit as his mother. She was five years older than Cassara, and nine years older than Jayden, and had always taken care of him. She used to tuck him in at night, until Cassara took over when Altessa married Bestian. He missed his family so much, it bled like an open sore on his heart.

He had loved his father. And now he was gone, and Cassara might be gone too.

He wanted to see his sisters more than ever. He wanted to be back in Edoline, in his own bed, with the smell of the blossoms and the sound of the surf, and Altessa bidding him good night or Cassara promising to take him on one of her adventures.

She might never, now. He felt that was the greatest betrayal of all. He had always wanted to follow his sister down the tree into the village, to have fun and be free, to share another secret with her. To explore Edoline in the shadows of the night, and then Kosel, and then the whole of Graydon.

He supposed he was exploring now. He was somewhere near the Southern Coalition, or in it by now. He had been in Elihor and Siabala's Rage, two places few people had ever been and lived to tell about. If anyone could be called well-traveled, it was him.

But it didn't matter. He was alone, without Cassara and without anyone else with whom to share the adventure. It made it all less exciting.

He sat on a rock near the shoreline, the sandy beach long gone, replaced by shells and yellowing grass. He looked out towards the shimmering sea, enjoying the last of the sun on his skin as he pulled out what few provisions he had left. Some form of dried meat and other items from Elihor he couldn't even begin to identify. He wished he had bothered to learn more about the land and its people, but he had felt so sick the whole time that his memories were patchy at best.

He was ravenous and ate most of his supplies, except for some mushroom-like candy. He hated mushrooms with a passion. He stuck them back in his bag and resumed walking, feeling stronger now that he had rested and had food in his stomach. Without Elihor's magic assailing him, he could breathe normally again. He set out to find shelter before the night was completely smothered in darkness.

He was scaling a small hill when he spotted a few riders in the distance. He hesitated for a moment, but then waved and jumped to get their attention. He wasn't certain how far the city still was, and the night stirred to life old fears.

The horsemen spotted him and turned to meet him. As

they approached, he saw the orange and bronze colors of the Coalition, and a small sweat broke out on his brow. The men were well-armed and all huge, career soldiers under oath of the Coalition his father had warned him would one day try and take over Edoline.

Jayden swallowed hard as they thundered to a stop near him. They were a scouting party, wearing short swords and bows and lighter chain mail. One of them was obviously their leader from the pins marking his collar. He stayed on his horse as he addressed Jayden.

"We didn't expect to find anyone alive here, boy. What is your name and where is your family?"

Jayden hesitated for a moment. He could lie. He was certain no one would recognize him, and he had no idea how hostile they would be towards him. But then he thought of his father and tried to imagine what he would do, and he immediately knew what he had to do. It wasn't the easy choice, but it was the necessary one.

He stood tall and looked unflinchingly towards the leader of the scouts. "My name is Jayden Edoline, son of King Alexavier Edoline and heir to its throne. I demand to speak to your leaders at once."

The scout's eyes widened for a moment as he looked at the dirty boy who stood before him, with his foreign black clothing from Elihor. A flicker crossed the man's face, as though he was debating whether or not to laugh the boy off. But when he met Jayden's eyes and the boy did not look down, he saw something in them that convinced him of the truth of Jayden's claim.

"I knew King Alexavier well," he said slowly, weighing his words. "My name is Colonel Simon Orliys, and I would be honored to escort you to the Council of the Coalition. Can you ride, your Highness?"

Jayden nodded and the colonel helped him up in front of him, Jayden hanging on to the beast as Colonel Orliys ordered his men to continue scouting before turning towards the East, riding away from the sun as it continued its slow descent in the Westland sky and towards Elihor.

Jayden gritted his teeth at the merciless pace, the colonel either eager to report his find or curious about the prince's request. Jayden hoped trusting the Southern Coalition would not prove his downfall.

He wished dearly for his trusted Edoline once more, an ache growing in his heart so deep he could have sworn it glided on the wind around him.

13

By the time they'd found shelter in a cave for the night, Avarielle felt better. Her body still ached, but her stomach had settled. There was no wood for a fire, so the two sat close in the darkness, Avarielle listening to the quiet night around them. She was exhausted, more exhausted than she remembered ever being. Fatigue weighed her down from her fingers to her toes. Her eyes were heavy and begged to be closed, but she resisted the urge to give in and sleep.

She didn't understand this fatigue. When in Graydon, she had easily been able to travel for three days with little to no sleep, unless she consumed too much magic. But regardless of the fact that she had slept the previous night and used no magic for several weeks now, she felt completely drained.

Even her fear of being found out and attacked by

monsters didn't pump enough adrenaline into her blood to keep her alert. The magic of Elihor was really starting to annoy her, and she refused to give in right away.

Keeping her voice low, she leaned in towards Kryde. "Tell me of your land. Before Siabala's attacks."

She could see the vague outline of his face, her eyes long ago trained to pierce the darkness. His strong jaw line caught some of the infiltrating moonlight, as did his straight nose, and his dark eyes absorbed the rest. Stubble shadowed his jaw. She saw a quick flash of white teeth as a smile spread over his features.

"It was beautiful, Avarielle." She loved hearing him say her name. He always stumbled on the third syllable, as though by then he thought her name should have ended, and his accent dragged on the syllable before that. It sounded foreign and like home all at once.

"There were three large cities, all working cooperatively through the capital to ensure enough resources for everyone. Farmland filled most of the center, and fishing villages lined the shore. The Circle assured ease of travel and communication through outposts, each no more than a day from the other, and each welcoming guests for the night, as long as they worked for their stay. The biggest battles we waged were in sporting competitions, a team per city and one for the central farmlands, which usually won the biggest awards."

He gulped a bit of water before continuing. "It wasn't perfect by any means. Petty arguments kept families apart, land battles made enemies of neighbors, and failing crops aligned cities against farmers. But it was beautiful, Avarielle. It was green and fertile, and full of rolling hills and flowers, and the smell of the sea swept across the land every now and then, sometimes even reaching the capital, which was in the center of the land. We used to say Elihor was sighing when that happened. When the breeze was so soft yet carried the scent of salt with it."

He paused, and Avarielle thought he was done when he began again. "I smelled it, on the day of the attack. I was heading towards the capital when I smelled it. I even smiled at my brother and we laughed. It meant good things would come on the day."

"You don't have to go there, Kryde."

"I know," he took a deep breath, interweaving his fingers with hers, as though borrowing her strength. "It sounded like the heart of Elihor thudded loudly before the flames struck. My brother had some magic, unlike me, and he tried to protect us. He saved me, but..." Avarielle held his hand more tightly, "he couldn't save himself. All I really remember from that day is the smell of burning flesh. That was it. It was over as quickly as it had started. Burning flesh, and death."

He took a deep breath and leaned back against the wall.

Avarielle swallowed hard and touched the side of his face gently. She tried to imagine the same chaos being unleashed on her people, the pain and fear, the terrible stench. Her heart pounded in her chest.

As though sensing her fear, Kryde brought her hand to his lips and gently kissed it. "We have little left to do in Elihor. The attacks will continue unless we find a way to stop them. If we don't, all of my people will become monsters, and then your land will fall."

"I can't let that happen, Kryde. I have to stop it." Her hand itched for the familiar feel of Graysword in her grasp. But all that she had was Kryde's hand, and so she squeezed it gently. He squeezed back.

"We've been on the defensive for too long, trying to save whatever civilians we could. But it's too late for that now. It's time to go on the offensive, and see if we can help your people where we failed to save ours."

Exhaustion crept back into Avarielle's muscles as the mantle of responsibility settled back on her shoulders as easily as it had slipped off. Her people needed her and, despite her assailed body and lack of magic, she still believed she could make a difference. She leaned forward and rested against Kryde's chest, letting herself be held by him and sharing warmth in the cool night. She fell asleep listening to his steady heartbeat, wondering what the shattering thump of Elihor's heart had sounded like seconds before her land had been consumed by fire and death.

∾

After three weeks of travel, Kryde informed Avarielle that they would clear the passage in two more days. The further down they went, the quieter the landscape became. Avarielle took deep gulps to fight back the nausea, intent on not letting it slow her down. More than a few times, she lurched to the side of the trail to empty the contents of her stomach. Each time, she immediately resumed walking without anything being said. Kryde simply stayed closer to her and helped her more than she was used to. She was touched and annoyed all at once.

The rocks down here had been seared, like the land below, making the ground more treacherous to tread on. A fine layer of ash shifted under every footstep, clinging to their boots and pants and leaving an easy trail to follow.

"Let's hope no one's looking for us here." He looked back at their trail. It practically shone in the daylight.

Avarielle shook her head and was taking another step when a shadow caught her eye. She whirled around, short sword pulled free in one swift motion.

Kryde pulled free his broad sword and was by her side.

She could feel her body slow down, readying for the attack her instincts told her was imminent. Her heartbeat slowed, her hearing sharpened and her muscles grew limber. The pommel of the short sword felt small but solid in her grasp.

The sun was setting. They waited a few more minutes, but still, no monster showed up.

Avarielle timed her breath to Kryde's as they stayed at the ready, neither one of them willing to put their weapon away just yet.

A gust of air threw ashes into their line of sight, and Avarielle felt more than saw a srock land between them, its wings knocking Avarielle down before she rolled to her side, avoiding the blow. She heard Kryde shout her name, followed by the ringing of steel against rock. Grabbing her short sword she leapt up, screaming as she swept down with the blade. But where Graysword would have cut off the wings as easily as a warm knife through butter, the short sword embedded itself in the creature's limb and stayed stuck, refusing to budge.

She jumped sideways to avoid a blow as the creature turned around, flailing arms and wings, the weapon still trapped in its flesh.

"How do we kill it?" Avarielle screamed as Kryde avoided another blow and struck down with the broadsword, taking off a piece of wing.

"Working on that!" He moved fast, but Avarielle knew it was only a matter of time before he tired.

She jumped up and reached for her sword, barely getting out of the way before the creature turned towards her. She tumbled out of the way, Kryde striking it from behind and managing to mangle the wing further.

The creature howled, its eyes growing red as its anger increased. It whipped around with a speed neither of them expected, sending Kryde flying against a jagged outcropping of rocks. Blood trickled from his hairline and he struggled to regain his sword and his footing as the creature charged him. Avarielle leapt up and placed herself between the wounded Kryde and the angry creature.

"Out of the way, woman!" he screamed, but Avarielle stood her ground, pulling free two knives and letting them fly towards the creature's red eyes. One bounced uselessly off the stone, but the other one struck home, breaking the thin layer that contained the creature's magical energies.

It stumbled as red flames leapt from the shattered eye, seconds before an inferno exploded. Avarielle threw herself back, protecting her face with her arms, feeling the hairs on them begin to singe. Then Kryde's arms wrapped around her and he crouched above her, the heat of his body suddenly greater than that of the fires.

Avarielle chanced opening her eyes, a black shield tingling around them as the red flames danced wildly and then vanished.

They both remained crouching for a few moments. The fresh burns had actually removed some of the ashes from the ground, or at least blown them away with its intensity.

"Was that your magic?" Avarielle whispered, putting her hands on his, where they were still wrapped around her.

He laid his head against her back. "I believe it was. But…"

She took his hand and kissed it, to stop him from saying what she knew he was thinking. He didn't need to voice it, making it more real by uttering words that already cut deeply with their truth.

But I couldn't use it before. Not to save myself, not to save my brother, and not to save my people, who depended on me.

He hadn't been able to use it until Avarielle's life had been in danger.

She could smell burnt flesh, and disentangled herself from Kryde's hold.

His back was burnt and blistered, singed black in certain spots.

She clenched her jaw and took out her water skin, gingerly trying to clean the wound, or at least remove some of the burned pieces of clothing encrusted in it.

She thought about his brother, and how he had died protecting Kryde, realizing Kryde might have done the same for her.

"Most magic is difficult, at first," she whispered as she pulled free burnt fabric and cleaned dirt from the wound, his blood as red as hers under the setting sun.

"Tell me about yours, this Graysword the Elder Tan spoke of," he asked, not uttering one complaint, only groaning slightly from time to time.

Avarielle cleaned another section of his back. "It's an ancestral sword, and it's beautifully weighed and crafted."

She imagined the feel of the sword instead of the bandages she now wielded. "But it's difficult to wield at first, like any other magic."

She bit her lip and forced herself to continue. "The first time I used it, Eloms were attacking." She paused, finding the memories difficult still. But Kryde needed to know that he might yet control his magic. "I lost control of it and I killed some people," Avarielle ended in a whisper as she finished cleansing the wound, remembering the death of her dance mentor that day. The memories were blurry. She remembered her fear, and her need to stop the Eloms. And then, the blood. She swallowed hard. "Some people that I loved too, Kryde."

"I'm sorry, Avarielle," Kryde said as he remained seated with his back to her. "But…thank you for telling me."

Avarielle nodded, knowing he couldn't see her. She rested her forehead on the nape of his neck where no wounds festered, wishing she could take his pain away even though she had failed to deal with her own.

They moved further down the mountain, away from the remains of the srock, in case anyone should come looking for it and find the battle site. Avarielle followed Kryde closely, his features drawn and movements stiff.

Fatigue clung to her limbs as well, held at bay only by adrenaline, even though she had slept a good portion of the previous night. She couldn't recall ever feeling so tired. Her fingers tingled, her lips were numb, and she wasn't positive she could lift her feet over the earth, half-dragging them instead.

It was more than tired. She felt *worn*. Even the magic of Graysword didn't usually drain her so.

She would have lain down to sleep, regardless of the danger, if not for Kryde. Wounded though he was, he found the strength to continue. The fresh blistered burns on his back looked painful in the setting sun.

I can't let this magic of Elihor drag me down when he's fighting his own wounded body!

She grinned. Pride, if nothing else, would keep her moving. And she was fairly certain that was the only thing keeping Kryde moving, too.

"This looks like a good spot," Kryde said as he ducked into a cave, the rays of sunset lighting it just enough for them to see it was empty. Whatever animal used to live here had long been killed or had fled from the monsters crawling across these mountains.

Kryde sat down and Avarielle joined him. He crossed his legs and pulled his sword free, laying it across his thighs.

He examined her. "You look terrible."

Avarielle mumbled a reply. "You know how to flatter a girl. And you're hardly one to talk. You look like a half-cooked roast."

He grinned and then winced in pain, taking a deep

breath before speaking again. "I'll take first watch, you rest."

Avarielle was starting to shake her head in protest when he held up his hand to silence her.

"Do as I ask, Avarielle." Then he added, more gently, "I won't be able to lie down or sleep anyway. One of us might as well be ready for whatever battle the morning brings."

"I'd be ready with or without sleep," Avarielle grumbled, wishing she wasn't so exhausted. She wanted to argue with him, but the grim determination on his face betrayed his pain.

"Why were the srocks more easily defeated?" Avarielle asked, trying to get him to focus on something else.

"We hadn't realized their eyes were so vulnerable," Kryde sighed. "That could have made a difference."

"What's done is done," she said gently, too tired to formulate another question. She sat up with him for a while regardless, until she grew too tired and, despite her claims to the contrary, knew full well she wouldn't be good for a fight unless she rested a bit. She lay down, watching his chiseled profile as the light grew dim and sleep claimed her, his head proudly held up and his hands resting on his weapon, at the ready.

She hoped she would never have to smell burning flesh again.

A few hours later, lighting splintered the darkness. It was dry, and no thunder trailed it. Avarielle didn't even move with the flashes of light, her face illuminated for a brief instance, highlighting only deep slumber.

She looked younger when she slept, despite bearing the wounds of many battles, her tanned skin etched with the scars of a lifetime of fighting. That all of her limbs were still attached indicated she was good at what she did.

He shifted slightly and winced as the dry burnt skin of his back pulled and cracked. The wound was bad, and would only get worse unless properly treated. Avarielle had done a good job of cleaning it, but the sores were deep and would require proper disinfection.

But still, he had done it. He had wielded his family's magic.

Fatigue and adrenaline competed for his body's attention. He was exhilarated at his success, and disappointed at his failure to protect himself. It had felt strange, like a dam bursting inside of him. Years of fighting and conditioning his body to take a hit, to continue despite all odds, to remain standing when normal men would fall, had not prepared him for the physical blow of Elihor's power flowing through him.

His heart still beat wildly with the rush and his chest felt wider now, as though being a funnel for Elihor's might had forced him to become more than he was. But still, like his brother, he had not managed to protect himself.

He could feel the burst of magic as it escaped him, but he couldn't force it to do what he wished to.

Though I suppose, he thought as he glanced at Avarielle's sleeping form, *that my main desire was to protect her.*

Just as his brother's must have been to keep him safe. Kryde tried not to wonder why the magic had only worked now, and not during the months of being under siege, of watching his people die. He tried not to think of why he couldn't even protect himself, but today, he had been able to protect Avarielle.

He tried not to think about it, but he knew the answer as surely as he knew the sun would continue rising, even if he was no longer here to witness its glory. The reason he had been able to protect Avarielle and no one else before was because he truly believed they could make a difference.

He had seen and tasted so much death, been covered in the ashes of his land and people, that he simply hadn't believed that saving Elihor would come from her people. That's why he had escaped to Graydon, to find answers or allies. He had found some answers, and one ally he knew could make a difference.

Or at least enough of one for him. To reinvigorate his desire to fight and to protect what he loved. To give him a reason to get up in the morning and to want to come back from the battlefield. To want to see the sun rising again, and every sunrise until the end of days, if she was by his side.

He shifted and grunted. No matter what his thoughts or feelings on the matter were, apparently he cared more for her than himself, as his brother had for him, unable to shield himself from the onslaught.

His head snapped up as he heard a rustling noise from the left. Avarielle still slept soundly.

His fingers closed around the pommel of his blade and he shifted to a crouch, ready to pounce.

Then he heard it.

The eerie song of a kealer, come to take him home.

Avarielle woke up as a strange song filled the entire cave. She opened her eyes to see a ghostly figure hovering over her face. She threw herself back, drawing her sword, leaning against the wall.

"Bloody Circle!"

The kealer merely floated away from her, towards Kryde, who remained seated as though in a trance.

"Move, Kryde!" Avarielle screamed as she launched herself at the creature, swinging full force with the blade. Meeting only air, she flew forward, through the creature, and landed on the rocky ground.

A chill ran through her entire body and her hairs stood on end. The core of her being was lit by a glow, like finding a warm fire after a long, cold night.

The ghost simply continued hovering, as though

drawn by Kryde's suffering as much as Kryde sat frozen by her presence.

"Kryde, use your magic!"

But he didn't seem to hear her, and Avarielle wasn't certain he would even know how to save himself. He hadn't ever managed to use his magic until she had been in danger.

*Until I was...*Avarielle suddenly understood what she had to do. It was a need so sharp and clear it forged her plan. She couldn't live without Kryde in Elihor. There would be nothing left then.

Before she could think of anything else, she knelt by Kryde. The kealer began attaching herself to him. Avarielle tried to touch her, but her hand simply cut through her, tingling with the warmth of Graydon's magic. The ghost looked so sad, its eyes closed as its hands were on Kryde's face. His features were drawn and pale, his eyes closed, his arms fallen uselessly to his sides, though he remained seated.

She was killing him.

Avarielle leaned forward and swallowed hard, her lips lingering near his ear as she whispered words she had once vowed she would never speak to a man.

"Save me."

Then she dropped the short sword, grabbed her long knife and turned it around. She took a deep breath and jabbed it through herself, near her heart, gasping at the sharp pain.

She tasted her own warm blood and fell to her side, the song of the kealer descending with her into the abyss.

Kryde felt Avarielle's hot breath against his ear, but was unable to respond, frozen by the kealer's magic. He had watched others perish at the hands of kealers and understood there was no way to fight them. Still, he forced his muscles to respond, to react, to at least twitch and assure him he still lived.

He had felt her hot breath, heard words he couldn't fully grasp, and then he saw her fall. Just from the corner of his eye, he saw her tumble, slowly, her dancer's body graceful even as she fell, red hair vivid in the kealer's light. Like a pulsing star, he felt her pain vibrate in the air around him.

Avarielle! She had asked him to save her. He could feel his heart shattering at his own ineffectiveness, seconds before his magic burst through him, shoving the kealer away.

The ghost seemed stunned, but it was not dead. If ghosts could even die. He shifted his legs, feeling groggy, and grabbed his sword. It was useless, he knew, and his magic would prove a better weapon, but he needed the comfort of the blade. A familiar weapon while facing an unfamiliar foe.

He stood, weakened but whole. Avarielle coughed, and

blood spurted from her mouth. It was then that he noticed the blade sticking out of her chest.

Forcing his eyes to break away, he faced the kealer instead. The creature looked at Avarielle with sad eyes and then began hovering towards her, its robes and loose hair dancing in the windless cave.

Kryde hesitated. He felt his magic dwelling within him, the dam reopened, and forced it to remain so. But he didn't know if he could heal Avarielle, and the kealer…*It might be able to heal those from Graydon.*

The Elder Tan believed it possible, and Avarielle had been healed by them once before. The kealer lay on top of Avarielle in a hug, as though a mother cradling a child. His muscles twitched in anticipation of a battle he didn't know how to fight, save by hurling magic he did not understand.

The kealer and Avarielle both glowed now, a soft, unnatural light.

Save me. Kryde clenched his jaw. Ready to fight his greatest battle yet, mostly against himself, Kryde sat down by the two, his sword still clenched more out of comfort than need, as he understood full well that winning this battle meant waiting and staying out of it.

The kealer would heal Avarielle. It had to. And all he had to do was sit and wait.

They were the longest minutes of his life.

～

Avarielle regained consciousness as she felt the blade slide out of her chest, an unnaturally warm sensation as though a knife cut through her like butter. She felt a warm glow all around her and managed to open her eyes just a bit.

The world was covered in a halo, but through the mists surrounding her, she could see Kryde nearby, sitting, watching her as worry etched his chiseled features.

Eli, he was handsome.

She wanted to smile at him and comfort him, to run her fingers down the line of his jaw and kiss him deeply, but her arms felt too heavy to move. She understood the warmth, suddenly.

A kealer was on her.

She wasn't afraid, partly because Kryde was right there, and partly because she could feel that the creature held no ill will towards her. She could sense it wanted to help.

Whatever magic of Graydon the Circle witch still possessed pumped into Avarielle, her body responding to the healing spell. She could sense it, the pain vanishing and blood no longer trickling in her mouth.

It did not hurt like the first time a kealer had healed her. But this time, she did not resist.

The mists dissipated and she sensed something substantial on her face, as though the ghost had come to rest its own cheek on hers. And then the mists were gone, melted away, and it felt like stepping out of a warm bath and into a cold night.

Kryde was at her side in an instant, gathering her into his arms, calling her a fool woman, a suicidal idiot, and a wonderful person all in one breath. He cradled her and she let herself be held, finding comfort in his arms.

As she found the strength to hold him back, finding a home in his arms. The loneliness of her travels, the choice to live in exile, the fear of always being alone dissipated.

With no ancestral oath left to fulfill, Avarielle Grayloft forged her own as she held the last heir of Elihor.

14

In the distance, she could finally see the high walls of the Lisal Gardens, a perfect circle etched above the stony gates, although normal eyes would not be able to easily spot the gateway. Shirina shifted on the horse. Less pain slithered through her now, but she still didn't feel quite right. Like a stranger in her own skin.

She would find some peace in Lisal, she hoped. Time to rest and gather her strength. And to figure out if she still had any allies.

The forest grew thicker as she approached, and she lost the walls from view for a few moments. Shadows covered the trail, and the path became increasingly treacherous with roots and stones, making progress difficult.

Shirina's senses perked to life with the increasing darkness. Sights, sounds, smells...they all became crisper.

As did her magical senses. She felt it pulsate and reach out from deep within her. It was vibrant and strong, and filled her with warmth as it always had, a connection to Graydon only a few shared.

But the strength of the magic was not as it had been. It seemed tarnished somehow, not at its full potential. She could sense the magic around her, the life force of Graydon left behind after his passing. Emotions so strong they had sustained the magic of this land for generations, like a ghost that refused to relinquish its hold on this world.

But where usually she would have grasped it and made it her own, weaving the powers to her own purpose and cause, she found that she could not reach out and hold it. A thin veil, almost translucent, had wrapped itself around the magic.

The more she fought to grasp it, the thicker the veil became, making her ill, as though she suffocated.

She couldn't access the magic of Graydon. Try as she might, the veil was too thick, and it wrapped itself around her. She willed her magical senses to life, forced the magic to come to her, to woo her as it always had, but it refused to obey, leaving her helplessly watching it wrap around every tree, every branch, every miniature life form, in a connected world she seemed to no longer belong to.

Her need for the magic became physical, she needed to *touch* it. She shivered, hands shaking, feeling as though her head would split and her stomach explode. She was thirsty for the magic, more thirsty than she had ever been, and it was within reach, but so far away.

So impossibly far away.

The horse stopped and whinnied, commanding her attention. Someone was here, of that she was certain. She resisted reaching for her sole weapon, the old rusty knife her cousin had given her. Regardless of how the magic seemed now, she was still a sorceress, and an Elite of the Circle, a highly regarded and respected rank. She would not be caught near one of their outposts wielding a rusty old kitchen knife.

Pulling herself straight in the saddle, pushing back exhaustion and pain, she adopted her most authoritative tone.

"Show yourself."

Shadows broke from the surroundings, collecting before her as the darkness melted away to reveal two of her brethren, blue circles embroidered over their hearts. Shirina did not feel relief or joy at seeing two from the Circle after such a long time away.

She was dressed in common clothing, returning from a failed mission, having lost her allies and disobeyed direct orders from the Covenant. Instead of warmly being greeted or welcoming them herself, she analyzed them.

Blue Circles meant a good understanding of Circle classes and magical systems, and the ability to manipulate light into illusions, perhaps some elemental work if they were particularly gifted students. Not enough magic to have developed the Sight yet, so they couldn't tell that she was unable to tap into the powers of Graydon, as they were obviously capable of doing through their illusion spell.

First, she had to make them understand who she was. She didn't care about who they were, and no Elite would.

"I am Shirina, Crimson Circle Elite. I have come to consult with whoever leads here now."

The slight shift in their stance was the only indication that betrayed their discomfort with the situation. She was getting to them already.

They would not make Yellow Circle quickly at that rate.

"Must I ask again?" She articulated each syllable like a drop of acid. She couldn't reach the magic and manipulate it, but she could still see and smell it, and they were both exhausted, their auras wild with fatigue and uncertainty.

She softened her voice a little, just enough to sound as friendly as someone from her rank would be.

"You're both tired, I see, and these are uncertain times we live in." Their auras responded in spikes, so eager were they to receive any type of sympathy or praise. She gave them both. "Lisal stands yet, proving you have done a fine job. But I need to speak to Grasky immediately. My business is urgent."

She could pull out her robes and show them what remained of the Crimson Circle, but she didn't want them to see the garment, as though showing the dirt, the blood and the rips to someone else would make it all too real.

The robes almost belonged to another era now, one of glory and purpose and direction. And magic. If she couldn't reconnect with the magic, perhaps she would never again wear the robes.

She pushed the worries deep within her. Just because she couldn't access the magic as a sorceress hardly meant she should stop thinking like a sorceress.

"If you will follow me," one of the urchins said, a girl with short brown braids.

Since when had the Circle used children to fight its battles?

Shirina followed the girl, walking beside her horse, remembering Avarielle and the fall of the West, knowing all too well the answer to that question was not one she was currently willing to face.

Shirina had always loved the Lisal Gardens. As a child, it was the first sight she remembered outside of Ravenhold. Closest outpost to the Covenant, it was also the first one most adepts visited on their first independent teleport. After visiting every other Circle outpost on at least one occasion, it was still her favorite.

Unlike most outposts, which welcomed you into a stark symbol-ridden cave or basement, the Lisal Gardens had been created with great care, the flowers and plants maintaining the correct flow of energy to welcome a teleporter. The Gardens created a beacon in the night for those who needed to know where to stop and reappear safely.

Lisal's beacon was so bright that the first time Shirina had teleported, she had believed she stood on the surface of the sun. Even when she teleported to other areas, she could often see Lisal's beacon, too far to reach, but still clear in the dark zone of teleportation.

It had always been beautiful and full of life, sustained by magic and the strength of the land alone.

As she crossed the gate into the gardens, the stark surroundings defied her memory. Plants folded in on themselves, their core yellow and dry. Trees had shed their leaves, their bark as brittle as old scrolls. Bushes had all but vanished, barren branches where once had grown leaves and fruit.

She looked away, up at the gray, cloud-covered sky, and waited as the youngling excused herself to get the Keeper of Lisal.

Her hands were clenched at her sides as she remembered the scent of a thousand exotic flowers, now lost in the smell of dead, dry earth.

She closed her eyes and let her sight adjust again, forcing them open to look down at the world around her. The magic was still there, but it was all wrong. All so wrong.

The harmony of the song of the Lisal Gardens had been let loose and wild, strands of magic whipping up towards the sky with unkempt power. The magic simply reached up and fell back down to the earth, unable to find anywhere else to go or anything else to maintain or inhabit.

The closer she looked at the sky now, the more evident it became that a lot of Graydon's magic had been let loose, not escaping for lack of life to breathe in its land, but rather set free without purpose by the dying life.

It was as though a thick white veil of magic attempted to smother the land.

"Elite Shirina, well met." The familiar voice of Grasky washed over her like a warm breeze. She turned around and saw his face, riddled with a relief he did not allow the youngling to see from where he stood.

"Thank you," he said to the girl, dismissing her. The youngling brought an open palm to the circle on her chest and walked off. It was such a familiar gesture to Shirina, yet it seemed ridiculously out of place here. She herself had not reaffirmed her Circle oath since leaving Ravenhold in pursuit of the cursed Grayloft.

She wondered if she ever would again.

"Well met, Grasky," she said and he extended his arms towards her, taking both of her hands in his in a gesture of friendship. Shirina felt so tired she wanted to break down and cry. But the time to be a child had long come and gone.

"Tell me Grasky, what of Ravenhold?"

He shook his head and sighed, squeezing her hands gently before releasing them again. He began to walk slowly to the side, his steps even more tired than before. He had lost weight, she noticed as she followed him. And he looked much older than the last time she had seen him, barely two months ago.

"It isn't good, Shirina."

She didn't say anything, waiting for him to continue, already knowing in her heart what he was about to say.

"Ravenhold has fallen. We don't know exactly what happened, or if anyone lives, but the few Circle younglings here were brought by the Elder Crimanon before she passed away from the sheer strain of transporting so many. She said nothing, but the younglings had all been warned not to return to Ravenhold. *Never* to return to Ravenhold."

He paused and turned to look at her, gauging her reaction. She had no difficulty keeping her features blank.

"I'm sorry, Shirina."

"Ravenhold died for me the day Tangia was exiled from it."

Grasky nodded, although Shirina could see he didn't believe her. She wasn't sure she believed herself, either.

He remained quiet, waiting for her to speak. She looked around first, searching for anyone hidden with her magical Sight and, seeing nothing and needing at least one ally, she decided to tell Grasky the truth.

"I don't know what I can do, Grasky." He went to protest and she lifted her hand to quiet him. Grasky had high faith in her, one of the youngest Crimson Circles to ever grace Ravenhold, but he needed to understand her limitations. She owed him, and herself, that much.

"I'm not the strength I once was, Grasky."

"None of us are now. Too many months of battles and demons."

Shirina shook her head. "No, I mean yes, that as well, but I've been…infected. By a magic I do not understand. I can't…" She sighed in frustration and lowered her voice to a whisper. "I can't touch the magic anymore, Grasky. I can see it," she reached out with her hand, the strands of magic just inches from the tips of her fingers, rippling away before she could touch them. "But I can't touch it or summon it. It's extremely frustrating."

She wished she could take back the last few words. Sorceresses endured and conquered. They did not admit to weakness or frustration.

"Truth be told, Shirina, I know little of your magic. I was not gifted in it myself, though the Circle was good to me and my family by allowing us to tend to these gardens and providing us with security. But it seems to me that if the way you've always done things no longer works, then you need to try something different, perhaps with a new tool."

"Go on," she said, to be polite more than anything else. He was still ruler here and she was his guest.

He changed directions to head towards the center of the gardens, picking up speed. "It's not uncommon, what you speak of, Shirina. Well, for someone your age it is, but perhaps too many battles have claimed their price." He paused and glanced sideways at her.

"Older sorceresses, particularly Elders, often find themselves encountering difficulty in channeling the magic. Not because the magic is lessened, but rather because their minds or bodies are too clouded by fatigue to grasp it. Perhaps this foreign magic is doing the same thing to you."

All central paths of the Lisal Gardens led to the great tree rumored to have been planted by Graydon himself, sprinkling it with his own blood to reinforce its connection to the magic. It stood before them now, the sapling Shirina had seen but a few months ago already growing bark that resembled an old tree.

"Did you never wonder why my family had been left in charge of the Gardens, Shirina?"

Shirina felt heat rise to her face. For all of her training in critical and analytical thinking, in questioning everything around her, she had never been encouraged to question anything the Circle did, and so she never had. Except of late.

Grasky spared her the need to answer.

"Generations ago my great, great, and some more greats grandfather was one of the best wood carvers in the land. He was good not only at carving a piece of wood, but also at taking a piece of a tree without killing it, an apt gardener and plant keeper. Circle Elders had always been afflicted by a loss of magic, but in their important positions, the last thing they needed was for others, particularly outsiders, to find out."

He walked forward, onto the stump that held the sapling. He ran his hand gently over it. "He helped them with this tree, as all of his descendants, myself included, have. It's a key, Shirina!" He held out his hand and she took it. He pulled her onto the great trunk and she gasped.

It felt as though lightning ripped through her entire body, a tingling sensation that left her numb and weak. She took a step back, struggling to catch her breath.

It had been Graydon's magic, she was certain. Wild, strong, warm, and undeniable. More of it than she had ever felt at any given time, and more than she thought even she could master.

"Circle adepts can't work with the tree, since it's too strong a conduit to the magic. But once a limb of it is crafted for its user, then it can be wielded to tap into magic. More magic than ever before, Shirina."

She nodded, not trusting her voice just yet. Her throat ached and she could taste blood again.

Grasky joined her. "Shirina." She had never heard her name spoken with such concern until she had met Cassara. "You don't look well. Your throat..." He glanced at it, and she raised her hand. Her scarf had slipped slightly, revealing the dark spot growing on her body where the magic of Elihor was eroding her.

But she had felt the magic of Graydon! She could still reach it, and use it, and make a difference yet!

Grasky ran a hand in his hair, ruffling it further. "Perhaps it's best to forget this entire idea. You're sick, and you could just stay here and rest. I make a wonderful chicken soup." He smiled tentatively at her.

She put her hand on his shoulder. "Chicken soup isn't the answer, Grasky. I need…I need to make a difference. To save what's left of the Circle, and to stop the darkness." She touched her throat absentmindedly. "It is the Circle's duty to maintain the Wall of Loss," she rhymed off, finding comfort in the familiar words. "If we are what remains of the Circle, then we must do what we can, until we can no longer."

She looked at the great stump, admiring the years of growth, of breaking, of regrowing and rebuilding and having the strength to push one more leaf out at a time, one sapling at a time, to still reach for the sun even after being burned so many times.

"I need to fight, Grasky, and I need magic to do so." She looked at the energy of the tree, so pure and white she had to look away, so tainted did she feel.

Impure.

"Give me a way to access the magic, Grasky, and I shall give them a fight they'll not soon forget."

~

When night had fallen on Graydon, Shirina woke up from a deep slumber knowing she was not alone in the room. Grasky would need until at least morning to finish his work, and he had no magic with which to cloak himself, and so she knew it wasn't him. She used the Sight, letting her eyes adjust first to darkness and then to the magic around her.

The user was fairly good, but Shirina was much better and she easily spotted her in a corner of the room.

"Show yourself!" she commanded as she stood up, the edge of her white night gown falling to the floor around her feet. The magic decreased and a woman stood before her, an orange Circle emblazoned above her heart. A bit more training, and she would be a Crimson Circle, like Shirina. She could do most things Shirina now could, except she didn't yet grasp the subtle nature of magic, and the finer spells like teleportation and Sight. It was like being fully versed in swimming without having ever been thrown in a turbulent sea. She would learn, quickly enough.

"I would like to know by what right you enter my room as I sleep?"

The Orange Circle lowered her head in acknowledgment. "My apologies, Elite, but I have just returned and thought it urgent that we speak."

"Oh?"

"The Harvest has begun."

Four simple words that sliced through Shirina like a fine blade. It was the year of the Harvest, after all. But, now? With monsters roaming?

"We've begun but a few weeks ago, to bring new strength to our blood." She looked proud. Not a confident pride from unmatched skill, like the Grayloft's, but rather a smug pride from gaining too much power at too young an age.

"The Circle will be strong again. But we'll need your help. No other Elite remains that we've encountered, and the Sight is not something we have yet mastered."

Shirina fought down her anger. *How dare they!* To perform a Harvest without proper Sight would mean false harvesting. The Circle did not take children lightly. They had to first be certain that the child could indeed wield enough magic to make a difference in the battle to maintain the Wall of Loss.

*The Wall is failing...*Shirina suddenly understood so clearly it was like a physical blow. The time to maintain the Wall was past. Now was the time to prepare for the ensuing battle, for when the Wall would fall.

They were too late. The Circle had failed.

"Tell me," she asked the Orange Circle, her voice a heavy whisper. "What is the role of the Circle?"

The woman was surprised by the question, but she simply answered, as she had been taught to do. "To maintain the Wall of Loss."

"And tell me," Shirina took a step towards the woman, who shrank back slightly. *Still just a child. When did I stop being one?* "What is the role of the Circle once the Wall fails?"

The Orange Circle stuttered a few words and then laughed proudly, as though what Shirina had said was so beyond what could be that she couldn't even imagine it.

Shirina raised a single eyebrow. The woman immediately grew silent and pale.

"Call back the Harvesters. I want them here by the next nightfall."

The Orange Circle was about to protest, but one glance at Shirina quieted her. She raised her open palm and placed it over her orange circle before walking out of the room.

Shirina remained standing, looking out the window, above the tree line, towards the Wall of Loss, which was at the other end of Graydon, yet still managed to shimmer on the sea of magic in the night.

She knew with certainty, now. Every fiber of her being knew it. The death of the land, the magic dancing just above it, refusing to leave it but also incapable of staying near it…it reminded her of a child anticipating a gift, so consumed with the future as to lose sight of everything in the now.

Or like a lover waiting for his beloved to return. The magic of the land already knew it, as surely as she knew that the sun would rise in the morning, regardless of whether or not the people of Graydon would be there to greet it.

It was no longer a question of *if,* but rather a question of *when.*

No matter how hard they had fought or how many in the Circle had already died trying to save it, the Wall of Loss would fall.

Shirina did not intend to helplessly watch from the sidelines.

She reached for her clothing to go find Grasky. She needed the staff now. The magic knew something was coming, and she could feel it in her gut. On the chair near where the Orange Circle had stood, a fresh Circle dress and cloak were laid out.

She took the robe and slipped it on, comfortable and familiar, and then she secured the cloak on her shoulders, as crimson red as the circle over her heart. She ran her finger over the embroidery, remembering the first time, more than a year ago, when she had first placed her palm over the crimson circle.

Not certain what she would be vowing to now, she laid her palm by her side.

The time to do the Circle's bidding was coming to an end. Unless Ravenhold still held secrets it refused to share.

oonlight streamed in through the sheer curtains, which billowed in the light breeze. The night was fresh and filled with promise. Cassara stood by the window, the curtains wrapping themselves around her dress, shimmering over the silver and gold details.

Her hair should have all been held up as would be proper in Rashim, but Cassara had only conceded to having most of it put up if she could keep some of the strands free at the back, wisps of a carefree time roaming the orchards of Edoline.

Her hair was carefully arranged to receive the crown of the High Princess of Rashim, wife to the heir of the throne of the most powerful kingdom of Graydon. Cassara looked down towards the small courtyard her balcony gave onto. The blossoms from the small fruit tree had all fallen, scattered on the ground like tears. Just like Cassara.

She felt lost. Groundless. As though she still had a future, but no past. This was it. Tonight, she wouldn't even have this room anymore, her small haven during her stay in Massir. Tonight, she would move in with her new husband and begin life as a wife.

She felt ill. She liked Dayshon, and she truly believed she could learn to love him, but it all seemed so fast. Her stomach churned under the corset of the dress and tears welled in her eyes. She closed them and fought the growing feelings of despair.

This was what she needed to do. Not only to help the West and repay Avarielle's kindness and unwavering loyalty, but also to help all of Graydon, to save it from the rising darkness. From the same darkness that had claimed her land and her family. The breeze smelled of rich earth and plants, and Cassara yearned for the sound of surf, for the smell of the sea, for Jayden's laughter to be carried on the wind, for the silhouette of her father pacing the night away, for the distant greetings of the villagers, for Kaden's strength and Carsyn's sarcasm, for Emala's fussing...for the Cassara that kept her hair loose about her shoulders and ran carefree and unafraid through the orchard, playing her flute without questioning if what she chose to do was wrong, when choices had been fewer and far simpler.

Anxiety gripped her heart and she took deep breaths

and stepped outside on her balcony. The moon was amazingly full in the sky, luscious and welcoming.

Her flute in hand, she stood by the edge of the balcony, alone. She could see no one in the courtyard, though they wouldn't necessarily be as easy to spot as her, all blond hair and white dress with gold and silver threads detailing flowers and vines, the life of Graydon.

She didn't care if she was heard at this point. She needed to lose herself deep in the music. She began playing softly, a song of Elihor and Graydon, who last met during a full moon night, the same moon under which Cassara would be wed. Elihor pleaded for him to stay. He pleaded for her to come with him.

They parted ways just before the rising of the red sun. The notes were long and slow and grieving. The story said that if the two had remained together until the rising sun, they would have seen it red and the omen would have been taken more seriously, and they would never have parted ways. The danger and the blood were evident, but by then it was too late, both their fates sealed.

The notes continued growing slower and more morose, and Cassara began playing the Traveler's song, easily woven into the final dips of the first song. A new journey. A world her mother would never have dreamed of seeing. *The West, the base of the Wall, Massir and all of the mysteries she would discover...*She focused on the adventure, not the fear nor the uncertainty. She had made it this far, hadn't she?

But I hadn't been alone.

Her fingers stumbled and tripped and the notes came out wrong.

I'm alone. She felt the ache so deeply it physically hurt and a sob choked the rest of the song. She was about to be married and to repay a debt to an old friend. She had allies she knew would stand with her until the very end. But still, the old treacherous feelings of being alone returned, refusing to release her heart.

A soft knock came at the door. Cassara closed her eyes and took deep breaths, composing herself. She remained on the balcony, her back to the door.

"Come in," she said, and the door opened. Still, she did not turn around. She heard Gragor's familiar voice.

"It's time, my Lady."

It gripped at her chest, the fear. It twisted and turned. Her hands grew numb. This was it. Of everything she had ever done, this was one of the most final. Nothing could take this act back.

Like killing Jesimae.

She felt herself grow faint and put her hand out to catch herself, only to feel Gragor hold her from behind. He helped her sit and knelt before her, concern lining his eyes.

"Lady Cassara," he swallowed hard. "I, I, um, wanted to tell you this earlier, but I didn't know how…I think you're doing the right thing. I can't imagine how hard it must be, to give up so much, but I think your father would be very proud of you."

Cassara looked at him and smiled, though her stomach still churned. Still, looking into his unwavering eyes, she allowed herself to think that he might be right.

"Thank you," she whispered and stood up. She still held her flute, but there was nowhere for her to bring it with her. The dress was too tight, and she didn't think a bag would be well-looked upon in court.

"I can bring it with me, if you'd like," Gragor said. "I swear I'll keep it safe." Cassara smiled and handed him the instrument, which he very carefully stowed away, as though it were some priceless jewel. Which for Cassara, being the only thing she still had of Edoline, it was.

She took a deep breath and focused.

"Thank you," she repeated, then smiled at him. "Nice uniform." He wore the full uniform of the Royal Protectors of Edoline, which she had asked to be custom-made for him. If she was to be a princess, she needed her personal guard. He stood straight and proud, wearing the weapons effortlessly like a seasoned warrior, the bands of green tumbling across his chest playing off the blue lining. The colors of her kingdom.

"Captain Klar would be proud of you, Gragor," she told him, and he flushed with pride.

"For Edoline?" he asked, a slight hesitation. Uttering a war cry when heading into a wedding was not common practice, but Cassara smiled as she confirmed it.

"For Edoline."

He nodded solemnly and stepped out. Cassara took a deep breath, feeling at peace again. This was right, and she couldn't afford to question herself so much. She had to follow her plan through, no matter how difficult or heart wrenching. Too many depended on their success, now.

She looked up at the night sky.

Some clouds traveled the night towards the West, where a storm seemed to be brewing, but here the sky was still fairly clear.

The full moon was an omen of good luck on a wedding night, and a storm, bad luck. At least it was not directly above her. It meant that the new couple could avoid the storm, if fate and choice agreed. Cassara looked up defiantly at the clear moon.

She would ride into the storm alone if necessary. If not to defend her beloved land, then to avenge it. And stop the darkness from claiming the Land of Light as its own.

Come fire or brimstone, demons or Siabala himself, Cassara Edoline was heading to war.

And she had no intention of losing.

She walked down the hallway towards the main court. The hall was deserted, bearing the colors of Edoline instead of those of Massir, a final nod to the bride's homeland before she adopted her new one. The banners had been quickly but finely made; her family's crest, marked by a sword crossing a flowering branch, flapped gently in the breeze of the high windows. Dust danced in the moonlight, the gold lining of the banners shining like that of her dress.

Her well-being was to be assured by her own guards as well, though Dayshon had offered to line the hallway with his own men since she had so few guards.

Cassara had refused.

Gragor and Loas were all she needed. They both walked behind her now, in full royal uniform, on the lookout. Queens-to-be had been assassinated here before, taken down before meeting their future husbands in the court beyond the closed doors up ahead.

It was a final test of will from the princess' family. To keep her safe at all costs. And Cassara had heard other, more dire rumors. That it was the last chance for the royal family of Rashim to be rid of princesses from weakening political alliances. Cassara didn't lend the rumors much credence. Other kings, perhaps, but King Darmir struck her as more straightforward. Which is where she believed his harsh reputation stemmed from. Honesty often led to misunderstandings and wounded feelings.

She walked from moonlight to darkness to moonlight, as she crossed the hallway and the great pillars rose around her, casting thick shadows. And then past the pillars and into the moonlight, the emblem of Edoline dancing within it.

Her father would have been with her, too. And Emala. Emala would have loved all of this, and Cassara had partly chosen this dress because Emala would have loved the detailing. And Kaden and Carsyn. And Klar. The two guards behind her kept their distance and were so quiet she could easily have believed herself alone.

She kept her hands clasped before her and walked slowly. It was a lovely night, after all, and she intended to enjoy it alone for a while longer.

A shadow broke free from the pillars in front of her and she heard a sword being unsheathed behind her.

"It's just me," she heard the loose Westland accent as Trevon stepped into a moonbeam to prove his identity.

Gragor sheathed his sword again. Cassara walked up to Trevon, who bowed deeply to her.

"You look like an oasis, Princess Cassara."

She blushed deeply. "Thank you, Trevon."

He stood straight again, so tall that she had to crane her neck up to look him in the eye. He spoke before she could.

"I wanted to thank you. For what you are doing for my people. You are a woman of your word." He bowed again, making her blush even more.

"There is something you can do for me in turn," she suddenly said, the idea forming quickly in her mind.

He nodded, waiting.

"Attend my wedding as one of my family. You need

only walk in with me and stand near the front, by me. The ceremony will be quick."

He looked surprised, but then a slow grin spread on his face. He seemed to understand her. She wanted to show the king that her claims had not been false. That the West stood ready to work with them, that their troops would not be ambushed, and that Cassara could help cement the peace to better prepare for battle, whatever form it took.

He nodded. "I can see why Avarielle likes you."

She smiled at that, a slow hesitant smile, tempered by his use of *likes* instead of *liked.* He still believed that she lived, whereas, Cassara realized, she had given up on her friend's survival, focusing on her people instead.

Trevon's smile vanished, as though he had just caught his own slip. He lowered his head but kept his eyes on hers. "I accept with honor, Princess Cassara Edoline." Then he added with a slight curl of his lips, "And I accept to someday follow you into more than just a wedding."

Cassara nodded. She indicated he should walk beside her. He took his place and the four resumed their walk. Trevon was hardly dressed for a wedding, still wearing traveling garb and his full weaponry, including the large broadsword crossing the sledgehammer on his back. But he looked like a Westlander, from his clothes to his weapons to his proud stature and red hair. She paused before the doors. She turned around and faced all three men.

She wanted to tell them how much their loyalty meant to her. That no matter what, she would prove as loyal in turn. But the words felt bitter in her mouth before she even spoke them. She couldn't make that promise. If she could betray Edoline, then it stood to reason that she could betray anyone, or anything.

For Graydon. She would save as many as she could. That was her goal. Instead of uttering a lie, Cassara just smiled at them.

"Thank you for being here with me today."

Gragor and Loas grinned and Trevon simply nodded. He was older, and she thought he understood what she was going through.

Of all the allies she currently had, she knew she could trust him the most, except perhaps her husband-to-be, though only time would reveal that truth.

She took a deep breath and stood before the final doors that would lead to her future.

The large iron doors to the royal courtyard creaked as someone tried to open them. Dayshon stood by his father and mother, the courtyard surrounded by guards and the guests of the court seated in the middle. Usually weddings took place in the next room, the old Circle shrine, but Dayshon had thought Cassara would feel more at ease in a courtyard, and it would give her something back of

Edoline. The banners of her homeland danced in the wind, intermixed with the silver and purple banners of his house.

The doors cracked and Dayshon looked up in anticipation. Then they began to open, a man in the middle pushing on them. Once momentum was gained, the two young guards of Edoline each pushed a door back. The man in the middle wore full weaponry and traveling clothes and, as he stepped out from the shadows, his hair shone red.

He looked defiantly towards the king and prince, and Dayshon hid a smile as he heard gasps from the guests. His father said nothing, nor did he react. As though pleased, the Westlander stepped to the side, revealing the princess Cassara.

She stepped forward into the moonlight, and Dayshon was too taken with the sight of her to even hear the sigh of the court. She seemed unreal, ethereal. She wore a dress of white, as customary, with gold and silver details, flowers and vines running down the long dress and glowing in the moonlight. She took a step forward, her skirt spreading behind her like a river surging through a plain after a long period of drought, and the entire court stood up.

She held her head high and did not look directly at anyone, keeping her eyes forward, towards her goal. Her steps were slow and calculated, and she walked alone, with no parent left to give her away to the King of

Rashim. Her hair was mostly up, but some strands still danced behind her, wisps in the soft breeze.

Dayshon realized he wasn't breathing when their eyes met. Hers had adopted the silver hues of the moon and her dress. They were clear and focused, without hesitation or doubt, silver from their steely determination born out of, Dayshon was certain, need and not love.

Looking at her walking with unfaltering steps through the court, silenced by her sheer presence, the Westlander and her guards following just as proudly, he found that he didn't care—she was the right queen for this darkness-riddled land. She stopped just before the guests, her guards flanking her, the Westlander moving to the side, where family would usually stand.

"Who will give you away?" the king asked, his voice ringing in the silence. Cassara did not look down as she answered.

"I will give myself away, your Majesty."

Dayshon's mother moved closer to him, slipping her hand into his to squeeze it. He squeezed back. He was surprised his mother liked Cassara so much. The two were like night and day, yet the queen had silently acknowledged her liking of the princess since their first meeting.

"Very well," his father continued, his voice unusually soft. He extended his hand for Cassara to take it. She easily accepted it and he brought her before his son.

There would be no fanfare of a ceremony. A full moon

was the only blessing Dayshon and Cassara had agreed they needed. In the morning, they would ride out to the West, to stop the Eloms from infiltrating further and save what remained of Graydon, so there would be no time for a celebration.

Tonight, there would only be a sealing of their choice.

"I agree with your choice, Dayshon," his father said with uncharacteristic kindness. Then Dayshon's mother came up on the other side of Cassara and kissed her new daughter gently on the cheek. Cassara's eyes welled up with tears. Dayshon wondered how long it had been since she had felt the kindness of a mother.

"I am pleased to call you daughter, and queen in my stead, when my son's time comes," Queen Traina said and, upon seeing the tears in her eyes, she hugged Cassara gently.

Then she released her and a servant brought the small crown that had once been hers, before she had been queen. Cassara knelt, skirts falling perfectly around her, her head held high as Dayshon's mother placed the crown on her head.

The silver crown held only a purple stone. The silver danced on the gold of her hair, reflected in her eyes. She stood again and faced the king.

"Welcome, daughter," he said and he gently kissed her forehead. When Cassara opened her eyes again, a tear escaped her, and the king reached up to wipe it away.

"Your father would be proud, as I am today to be gifted with that title as well."

Then he went to join his wife, who laced her arm into his as he held her hand. Cassara stepped up towards Dayshon. He smiled and took her hands into his.

It was sealed. She had been welcomed into the family, as one of their own blood.

The guests clapped and Dayshon was taken by surprise. The whole ceremony had been so intimate he had forgotten they were even there.

The wind grew and a cloud passed before the moon, casting them in darkness save for the few torches. Dayshon took Cassara in his arms and kissed her, and she kissed him back. He tasted her tears and felt her warmth.

He would keep her safe, regardless of dark omens, of monsters, or of the storm they would face in the morning.

The cloud moved again and Cassara looked up at him and she smiled, not a forced smile, but a genuine smile.

He thought he might be able to make her happy too, and she could in time learn to love him, once all the battles had been fought and won and their land reclaimed from the tides of darkness.

16

Shirina walked slowly, the scarf around her neck thick and uncomfortable. It seemed strange to wear one with her Circle garb, especially in the warmth of early summer, but she had little choice if she wanted to hide the growing dark mark on her neck.

Grasky would not be ready to receive her yet, the sun still hidden below the horizon. But she could no longer sleep, no matter how tired her body. Her mind was reeling at the possibilities, her body repulsed by them, her heart aching at the thought of them.

She summoned the Sight, looking around at the mist of the magic of Graydon. She wondered if it covered all of the land or just the Gardens. She had not noticed it until yesterday, but she had been so tired and battered, she could remember very little of the past few days.

Marguerite Monlie.

The name was a fresh wound on her already-broken heart. As she steeled it again, she wished she could remember nothing of the past few days.

She needed to focus. She needed answers. Circle younglings had been running the show, lacking Elder guidance, as apparently none remained. Shirina swallowed hard and continued to force her heart to become harder, to see only the light and the dark, not the shadows that tricked you into believing falsehoods.

But the Elders brought the downfall of the Circle! She knew it with certainty. Delora had been a catalyst, but other Elders had chosen to help her in her cause. They must have known the dark path they embarked upon.

And the Circle had not questioned. An army of sorceresses, of Elites, of adepts, of sproutlings even, and no one had stopped them. There were those that had quickly vanished, but what of the others? Were so few in Ravenhold willing to stand up to their leaders to stop them?

Is that why the Harvest was allowed to continue? Is that why she herself had harvested others?

Leave my child, leave!

She stopped and closed her eyes, the weight of memories almost more than she could bear. She had used the Sight, scouted magical potential and taken children. Just as she had been taken.

She had become the enemy of her youth, the

harvesting witches she and her brother used to tell scary stories about at night.

And now, even with no Circle or orders, young sorceresses and sorcerers had taken it upon themselves to ensure the Harvest would continue. It seemed so…*wrong.* She curled her fists, a gesture so physical it felt strange yet welcome. *Human.*

A shadow caught her attention, and she looked up to see a young girl, at least ten years younger than her, standing near. A product of the last Harvest.

"Yes?" Shirina asked, annoyed at the interruption, annoyed at the girl's defiant yet frightened glance, annoyed at herself for expecting her to be a sorceress and not a child.

"I wish to continue my training," she said in a small voice, looking Shirina in the eye nonetheless. She bore a blue circle, and so was just one step above green, the lowest rank in the Circle.

"Then continue it." A typical Elder response.

"There is no one else," the girl whispered. "No one left to teach us, Elite."

Shirina turned to look at her. She was right. There was no one else left in the Circle to teach them. If the Elders were all lost, and there were precious few Crimson Circles to begin with, then that could mean change. But was change really what the Circle needed now? Could she afford to follow emotional callings on the whims of a memory? Of a chance encounter when her mind and body were weakened and more susceptible to turmoil?

Could she afford to weaken the Circle when it needed to be at its strongest?

She looked at the young girl, full of hope, apprehension, fear, the desire to accomplish, the hope to succeed…Shirina called upon the Sight to see more than what her eyes would show her. The young girl's magic was wild still, flowing and ebbing towards the magic of Graydon around them, the mist clinging to her like specks of pollen.

Shirina did not know if she had been the one to harvest the girl. She might have been but, truth be told, she had harvested so many that she couldn't remember them all. Nor did she dare try.

Dawn began to rise and Shirina spotted Grasky from the corner of her eye.

He motioned for her to follow before vanishing between some tall bushes.

She nodded to the girl. *Where do you come from? Is the Circle all that you dare remember as home now, too? What happens when you realize there is no more Circle?* She bit back the questions she yearned to ask. The Circle had to survive, for Graydon to survive.

"We will continue your training, then. But first, there is something I must tend to."

She crossed through the thin bushes and exited on the other side, amidst rows of dying roses. She followed the path they laid out for her, until they opened up to reveal rows of marigolds, hues of gold, orange and red dancing in the slight breeze. Grasky stood in the center of them.

"These fields were seeded by the first Yellow, Orange and Crimson Circles. With the few green leaves and blue skies, they represent every level of the Circle, except for Elder. I thought this was an appropriate place to give you this, Shirina, to remind you of what you've accomplished."

He held out a staff in his hands. It had been quickly carved, only the top portion freed from bark where she could safely grasp it. The end resembled that of a bone, and Shirina felt a shiver just looking at it.

"Like a bone of Graydon himself," Grasky said gently, as though reading her mind.

"I couldn't finish it all," he said in apology. "The wood took longer to prepare, the tree more temperamental than before. It too, is changing, like the rest of our land. I wonder how long before the magic that keeps these flowers alive will begin to fail."

He smiled sadly at her. "Just an old man rambling of days gone by, Shirina. I gift this to you, Elite. May its magic serve you, and Graydon, well."

Shirina noted he did not mention the Circle. "Thank you," she said.

"You should know," Grasky hesitated to give her the staff, "that it will test your magic. A few seconds that could save you or kill you, Shirina."

Shirina nodded and did not hesitate to take the staff

from his extended hands. The second she touched the wood, it felt as though lightning coursed through her entire body. It tingled from the tips of her toes to the ends of her hair, and left her with a sickly warm sensation, like honey drizzled all over her senses.

It was sweet and promised what she craved, but the staff taunted her.

She could sense it fighting her!

She could no longer see Grasky, her head buzzing with the power of Graydon's magic, filling her mind like thick cotton. She forced her breath to grow long and focused on the magic, on bending its will. Her head turned to fire, a raging fever devouring her entire body.

Her grasp on the staff was growing slippery with sweat. She clutched it more tightly.

Think, focus, aim, Tangia's voice rang in her head, and Shirina tried, but the heat and stuffiness made her own skin unbearable.

She couldn't breathe. She needed to breathe.

Panic welled in her and she tried to calm her breath, to focus, but she couldn't. Just like the first times she had used magic. She clung to those memories. That sensation had passed.

She just needed to control this magic. *But I can't!* It was stronger than her! *It's killing me!*

Suddenly she didn't want the magic. She wanted to be back home, without fear of failure or expectations of success, without the need to struggle to master Graydon's powers again, without the overwhelming pressure that made her want to escape her own skin.

She saw her own tombstone, so small beside her family's, finishing a perfect row to an imperfect ending.

Marguerite Monlie died that day, she had told her cousin.

But she hadn't. Her future had died that day. And her hope. The Circle had taken it from her, and replaced it with magic and purpose.

It was not enough. It had never been enough. She wanted to be back home. She wanted to be Marguerite again, with no suffocating magic, no need to fight, no need to die for a cause not even her own.

It's mine now. Everything will die unless I fight this! Shirina felt the jolt of hope and anger, seeing her family's graves and her cousin's uncertainty at dealing with her. She wanted a future. She needed to ensure their survival. And only the Circle offered her the ability to do so.

Marguerite Monlie may have died that day, but Shirina will not die this day!

She channeled the magic with her emotions instead of with her mind, leveraging her anger as a fine weapon, sensing the magic react to her need. The pressure dissipated and she heard herself gasp as she could breathe again. Her skin no longer felt foreign to her.

Fight.

It was like a command in her mind, whether from her or the staff, she did not know.

She forced her hand to remain on the weapon as the

magic of Sight was triggered and she could see every magic strand much clearer than ever before, as though a veil she had not even known existed had been lifted from her eyes. Keeping a hand on the staff, she raised her other hand and stroked the nearest strand, her heart racing at its potential. She could grasp it.

She could grasp all of it. Even magics she had not known to exist beforehand danced before her, so subtle and faint she couldn't even guess their purpose.

She closed her eyes and forced the Sight to stop. Stronger magic would be useful, but only if she could control it. Otherwise, it would prove more dangerous than useful.

May your steps be steady.

Her steps would be steady. But they could no longer march to the beat of a Covenant that had betrayed all of Graydon.

Shirina had intended to sleep some more, but as she headed to her room, three Orange Circles blocked her path. She recognized the one from last night, and the other two she did not know.

They were trying to be impressive, their heads raised proudly, their arms crossed before them.

Shirina supposed others might be impressed, but she did not pause or slow down as she neared them, not even acknowledging them with the slightest nod of the head.

It ruffled their feathers.

"Why did you call off the Harvest? The Circle needs new blood!" one of them cried as she passed him, a male sorcerer. She turned and faced him, their noses barely a breath apart. He tried and failed to hide his panic. She ignored his question. If the idiot was too stupid to realize that his training was incomplete, as was that of all other Circle adepts here, and still wanted to bring new trainees into the mix, he would probably never become an Elite, anyway. You required some ability to think for yourself as an Elite.

"What of Ravenhold? Has anyone returned since you left?"

Taken aback by her ignoring his question, he stuttered the answer. "No, not here, anyway."

"Ravenhold has fallen," the Orange Circle from last night said. Shirina turned to face her. She was tall, as tall as the Grayloft, and seemed just as smug.

"You believe," Shirina said, exhausted by their childish stupidity. "What are your names?"

They hesitated for a moment, but the woman from last night, obviously the leader of their group, spoke up. "I'm Shala, she's Pola and that's Trit." Shirina nodded.

"Well, Shala, Pola and Trit. As the three Orange Circles here, you now have the duty to teach every Green, Blue and Yellow Circle here. Once they've each gained a rank, then we'll re-open discussions on a Harvest."

Shala stammered. "But, it'll take months, maybe years to train all of them to reach a new rank! And we're," she stopped herself and flushed, but to her credit, finished the sentence. "We're Orange Circles. It is not our place to train others."

"I agree, it is not your place. So, what would we do with the new Harvest, then?"

Their eyes widened, as though they had not even considered the possibility beforehand. The situation at the Circle must have kept most Elders busy if that was the type of thinking and behavior now allowed.

She continued walking, but turned around when she had passed them all. "Remember your place. I will remind you, if necessary."

She met each of their eyes and held them until they lowered theirs to the ground. She turned around and allowed herself a half smile. They were inexperienced and brash, but she still needed them.

Or she would, when the time for battle came.

But now, she had to master her new talisman to reach Ravenhold and see what secrets the keep still held from her.

17

The clouds had gathered towards the West during the night and they could see the blur of rain in the distance. Cassara watched with passing interest, hoping the rain would not catch up to them.

Trevon, Dayshon and Jiles had been in deep discussions for over an hour now as they prepared the troops, the sun barely risen. Part of Cassara wanted to participate in their strategizing, but another part of her was too tired to care.

"Your Highness." A guard came up to her, bowing. Cassara flushed. She still wasn't used to the formality of Massir, and she hadn't yet managed to convince any of the guards not to stand on so much ceremony. And it was nearly impossible to engage them in conversation.

"Your mother the queen wishes a word with you." She nodded and followed him. Glancing back once at the chatting men, she wondered if she should grow used to the exclusion, knowing full well she wouldn't let it go on too long, not once she was more awake, anyhow.

The guard led her through part of the palace and Cassara was soon completely lost. She would need years to grow used to the layout of this vast place. She supposed that she would have all the time to explore in the future, once they had returned. Her heart fluttered at the thought of being inside these giant stone walls for the rest of her days, her ears still aching for the sound of the surf.

"She awaits you in there." The guard motioned towards the great hallway Cassara had been made to cross last night to join her new family in the courtyard. Edoline's banners were already gone and replaced by Massir's royal banners.

Spotting the queen near one of the columns, gazing out a window, Cassara walked towards her. She was beautiful, the queen. She did not show her age like her husband did, though Cassara suspected part of it was that she took little interest in the troubles of the court. Her dark hair, graying in places, was swept up in a knot as was proper in Massir, framing her dark features. Half of Cassara's hair was down today. No one mentioned anything, and Dayshon had simply smiled at her.

Maybe that was why she wanted to see her today. To reprimand her girlish and independent ways. Cassara steeled herself for a confrontation as she approached the queen. But then she turned, and her large brown eyes were filled with tears. She quickly brushed them away before smiling at Cassara, greeting her warmly by taking her hands and kissing her cheeks.

"Thank you for coming," she said, turning back towards the window. Cassara joined her. From where they stood, they could see the army mobilizing in the distance.

"You will be leaving soon," the queen acknowledged. Cassara nodded, careful about what she said. She still wasn't certain how to deal with the royal family.

"I am certain with Dayshon at my side that I will be safe," Cassara said softly. The queen smiled and seemed to relax.

"Do you love him?" she suddenly asked and turned to gauge Cassara's reaction. Not expecting such a bold question, Cassara did not manage to hide her surprise.

The queen raised her hand. "It doesn't matter, Cassara. Love grows, you know, it doesn't just happen."

Cassara gave a small smile, feeling like a little girl again. "I'm certain in my heart that I will someday grow to love him."

The queen seemed satisfied with her answer, favoring her with a smile and turning to walk down the hallway. The hall was much less imposing during the day, though it was still filled with secrets and history.

"I remember crossing this hallway too, a long time ago, Cassara," the queen said as Cassara matched her speed and walked beside her. "I was about your age, and terrified. I had never even met the prince!" She gave a short laugh. "But he was handsome, and that was enough at the time. I knew they wanted to strengthen ties with the Southern Coalition, which was why I had been shipped off for marriage. Now, I wouldn't say the Southern Coalition and Rashim are stronger allies for it, or that they ever will be, but my husband and I found each other, and learned to love each other, and that proved enough."

She was silent for a few steps and Cassara waited, wondering if that was why the queen had called her. The princess doubted she just needed a friendly ear.

"It was easier when we were just prince and princess, Cassara. Before the troubles of the court began haunting my husband. I love him still, perhaps even more, but it's… lonelier, now." She stopped and turned to face Cassara, cupping the princess' right cheek with her hand as she spoke.

"And I regret that you and Dayshon will not have the chance to know each other free from those responsibilities. You will have to be strong for him, Cassara, and he for you, as you will be a much more involved queen than I chose to be."

Cassara smiled as the queen removed her hand. "Don't worry, your Highness. When we return from the West, we will learn to know each other free from responsibility, as you had the chance with your husband."

The queen's lips trembled slightly and she turned and continued walking, her hands clutched before her.

Cassara followed, curious. Something obviously troubled the queen, but she wasn't sure what. She doubted it was her marriage with Dayshon. The queen had already taken a liking to her, and Cassara liked the soft-spoken queen as well, though she didn't quite understand her desire to stay out of the court's business. She supposed the queen must find her difficult to understand, as well, wanting to ride into battle in an unknown land, allied with old enemies and fighting creatures of insurmountable might.

The queen suddenly spoke again as they reached the iron doors, fully open now, the sunlight and the courtyard just a few steps away. "The king is dying."

The words, barely a whisper, sliced through Cassara. "What? How? He seems healthy to me."

The queen shook her head and refused to meet her eyes, her hands clutched tightly and her lips set.

"We don't know, but we suspect Circle magic. Some form of poison. It's taking its toll."

She paused and unfolded her hands, limbs falling uselessly by her side, as though she was too tired to hold them firm.

"He will be dead by the time you return, Cassara."

Tears welled into Cassara's eyes. He had been so kind to her last night, welcoming her into his family as a daughter. And she thought they might get along, once she got beyond his hard exterior.

But it seemed she would not be given the chance.

"Dayshon does not know. Not yet. He needs to

concentrate on the battle ahead, and not worry about his parents. But it's taking all of the king's strength to even remain standing." The queen took a deep breath. "I will keep things going here until your return and until I can step down from my position. I may have stood in the shadows, but it does not mean I did not pay attention. I will be fine, as will Rashim, but…when Dayshon is returning, once he has celebrated victory with his men, give him this." The queen handed Cassara a letter. She took it and stuffed it in her bag with her flute, a lump forming in her throat.

"I'm sorry to do this to you, Cassara, to burden you with a secret from your new husband, but I need you to keep him safe. You said you had magic. Please, use it to bring him back. Without him, there is no other heir to Rashim, and I do not have the strength or standing to lead our kingdom through one of its darkest periods. Eventually our storehouses will empty, and they will not refill without the help of the dying fields…" The queen turned and placed both of her hands on Cassara's shoulders, holding her eyes captive with the fear in hers. "Cassara, Dayshon will be needed. Keep him safe. Bring him home in one piece, quickly, and with hope."

Cassara nodded and swallowed hard, the queen composing herself and smiling kindly, as though nothing had been said. She then leaned forward, kissed her new daughter on the forehead, and walked out into the sunlight, humming gently as she examined the few remaining flowers, kept alive by tender care and willpower.

Cassara hesitated for a moment before walking back down the hallway, the banners of Rashim snapping in the high winds, as though screaming at Cassara not to forget that their survival depended on a magic she no longer had.

King Darmir had never been one for flights of fancy, but on this day, he found himself wishing for many different things. He wished he could control his limbs and feel strength flowing into them like he used to. He wished he were still strong enough to ride to war instead of his son.

And he wished the girl before him would stop whimpering like a child. "Princess Malir, you shame yourself. You have already proved poor of judgment. At least prove yourself strong of pride."

She did not stand, remaining crumpled on the floor. Darmir sighed. He had killed a few as examples, mostly. Delora had made his blood boil like none other. She had left his land and people weakened and scarred, and he was certain that even if Graydon survived, Rashim might not.

His kingdom was battered, and his sole heir was riding to a battle he very well might not win.

And Darmir was dying, another legacy of Delora, of that he had no doubt.

He wished he still had the strength to care.

The least he could do was try and garner allies for his son. He wished for the thousandth time he had not relied on the Circle for news on his land. He wished he had known his people suffered so as his kingdom slowly perished. The walls of Massir and its court had grown too thick and difficult to see beyond. He felt confident his son's wife would see to their thinning.

"Princess Malir, I will not kill you," he said. His left leg began to shake, and without his wife here to lean on, he needed to end this now.

"Listen to me, and listen well." The princess had stopped sniveling, for which he was grateful. "You will go back to the Southern Coalition, and you will convince them to gather an army of at least one thousand men, and they will ride west and help my son. Do this, and I will spare your life."

She didn't dare look up, but he could tell she was thinking about the offer. "How shall I get there, my Lord?" Her small voice only added to his fatigue.

"I don't care. Find your own way. But leave as soon as my son has left, and make sure I don't see you again unless there is an army at your back."

She folded in on herself and he added, "Consider yourself lucky, princess. Yours is a fate you might survive."

He found himself wishing that she would, which took him by surprise.

Dying was apparently turning him into a softer man.

He laughed softly as he walked away, to find his queen and her strength before having to bid farewell to their son.

Within the hour, the army was moving. Five units, each boasting five hundred well-armed men riding horses. A cavalry force was needed for speed. The rest of the army would remain in Massir, just in case.

No one specified in case of what.

Dayshon rode at the front on his brown steed, with Cassara at his right, on a white horse. Gragor and Loas rode with Jiles near the front, still bearing the colors of Edoline, Gragor holding the emblem of Cassara's kingdom proudly. The rest of their emblems were from Massir.

Trevon rode as well, though he looked extremely uncomfortable on a horse. Cassara waved at him, and when he tried to return the greeting, he almost fell off the horse. Cassara bit back a laugh and turned around.

The king and queen waited for them at the gates. Dayshon jumped off his horse and helped Cassara off hers. They went together towards his father.

"We ask for your blessing as we ride towards the West, father," Dayshon asked, bowing slightly. Cassara lowered her head in acknowledgment. His father stood proudly and nodded. Now that she knew he was dying, she could see the weakening of his left leg, how he clutched his hands together behind his back so his son wouldn't see them shaking, and his sunken eyes and cheeks. When she had first met him, she had attributed those to the demands of rule, but now she could see the yellowing of his eyes and the ashy undertone of his skin.

She doubted Dayshon noticed. She would not have, had she not known what she did.

The queen stood near him, a little bit behind, and Cassara now saw the concern behind her smile, and how closely she kept an eye on her husband, ready to cover his sickness when necessary.

When the king did not speak, the queen did.

"Be careful, my son, my daughter. You both make Rashim, and us, proud." She took a step forward and embraced both of them, Dayshon kissing her on the cheek. She stepped back and the king extended his hand and Dayshon took it, shaking it firmly. Cassara marveled that the king, so near death's door, still found the strength to give his son a firm handshake.

The king simply squeezed Cassara's arm and met her eyes. She nodded and swallowed back the tears.

"Thank you," she whispered. He nodded in response, and in that simple gesture conveyed more than any words would have. She felt welcomed and loved and thanked all at once, while the burden of their responsibility for their son was placed on her shoulders.

She met the queen's eyes once and nodded.

Dayshon led her back to her horse and helped her mount, smiling up at her as he jumped on his own steed, ordering the army to march. Graysword was secured to her saddle, and Cassara gently ran her gloved finger over the detailing of the pommel. Whoever had crafted the weapon had poured a lot of love into it. But it would remain lifeless, useless except as a reminder to Cassara of why she had chosen this path.

Dayshon glanced back once at his parents and waved goodbye, not knowing it was the last time he would see his father.

They rode out of Massir and set a steady pace west, towards the eye of the storm.

18

"Tell me you didn't just suggest that we head out now," Avarielle said incredulously as she peered outside the cave. The storm that the lightning had promised had finally appeared, rain pouring down. Not torrential, but enough to drench anyone who stepped outside.

"We need to keep moving," Kryde said as he struggled to his feet, trying to disguise his pain and fatigue by moving slowly.

Avarielle felt almost normal by the morning, the powers of the Circle ghost having healed her self-inflicted wound and revitalized her body. Though she still wanted to throw up, thanks to the blasted magic of Elihor. But Kryde had only been partly healed, and his energies had been drained by the intake of Graydon's magic.

He would have probably been fully healed had the kealer completed its task, but then he would also be dead.

"Really?" Avarielle raised an eyebrow as he finally straightened up.

"Yes," he growled, growing more and more annoyed. She could understand him. He wanted to save what he could of the survivors, which required getting to Stormhold sooner rather than later, before they were completely turned into Eloms and let loose upon Graydon. Plus, he was clearly deeply worried about the effect of Elihor's magic on her. But she could take it, and would, as long as she needed to.

Kryde was hardly in any shape to fight, and the rain would not help his weakened body.

Avarielle grinned and took a quick step towards him, grabbing his arm in hers and twisting him as she placed her leg behind him. He swore, though she absorbed most of the shock by holding him as he fell. He was a heavy brute, and she knew his back still hurt, despite his claims to the contrary.

He took a deep breath as they both lay on the floor.

"Point well taken," he said, his muscles relaxing as he shifted. "Perhaps another day would see me more fit for battle."

Avarielle laughed again and then shifted, placing her arm around his chest and her head on him. He gently played with her hair with one hand while he held her with the other.

She wrinkled her nose. "You smell like burnt flesh."

He gave a short laugh. "And you smell like dead fish. Between the two of us, we're a wonderful couple." He stopped laughing and paused, growing serious. She could feel his heart accelerate. "What are your customs, in your land? For couples?"

Avarielle raised her head and looked at him with a coy smile. "Are you propositioning me?"

Kryde smiled broadly. "Technically in my land we're pretty much sealed together by now, but I just realized that I have no idea what your people do."

Avarielle laughed and stole a quick kiss from his lips before resting her head back down. "We travel a part of life's journey together, forging a common path and allies. And when comes a time that path is no longer shared, we part ways. Sometimes we find each other again, but that's all up to the Fates."

"So we're traveling down a path together, then? Sounds nice."

Avarielle smiled. "I never found anyone I was even remotely interested in traveling this path with before you."

"I'm honored then. What would make you part ways from me?"

Avarielle gave a short laugh. "Already trying to get rid of me?"

"Hardly. Just trying to understand your ways."

She pondered the question, wondering what would

make her leave him. He'd proved loyal, dependable, and fun. She didn't feel the need to lessen herself for him, nor did he for her. Old responsibilities tugged at her heart, but she ignored them. They were too far, and she'd finally found some form of peace.

"I honestly can't think of anything," she whispered. "You got me out of Siabala's Rage, Kryde. That's a solid start to our union."

"Well, I cut you down and gave you a sword, then left you as you foolishly ran back in," he laughed softly. "But I know you'd do the same, which heartens me."

"Of that you have my word," she grinned. "If ever I think of anything that would make me leave you, trust me, you'll be the first to know."

He held her more tightly. She wondered if he was in pain, but didn't ask. He wouldn't tell her, anyway. His breath grew long and he fell into a deep slumber to help his body heal and regain his strength.

Avarielle wasn't tired at all, but still she stayed near him, her head on his chest, standing watch while guarding the slow beating of his heart.

Kryde slept most of the day and night, and by morning his fatigue and the rain had vanished.

The storm had done Elihor a world of good. It had dragged the ashes down the mountains, black rivulets on tainted stone, and most of the rock face was now gray instead of black. With the rising sun, they could see Elihor spreading far below them, puddles shining black in the new light. But beyond them, in some spots of the burnt land, Avarielle could see patches of green beginning to emerge.

She turned to point them out to Kryde, but when she looked at him and saw the pride on his face, she knew he had already seen them. Avarielle took a moment to look at all of Elihor. The land was smaller than Graydon, or at least narrower. The sea shone brightly on either side. They were high enough that in Graydon, at the same height, you could probably see the whole land as well, but in Elihor the land thinned and stretched out, whereas in Graydon it grew wider.

Avarielle wished she could have seen Elihor in its prime. With some of the ashes washed away, she could make out more of the lay of the land. Some roads, or rivers, crisscrossed below. It was difficult to tell.

And from the way the sun hit Elihor, over the mountains behind them, she could see shadows that revealed where a large forest once stood, just to the north. She wondered if that was their Kosel.

The horizon became a blur, stretching far beyond what she could see, vanishing in a misty haze.

"On a clear day, you can see all the way to the end of Elihor," Kryde said. "I came up here once with my grandfather. We climbed, higher even, all the way to the

Wall of Loss. I wanted to touch it so badly and, even though my grandfather had made me promise not to, I did it anyway."

He paused and looked around, a slow grin spreading over his face. "He was so mad, Avarielle, I thought he was going to take off my head or just throw me off the mountain." Avarielle smiled at him. "I only grazed it, really, the Wall. Just for a second. And it didn't hurt, it just…it was wrong, Avarielle. It was like sorrow and pain combined into one powerful magic. I cried, I remember, which stopped further scolding from my grandfather as he comforted me, instead."

He looked up towards the Wall, which danced with sunlight, the light piercing in from Graydon and the East. "Now that I think of it, after he got over his anger, he seemed to understand. I wonder if he'd touched it once, too. Probably."

He looked back down towards Elihor, stretching his back. "Last night, when the kealer touched me, Avarielle, it was the same type of magic. The same sorrow mixed with warmth. I think that whatever magic built the Wall, it also helped create the kealers."

Avarielle looked at him questioningly. "You mean Siabala? But Siabala had nothing to do with the Wall. It was Elihor and Graydon."

"Or so the stories say." He began walking down and Avarielle followed. "But what if he had something to do with it? What if his magic was part of building the Wall? I mean, the stories are so different in our lands already, isn't it possible neither one of them is right?"

Avarielle had to admit he had a point. "But why would Siabala have helped create the Wall? What do we even know of him?"

Kryde looked over his shoulder at her. "Not much, really. We thought he was just a story until recently, to be honest. What little we do know is that Siabala was imprisoned below the Wall by Elihor and Graydon, who were too weak to kill him."

Avarielle nodded as she jumped off a stone. The fresh morning sun felt amazingly good on her damp skin. It promised a warm, dry day. Just the way she liked it.

"We have the same story, actually. The first victory of Elihor and Graydon. The first real battle, where the two of them survived but many of their brethren perished."

"What brethren?"

"What do you mean?"

"The Circle didn't exist then, unless your stories tell it differently."

"No. Our history says the Circle was built to maintain the Wall."

"Same here. Good. But our stories also indicate that Elihor and Graydon were the last of something, and it wasn't the Circle, so what was it? Another covenant? Siabala killed most of them in the battle that imprisoned him, but who were they?" He ran his hand through his thick dark hair, ruffling it even further. "It might not even matter." He looked towards his burnt land and added in a whisper, "I'm just trying to make sense of it all."

Avarielle kept silent, wishing she had the answers he sought. The simple fact of knowing why it had happened, of knowing it wasn't just a random act of evil, might ease his pain a little.

"There it is," Kryde said, crouching as he neared a cliff. Avarielle crouched beside him, sucking in her breath as the valley spread below her.

The mountains jutted down in a straight line, as though something had cut through them with a knife and pulled out a chunk. It was perfectly circular, with slits in the easternmost mountain allowing the sun to wash the center of the stony basin in morning light. Its middle was absorbed in the Wall of Loss, the keep spanning the two worlds. The shimmer of the Wall danced in the light, specks of blues, purples and yellows sparkling in the air below.

In the center, on a great pillar reaching into depths too deep and dark for them to see the bottom, a stone keep rested, like a cenotaph to a great era long gone. A large stone building had been carved directly out of the pillar to form the central Circle Keep, intricate designs Avarielle could barely make out forming windows and pillars.

A great stone bridge connected it to the mountains, impressive for its length and its thin, almost fragile-looking carving.

Avarielle couldn't see inside the tall building, but small

windows on the top towers suggested they could be climbed. The towers themselves were so big that they could house a small village of people on both sides of the Wall. She wondered if the magic of the Wall cut into the keep, or if it was somehow stopped, allowing for safe passage between the worlds. Safer than Siabala's Rage, anyway.

She turned to Kryde and whispered. "Do we have to cross that bridge? How do we reach it?"

Kryde pointed to the left. "There's a path leading to that section down below. We have to climb lower than Stormhold and then cross the valley. At least, I assume the path still exists. No one has been here in a very long time, not that I know of, anyway."

"Let me guess, your grandfather came here?"

Kryde grinned. "Yes! As a young man though, when this Covenant still existed too. The way he told it, he would have been thrown into the abyss if he hadn't been a descendant of Elihor."

Avarielle smiled. "I think I'd have liked your grandfather."

"I think so too. He'd have definitely liked you." He smiled and indicated that they should go back a bit. She followed him, remaining crouched until they were both out of sight of the keep.

"All right, so how do we get down there?" Avarielle asked once they were far enough.

"We climb down, that way," he pointed towards the right. Avarielle nodded.

"Sounds fun. And then we cross a bridge, ripe for the picking?"

He shrugged. "We'll see when we get closer, but I imagine so."

Her stomach gurgled and she winced. At least the nausea was already dissipating, and she had managed not to throw up so far today. A rare occasion in Elihor.

"Lunch first?" Kryde asked, grinning.

"Probably not a bad idea, or my grumbling stomach will betray our presence long before we even reach the keep!"

Kryde checked his dwindling supplies. "We should hunt some. It'll still take a few days, maybe a week, to reach Stormhold. We don't have a lot of food left, and any bird will be higher up, not down there."

Avarielle grimaced. "But how are we going to cook a bird? You don't intend to eat it raw, do you?"

Kryde smiled. "That, my friend, is a secret I'll reveal to you only after we've secured the meat."

"Wonderful. But I'm not eating it raw, just so we're clear. That's disgusting." Kryde gave a short laugh.

"It'll go faster if we split up to hunt. Let's meet back here within two hours, successful or not."

Avarielle nodded. She hated the idea of splitting up, but it was the quickest way to proceed. And time was of the essence. "Be careful. Don't go far."

He smiled widely, baring perfect white teeth, a sharp contrast to his black eyes. "Without me, you won't know how to eat those birds the right way!"

"Not raw is usually the right way."

"You'd be surprised."

"No, I'm pretty sure I wouldn't be, but I am curious, I'll give you that."

"Well, as long as I get something." He closed the gap between them and kissed her fiercely before releasing her.

"Two hours!" he called back and headed towards the northeast, closer to the keep. Avarielle shook her head as she watched him vanish around some rocks.

The fool man seemed convinced she needed some sort of protection, even though they were fairly evenly matched in skills.

She smiled as she walked down the southeast path, away from Stormhold, but not intending on wandering too far from the man she had grown to love.

Kryde was securing his two catches on his belt when three birds scattered nearby, terrified by something. Dropping the birds, he took cover, drawing his short sword.

He heard shuffling before he smelled rotting flesh, so strong it made him gag. More shuffling, and some strange clicking noises. He flattened himself as much as he could against the rock, not certain what was coming around the corner, but confident it stemmed from Siabala.

Then he heard another noise and turned around. A figure stood right beside him. It was a woman from Graydon, bearing an evil smile. Half of her face was covered by rock, but her eyes betrayed her origin. He moved quickly, lifting his sword to strike her, but she sent waves of magic into him and he went flying, scraping his back against the stone as he was flung into the path of the incoming creatures.

Ignoring the pain of his freshly re-opened wounds, Kryde quickly stood up again, pulling his broadsword free. He looked at the monsters that now surrounded him. Where he had thought Eloms were disgusting, mostly due to the fact that he knew they were his people, these creatures were completely repulsive. They still looked human, but their flesh was rotting and their eye sockets were empty. Their jaws hung limply and their steps were more dragged than walked.

The clothing they wore revealed who they were. Circle garb, except their dresses had two Circles, one embracing the other, forming a continuous symbol of infinity. His grandfather had described that symbol. They were the keepers of Stormhold.

One lunged at him and he attacked, part of him wanting to defend himself, the other part wanting to ease the creature's obvious pain. He brought his sword down and stabbed it through the chest. The creature stumbled but did not fall.

Kryde swung again, aiming for the neck, decapitating it. What had once been a sorceress fell to the ground, unmoving.

Before he could down another, he was hit with a volley of magic, energy shackling his wrists and ankles. He held his sword as long as he could, but the pressure on his wrists forced his fists to open and he dropped it, the weapon clanging uselessly on the rocks. The invisible bonds pulled him down and he was forced on his knees, looking up angrily at the woman from Graydon as she approached.

He would rip out her eyeballs and make her eat them when he had the chance.

"Kryde Kolder, I assume? We've been looking for you, but you've been nearly impossible to find until you kindly used your magic two days ago. Thank you."

"Who are you?" he demanded, eyes blazing with fury. How dare a woman from Graydon interfere with Elihor, much less make him a prisoner? Now that she was closer, he could see a Circle above her heart, though her robes were red. "Where are you from?"

She smiled wildly, insanity tinting her eyes, black circles etched deep under them. "My name is Delora. I'm a friend of the Grayloft. And I represent a new Circle, the only remaining one. Ruled by Siabala."

Kryde wanted to hit the woman even more. She was

not only a fool, she was a mad fool, at that. He was about to tell her as much when an arrow shot out and struck the woman in the face. She fell to the side. Another arrow flew and hit the witch straight in the heart where she lay, unmoving. The creatures stood still, as though uncertain what to do without the witch's guidance.

Avarielle walked up to him, her bow held at the ready as she walked by the creatures.

"Ugly things," she mumbled, wrinkling her nose in disgust. She looked at the witch, her eyes narrowing. "I told you I'd eventually kill you."

"Glad to see you," Kryde said as he knelt.

"I told you I had your back," she said. "You don't have to kneel before me, Kryde. I would save you without the formalities."

Kryde grimaced. "Some sort of spell. I can't get up."

Avarielle's eyes grew wide and she spun towards the witch, shooting another arrow before she had even fully turned. It missed. The witch was no longer there.

Then magic flew into Avarielle, sending the warrior stumbling to the ground, until another blow came and she was lifted up, grasping her neck as the magic choked her.

"You have been a pest since the start," the witch said as she stood up, the arrows still embedded in her, blood dribbling near the shaft, the skin cracked and broken around it.

"Let her go, witch," Kryde grumbled the threat, his magic rising within him.

"If I didn't need her still, I would let her go, over the cliff. Unfortunately, I need both of you."

She dropped Avarielle, the warrior choking and heaving, her skin tinged with blue. Before the warrior could regain her senses, the witch cast another spell, sending her flying against the rocks behind them, her red hair covered with bright blood as she collapsed near Kryde, barely conscious.

"Don't worry. If you behave, I'll be much nicer to you," the witch said, and Kryde snapped, his magic lashing out at her. She managed to block it, her eyes gleaming with victory as she held up an amulet and absorbed his magic into the moon half of it, the silver glowing bright, even in the daylight.

I walked right into that trap! He suddenly understood that she had wanted him to use his magic, victory flashing in her eyes. He remembered Tan's words: *a fully activated amulet.* The witch smiled and concentrated on it, igniting the sun half with her powers.

It's one of the two keys. The sword and the fully activated amulet, and those with the power to wield it, can bring down the Wall of Loss.

Kryde had just handed her one of the missing pieces. Now all that she needed was Graysword.

And Avarielle.

"You have no idea how nice it is to have a magic that doesn't require a wielder in order to be effective. All I needed was for you to activate Elihor's portion of the amulet." She shot Avarielle a look filled with poison. "But don't worry, I'm sure Siabala will find something for you to do while I continue coaxing the Grayloft to summon her magic." She smiled so evilly it sent shivers down Kryde's spine. "Hopefully it won't result in her death."

Something inside him snapped again, the magic lashing out, but this time he directed it towards Avarielle, wishing her to be safe above all else. If the magic would not keep him safe, then let it at least keep the one he loved safe.

He willed it so, and the magic obeyed, surrounding her with a soft glow. The warrior snapped fully awake, her eyes wide through the shield of his magic. She was vanishing. *He was teleporting her!*

She reached out to grab him, to bring him with her, but the magic grew too thick, and she barely managed to touch his cheek with her finger, the light touch warm on his cold face.

Then she was gone, and he was left alone with the witch and the creatures, his magic abandoning him, casting him aside as though unworthy of being saved.

But it didn't matter. Come what may for him, he could die knowing he had saved her.

His only regret was that he could not save Pack or any of his people, and that he would die without a sword in his hands.

19

After two days straight in the saddle, Cassara thought she would never feel her lower body again. She desperately wanted to rub life back into her behind, but her tent was not yet up, and she could hardly do it out here, in front of all the men.

Sighing, she removed Graysword from her saddle, her arms also numb and aching.

"Can I help you with that, Lady Cassara?" Trevon asked as he walked up behind her.

"No thank you, Trevon. I can handle it." But when she turned to face him, her arms shook slightly from the effort of holding the blade, though it was fairly light.

"May I walk you to your tent then? I believe the men have finished setting it up on the hill."

"I would appreciate that, Trevon," Cassara said. He took his time as he pretended to look around with great interest, keeping the pace slow. Cassara was so grateful she wanted to cry. She was tired, but she didn't want to show it. Her bones and muscles ached, and her body had just started to recover from her last journey, and had hardly been ready to undertake a new one. She dared not complain that she couldn't keep up with the trained and seasoned warriors.

The last thing she needed was to be left behind like extra baggage. Especially now that Dayshon and Jiles had formed a warrior's camaraderie with Trevon. It was only a matter of time before they clued in that Trevon had been her only Westland ally, now that Avarielle was gone. Once they realized she also had no magic, she was certain she would be shipped back to Massir.

She couldn't bear the thought, yet she was conflicted. The only reason she had married Dayshon was for his army. She supposed she had accomplished her goal of sending help for the West and preparing for whatever was to come next. Now that she had done that, had she not repaid her debt to Avarielle?

Couldn't she leave Graysword with Trevon and return to Massir, to find help for Edoline? Why did she feel the need to head into this battle too, when she was even more ill-prepared than the last ones she had barely survived?

*Still...*It felt right. Her instincts told her to continue on this path. But her instincts had also told her she could trust Shirina, which had cost Avarielle her freedom and possibly her life.

They neared the tent, the soldiers having just finished putting it up.

"Princess," Trevon said as they stopped nearby, waiting for the soldiers to finish. Cassara turned to face him.

"I do not know the whole story of your allegiance with Avarielle, but I want you to know two things. The first is that I considered Avarielle's father to be a brother, and so any oath he took, through heritage or choice, I fully intend to uphold. And the second thing," he paused and looked down at Graysword, which she clung to, "is that Graysword will remain in your possession until you give it willingly. And the West will listen to one who holds Graysword, no matter that she is a young girl too afraid of being left behind to utter a complaint."

Cassara flushed and gave a slight smile. "Am I truly that easy to read, Trevon?"

He grinned. "If your husband does not give you a massage, he is a fool."

Cassara blushed furiously at that statement, making Trevon laugh. Then he sobered again. "Seriously, I need to know—he treats you well?"

Cassara gave a slight smile. "Yes, he does. He treats me like...like a queen."

Trevon nodded, pleased. "Well, your tent is ready, if you'll excuse me, your Highness."

He began to walk away, but she called after him. "Trevon!"

He stopped and turned around. "Thank you. For everything."

Trevon lowered his head in salute and walked off, his stride now long and purposeful. Cassara felt better than she had in two days. With Trevon at her side, she knew she would not be left behind. He had told her as much.

And she knew Westlanders kept their word, even if it cost them their lives.

By the next morning, Cassara was so sore she could barely stand. Dayshon didn't help, pulling her back down on the thin mattress.

"Is it time to go already?" he asked as he held her down, still half asleep.

She smiled and ruffled his hair. "It's sunrise. So time to get up. The men will wonder what we're doing!"

His head perked up at that and he grinned at her. "Let them wonder, then. They're all just jealous I get to sleep with the most beautiful woman in camp."

Cassara laughed. "With the only woman in camp, Dayshon, who also happens to be your wife. We really need to discuss giving more women swords in Massir. Now, get up!"

She slipped out of his arms and hopped away from him so he couldn't pull her back down. He rolled on his back and stretched, wincing.

Cassara lifted an eyebrow. "You're sore?"

Dayshon looked at her as though she was insane. "Of course I'm sore. I don't exactly ride all the time, not like most of these soldiers." He winked at her. "Though don't go telling them that."

Cassara laughed softly. "I was afraid of telling you I was sore, for fear…" she caught herself and stopped.

Dayshon sat up. "For fear of what? Of being left behind?"

She really was too easy to read, Cassara decided. She sighed and sat beside him on the bed.

"Yes. I don't want to be a burden or a worry, but I really need to come."

"Cassara." Dayshon took her hand in his and kissed it, sending a shiver down her spine. His hair stuck up wildly, he sported two-day-old stubble and his eyes were still filled with sleep. She had always thought he was good looking, but right now, she thought he might very well be the most handsome man in all of Graydon.

"I promised you I would let you go back home whenever you chose. And right now, I think your friend's home, the West, is the home you really want to go to."

Cassara bit her lower lip. If she closed her eyes for a second, she thought she might hear the surf. But they were nearing the desert, the land and the air growing more and more dry. She was just being silly. Edoline was gone, and she had to accept that.

"You don't have to tell me everything, Cassara, but when you're ready, know that I'll listen."

Cassara nodded. He wanted to know about Graysword, she knew. He had asked once and she had avoided answering, not certain how to explain the entire situation. She wasn't convinced herself it made much sense, and explaining it to someone else would probably not make her sound any saner.

"I promise I won't leave you behind, Cassara. I think any adventure could only benefit from your company, personally." He grinned at her and she gave him a quick kiss on the lips.

She stood up and started dressing for travel, Dayshon doing the same. *Traveling to battle together right after getting married certainly crushes dreams of romance,* Cassara thought as Dayshon and she changed, both in utilitarian clothing that had been worn for two days already.

When they were done, Dayshon turned to her. "Do you regret it, Cassara? Getting married to me?"

Cassara gave a short laugh. "Dayshon, it's only been a few days! I should think solid regret would take longer to form." She closed the gap between them and kissed him. She didn't know if she loved him, but she was willing to learn. She was fairly certain she could trust him, and she wanted him to know it, and to know that he could trust her, too.

She broke free again and held his eyes as she spoke. "The sword belongs to a good friend who was sent to

Siabala's Rage while trying to help me, Dayshon. A warrior named Avarielle Grayloft. She was also a leader in the West, and I hope that will bear enough weight to make a difference in solidifying alliances."

Dayshon looked towards Graysword and nodded. Cassara continued, so he would understand. "The Elder Delora is the one who sent her there." She didn't bother mentioning Shirina. That was just an extra complication, and she didn't want to spend all day explaining the whole sordid tale to him.

She just wanted him to know she trusted him, as he had shown he trusted her by not leaving her behind.

"Delora," Dayshon whispered the name like a curse. He turned to look at her again, his eyes blazing with fury. "So she cost you your home, your family, and your friend?"

Cassara blinked back tears, her next words but a whisper. "She's my aunt, Dayshon."

His eyes grew wide. "Really? Then why would she do all of that?"

Cassara hesitated at that. She had not intended to tell him about her magic. She had intended to keep herself at arm's length from the whole story. Just a passive witness. But then, she had mentioned in court that she had access to magic that might help them.

She steeled herself. If this marriage with Dayshon was going to be solid, if the two of them were going to work together to save Graydon, then he needed to know all of it. Or at least the broad strokes, until there was time for more details.

"My family had an ancient magic, Dayshon. Delora wanted it, and I was its keeper." She paused. "And now she has it."

Dayshon looked at her with calculating eyes for a second, as though weighing the truth of her statement. Cassara looked up at him boldly and prepared to argue. She had not lied and would certainly not let herself be accused of doing so.

But then Dayshon cracked a quick smile. "Cassara Edoline, you are simply full of surprises, aren't you?" He bent down and gave her a quick kiss.

"Thank you. For telling me. I have to go now, or the men *will* begin to wonder." He grinned at her. "Not that anyone would have a difficult time understanding my whiling away the time here with you…" She blushed and he laughed as he stepped out of the tent, leaving Cassara alone to finish getting ready.

Cassara felt a bit relieved at having shared some of her story, from the blood relation to the betrayal, and the loss of both magic and friend. Though it also made it more real, which left her feeling numb.

She tied her hair back and picked up Graysword, the jewel of the blade glowing dully in the light of the tent, as though waiting for its chance to shine in the darkness once more.

20

She would take down Stormhold, even if she had to bring it down one stone at a time.

Her hands were bloodied, scraps of torn shirt tied around them in a vain effort to stop the bleeding. Smears of blood marked the downward climb. She gritted her teeth and continued gripping the rock, not resting, no longer giving in to the fatigue of her battered body.

Not the magic of Elihor, not this mountain, nor her bloodied hands would stop her from moving fast, faster than even Kryde would had believed possible.

Kryde.

She clenched her jaw and anger energized her muscles. He had been captured over two days ago now, but he was tough, and he would withstand whatever Delora had planned for him.

Oh, Avarielle had plans for Delora, too. Not her own

torture, nor Jayden's imprisonment, nor threats against Cassara had lit the fire she felt now. By the time Avarielle was through with her, the witch would regret ever having taken her first breath.

The sun was setting for the second night of almost relentless climbing, and Avarielle could feel that she needed to stop and rest. But she refused to give in to her body. Even once she cleared this cliff, she still had a few days of constant walking to reach the bridge, which would undoubtedly be guarded.

Try and stop me.

Avarielle grabbed another rock, using her stomach muscles to spare her arms and legs the fatigue of climbing. The darkness impeded her sight, but she had managed one night of careful climbing and she would manage another. Or she would plummet to her death and die knowing she had robbed Delora of the precious Grayloft heir she needed to bring down the Wall of Loss.

She knew she was playing right into Delora's hands. The witch waited for her, traps in place, ready to capture her and force her to summon Graysword to save Kryde.

She knew it as clearly as she knew her own name. And she didn't care.

She reached for another hand hold, and the rock she still held onto came loose. Avarielle began to tip back, using the strength of her stomach muscles and legs to push herself towards the stone, where she could find another handhold. One of her footholds gave way too, and she began to slide, hitting rocks until she found a handhold again and stopped herself, so calm it seemed as though she had never been afraid of dying.

And she knew she wouldn't die now. Not before the witch had breathed her last.

Avarielle ignored the deep bleeding gash on her leg, grabbing the next rock as she continued to lower herself, no more careful than before.

By the third day she hit level ground again. Her entire body throbbed with pain, so tired she could barely see. She half-fell and stumbled the last few meters, not caring that her hands were so raw blisters formed within the wounds, infection deeply warming the cuts.

Nor did she care that the cut in her leg was deep and full of shards of sharp stones, which dug deeper and ground somewhere near her bone. She'd worry about that later.

I'll just have Kryde nurse me back to health. She grinned at the idea, feeling light-headed and dizzy. She finally needed to sit down and rest, at least for a few hours.

Not finding any shelter, Avarielle just lay down to sleep on the path. It wasn't wide, and if she stumbled off of it, she would plummet to a quick but unpleasant end.

She was an easy target, but she doubted Delora would attack her here. The chances of her stumbling off the precipice were too great. Why take the chance when it was obvious where she was headed?

Avarielle leaned against the cliff and slid down, sitting

and looking out towards Stormhold. She could barely see the keep, only one corner noticeable from where she was. The stone was intricately worked and the sharp lines of the building looked out of place in the valley. She briefly wondered who had built this place, then wondered if Ravenhold would look the same, never having seen the keep with her own eyes.

She would find out eventually. She intended to see Ravenhold yet.

After rescuing Kryde and dealing with Delora, she intended to find Shirina and make her pay.

Ghosts haunted her dreams. Usually sapped by Graysword's magic, dreams now roamed freely in her mind, whispering of doubt and shame, fueled by the hatred ignited deep within her heart.

She was fourteen again. She remembered the day clearly. The sky was turquoise and she had been on the edge of the great mountain that led to the Wall of Loss. Lilies bloomed amidst the cracks, sending their perfume into the air all around her.

The dandelions had exploded into puffs of cotton that very morning, the white seeds blowing in the wind. Avarielle had not been that happy since before the deaths of her father and two of her older brothers. Their deaths left only her and her youngest brother, Rojon, who was still several years her elder. The sun allowed her to forget their deaths, if only for a few precious moments. The chances of dark creatures attacking were non-existent, and Rojon's sword practice was far away. There was no striking of metal on metal, no grunting, no promise of upcoming battle.

All that she had now was the dance that Eliya, whom she loved like an older sister, had taught her.

In the past year, Avarielle had grown tall and straight like a stick, but with none of the awkwardness of some of her other friends. She had understood her body immediately, her limbs following new graceful arcs with their length, her legs stronger and better able to support her in jumps and twirls.

She felt so free as she danced, to a music entirely her own, fueled by the wind, the blowing dandelions, the shifting grass, the leaves of the few trees. She had kicked off her boots and just danced, in the space where the sand met grass, near the base of the mountain.

She lifted her arms in arches, she jumped, she let her body move to its own rhythm. It had been so long since she had just danced, for herself.

Night snuck up on her. The music was interrupted by the cry of a coyote, before it was silenced. Avarielle stumbled and opened her eyes.

The wind no longer blew and the sun had all but vanished.

Then she smelled it. The odor of rotting corpses.

She ran. Still feeling light from the dance, her legs moved of their own will, fueled mostly by fear. She felt as though she glided on the sand, but still, she could hear them coming. She had seen them a few times, before they had met death at the hands of the warriors who defended the borders of her town.

One of them came into her peripheral vision, running on all fours. Avarielle stumbled but managed to remain standing and running, the fear now turning her limbs to lead.

She was going to die. She couldn't outrun them. She couldn't get away.

Then she saw them. Warriors running towards her, her brother at their head, running so fast her own speed increased at the sight of him.

But then one of the Eloms leapt sideways and knocked into her. She heard her brother scream and felt the bite of the creature on her upper arm.

He was going to eat her!

And then a quick flash of Graysword, and her brother screamed a war cry, and the other warriors were there.

He was over her, calling her.

"Ryle? Avarielle, come on, are you okay?" She had never heard such fear in his voice.

"We have to move back," said one of the warriors, a man Avarielle knew only in passing. He was from another village, one of the fallen villages whose survivors had come to seek shelter in the magic of Graysword.

"Right," Rojon said as he picked Avarielle up in his arms. She felt woozy, but her brother's strength would keep her moving.

"That sword's powerful," the warrior said. "But it would be better if it was wielded by someone older and more experienced."

She remembered her brother gently putting her back down, grinning at her and telling her everything would be okay. And then even her dreams refused to show her what exactly had happened.

But she did remember wailing that night, screams so guttural part of her didn't even believe they were hers. Alone, clutching her dead brother, in the desert of the West, left to be eaten by Eloms.

And she would have been, had Trevon not found her and carried her to safety, leaving her brother's body to rot, unable to carry both siblings.

Just hang on to me, it'll be all right, he had whispered, over and over again, until she had quieted and fallen asleep.

She had awakened at home the next morning. Alone in a big house.

Trevon had come in later that day, checking up on her, his face grim as he placed Graysword back on her family's wall.

It would be a few years before Avarielle had the courage to even touch the sword and, even then…

She woke up drenched in cold sweat, dread in the pit

of her stomach. Her body was sore from resting, her muscles beginning to seize. Standing up, she felt dizzy as nausea struck hard, giving her just enough warning for her to bend down and retch.

She wiped her mouth with the back of her hand.

Where was a bloody kealer when you needed one?

Night had fallen and she forced her weary body to move. Having very little food and water left, she was fueled mostly by hatred and need.

She had to save Kryde.

She didn't want to face the rest of her life alone, in a big empty house, with only her nightmares to keep her company at night.

21

The vegetation had been growing thinner the further West they headed, the men growing quiet as the destruction scarred the land around them. They had not encountered Eloms since heading out on their journey, which only served to make the men more jittery, the lust for battle flowing in their veins unspent and turning into apprehension at what exactly their enemy was planning.

Some men had begun whispering that it was just a trick by the West to lure them out and slaughter them. As the champion of this mission, Cassara was implicated in some stories, some soldiers even suggesting she and Trevon were lovers leading their future king into a trap.

Captain Jiles had punished a few, but still Cassara could sense them staring at her as she rode ahead. It took all of her will not to hide in the evenings but to mingle amongst the troops.

She tried to think of it as a game. To meet stares unflinchingly and let the soldiers lower their gaze before her. She had won every round, so far. The fact that she would eventually be their queen gave her a wonderful advantage. *I'll be their queen sooner than they think*, Cassara thought. She felt guilty for not telling Dayshon that his father breathed his last, but she respected his mother's wishes. Dayshon had more than enough to worry about right now.

He knew of the rumors and he showed his support of her every chance he could. Jiles kept near her and she could see him now as she walked near the troops, on the periphery of the camp. The horses were tethered nearby, stomping their legs anxiously. The restlessness affected everyone.

Cassara walked with her arms crossed around her, the night promising to be chilly. Graysword was tucked safely in the tent, and she wasn't worried for its safety, not with Trevon nearby.

Stopping near an old, desiccated tree, she leaned against it, now hidden from view from the troops as she stared out toward the Wall of Loss. The rays of sunset still broke through the Wall long after the sun had dipped below the horizon, beyond the Bloody Mountains, which formed the base of the Wall. Darkness had fallen on Graydon, but beyond the Wall, in Elihor, the sun still embraced the land, sending only a few rays to dance in the shimmer of magic.

Cassara stared at the Wall for a while, until she realized that it was now dark, the sun having been swallowed by Elihor. Yet she could still see the Wall of Loss, shimmering as brightly in the distance as it would in daylight, specks of dark purple and red dancing within it, reminding her of Avarielle's graceful movements. She felt as though she could reach out and touch the Wall, its magic like a fine mist that coated this land.

She jumped when Trevon appeared beside her.

"Apologies, Princess. But I wanted to tell you we have been spotted."

Cassara looked around quickly. "By whom?"

"My people, of course. They know we approach, and will be ready."

She nodded, seeing no reason to distrust him. "Have you informed my husband?"

"Not yet. I saw you first." He paused. "Perhaps it would be best if you returned to your tent, my lady, seeing as darkness has fallen on the land."

"Do you believe we are in danger of being attacked?"

Trevon scratched the back of his neck as he looked towards the horizon. "I can't say, to be honest. I would have said no even a few months ago, but we are so few..." He sighed. "I doubt they would, simply due to our number, but they will not welcome us tomorrow. And I'm not certain Graysword will be welcomed either."

Cassara looked towards the horizon, towards the Wall. Siabala's Rage was reputed to exist between the two worlds, under the Wall itself.

"What do we tell them of Avarielle?"

Trevon took a moment to answer, turning to face her, his eyes shining with moonlight and determination. "The truth, Cassara. That she found allies for the West. That she sent Graysword and me to prove their good intentions. And that she fights for us still, somewhere out there."

A lump forming in her throat, Cassara nodded. It was a truth she could embrace.

"Now let's go find your husband and see you safely to your tent, Lady Cassara."

"Tell me Trevon, is the Wall always lined with specks of purple and red? I have never seen it this close, before."

Trevon looked towards the Wall and then back at her as though weighing her sanity. It was a look she was growing accustomed to.

"It's white, princess, and it's impossible to see in the darkness, not from this far, anyway, and my eyes have been likened to those of an eagle."

Cassara looked towards the Wall, the white dancing with the purple and red, so vibrant it made her eyes water in the darkness until she had to look away. She could see more than Trevon, just as she had seen Delora's magic.

Her magic, or at least some piece of it, was still a part of her, she was certain.

But how do I tap into it without the amulet?

Or was this simply leftover power from her amulet, which would dissipate with time?

"Shall we go?" Trevon asked, eager to find Dayshon and tell him that scouts had found them. It hardly mattered though, as within a day they would reach the settlement, if it was still where Trevon indicated.

Cassara nodded and followed him back to camp, glancing back at the Wall of Loss, still as vibrant as before, except now she also noticed specs of black dancing amidst the glow.

"I am not staying behind, Dayshon." Cassara brought her horse up to his, staring stubbornly at him. They were far enough away that the men couldn't hear them.

"Cassara, it's for your own safety. We don't know what we'll be riding into."

"If it's that dangerous, then you shouldn't be going either. You are the heir, after all. It's your bloodline the kingdom is concerned with, not mine!"

Dayshon's eyes narrowed and Cassara thought she might have gone too far, but when he spoke his voice was calm and firm.

"You will stay here if I need to tie you to a tree myself."

Cassara raised an eyebrow. "You would tie your wife to a tree and leave her with an army of men? That seems reasonable to me."

Dayshon sighed and might have cracked a smile, though he hid it quickly.

She placed a hand on his arm.

"Dayshon, you need me there." He looked down at Graysword, and for a moment she thought he might take it from her. But instead, he called out.

"Trevon!"

The Westlander walked towards them. He had been looking with interest at the altercation.

"Trevon, how safe would it be for Cassara to ride in with us? What are the chances of our being attacked?"

Trevon shrugged. "I'm not sure, but I'm guessing not too great if you just go in with a diplomatic party. I'll be there, after all. Besides, if you are attacked, Westlanders don't attack unarmed women."

"I have Graysword with me," Cassara said.

Trevon gave her a half-smile. "Let me reword what I said. They don't attack women who are not warriors. You are many fine things, Princess Cassara, but a bloodthirsty warrior is not one of them."

"I'd care to agree with that," Dayshon said, apparently satisfied with Trevon's answer.

He looked Cassara in the eye. "If there is any sign of trouble, you turn around and head back to camp. Promise me that, and you can come."

"I promise," Cassara said, vowing to use her own definition of trouble. Dayshon was so skittish over her safety right now that someone looking at her the wrong way might be seen as trouble.

He nodded as though satisfied and pulled his horse around to head towards Jiles, who had gathered fifteen men for the expedition.

"Trevon," Cassara said. The warrior looked up with interest.

"If anything does happen, I need you to protect Dayshon. Not me, but my husband." Trevon raised an eyebrow, but he asked no question. "Please."

He pondered for a moment and nodded, though Cassara wasn't certain he would risk breaking a Grayloft oath to save Dayshon, despite Cassara's wishes.

But she had made a promise too, to keep Dayshon safe, to ensure Rashim's royalty was secured and the largest kingdom in Graydon would have a leader in the upcoming battle, no matter who the foe might prove to be.

As Trevon had suggested, Dayshon, Cassara, Jiles and himself left their horses and the extra guards within sight of the camp, but far enough away so as to not be a threat to the Westlanders. Jiles had fought to come with them, with such determination Cassara had been convinced it would come to blows. In the end Trevon had laughed and clapped the captain on the back, telling him to keep his temper in check if he was going to be of any use.

Jiles had made no promises.

They walked into the camp, and a beleaguered and battle-worn people greeted them, though fire and pride lit every movement. The women all seemed extremely capable of holding a sword, though none quite so tall and wiry as Avarielle, and none with hair quite as red in the sunlight. Cassara guessed that even amongst her people, the warrior stood out.

Their faces and skin were all sun worn, and men and women both walked around sporting weapons. Children played with wooden swords and bows that were small but real enough to hurt.

Several of them pointed to Cassara, her golden hair even more out of place here, shining brightly in the sunlight. She was glad she had opted to tie most of it up, to keep some of its length off her neck while still warding off the warmth of the summer sun.

The camp consisted of only a few houses, where an entire village had once stood. The buildings looked more eastern, unless Westland architecture was similar. A few tents had been scattered amongst the houses, and campfires set up generously around the encampment.

To ward off the darkness and its demons. Cassara felt a chill despite the summer heat.

A man was walking towards them, a sword that made Graysword seem tiny dangling from his back. Cassara couldn't imagine wielding it effectively in battle, though its bearer was well over six feet in height.

Trevon stepped forward to greet him, extending his hand, which the tall man warmly took.

"Breck, you old goat! Are you running the camp now?"

"Old goat? I'm younger than you, you useless swine! Ya, Bryson got himself killed, thank Eli." Trevon broke out laughing.

"Well, that's one blessing for our journey!"

Breck looked suspiciously towards the Eastlanders. "You bring the East to us, Trevon? I didn't expect that of you."

Trevon shrugged and turned to them. "They're here to help." He motioned them forward. "This is Prince Dayshon, heir to the throne of Rashim, traveled here to help and share resources, and this is his captain, Jiles."

Breck spit on the ground, as though annoyed, and before Trevon could introduce Cassara, Breck spoke up.

"We don't need Eastern *help.* The only thing the East has ever brought us was pain and death, but I'll be kind enough to let you run now before I gut you where you stand."

Dayshon took a step forward, his hand going to the pommel of his sword. Cassara quickly stepped in front of him, smiling warmly as she extended her hand to Breck.

"I am Princess Cassara, wife of Prince Dayshon, and it's a pleasure to meet you, kind sir."

Thrown off by her bold move, he took her hand and

shook it, Cassara trying not to wince as her hand was lost in his big one. She continued, smiling as though no ill-intended words had been spoken.

"I was a friend with someone you may know, Breck. Someone who asked me to help you."

"Oh?" he asked disinterestedly.

Cassara lost her smile as she spoke, her eyes holding his prisoner. "Avarielle Grayloft."

At the mention of the name, the camp grew so quiet you could hear individual specks of sand shifting in the wind. Cassara couldn't gauge if that was good or bad, but Trevon wasn't stopping her or stepping in, and she could only assume he wouldn't let her say something completely suicidal.

She hoped.

"She has given me a token to bring to you, with her good will." Cassara pointed to her horse, the gold of Graysword's pommel reflecting the light, the red jewel like fresh blood.

Breck looked questioningly at Trevon, who smiled broadly. "These are interesting times we live in, Breck. Now why not greet our guests properly. They have come a long way, and have yet to be shown some Westland hospitality!"

Breck hesitated, staring at Graysword and at the faces of his people. He then nodded and the two men shared a smile, leaving Cassara to wonder what exactly this Westland hospitality entailed.

2 2

Shirina stood in the middle of Lisal's teleportation circle. The flowers, fed by magic and not solely on the strength of the land, still shone vividly all around her. She clutched her staff, the wood strong and brimming with energy under her hand. She gazed at it, the ancient symbol of Graydon etched in by Grasky, carved quickly in the fresh wood. The same symbol which Cassara's amulet had mimicked.

Distracted for an instant, she thought of Cassara, wondering if the prince had found her. Shirina had tracked Cassara with her magic until she had sent Dayshon after her. Then it had become too tiring, and she had made peace with deserting the princess. After betraying the Grayloft, she doubted Cassara would want much to do with her, anyway.

She pushed back the thought of the princess. She

didn't need the distraction now. Cassara had sealed her fate the day she had chosen to follow the Grayloft, anyway. To each their own path.

She took a deep breath and focused, honing her will to the staff.

Standing in the midst of her gathering spell, she used the Sight. The energies around her seemed stable, swirling in a haze of magic.

A flutter danced in her stomach and she pushed it down, ignoring the fear. But she knew that if she couldn't control the staff or her powers, she could be lost forever, in the magical energies of Graydon.

But she had been practicing lesser spells for a week now, and the staff seemed to have heightened them, and didn't demand as much from her physically. Which was good, considering she had not managed to heal or stop the dark magic growing within her.

A dark magic that sapped her body's strength, and her hopes, as well.

There will be answers in Ravenhold, Shirina thought, keeping a close eye on the energies until they grew thick around her, the colors of the flowers swirling into the magic until the mists grew strong and silvery-white strands covered Shirina's entire world. Knowing her spell was set, Shirina willed herself to the keep, her body shimmering as it broke down into magic.

As always, she kept her eyes open, watching the world

vanish into a haze of light, as transitory as a winter storm, as temporary as morning dew.

The first time Shirina had teleported was the first time she had truly felt a part of something bigger. She could sense not only all of Graydon's magic, but also all of the points of contact. The hundreds of Circle adepts, half in Ravenhold, the other half spread throughout the world in outposts, in villages, some covert, some not, shining like bright lights on the canvas of Graydon.

Their connection to the magic was so strong that even when not using a spell, they still left a mark on the magical plane. And when someone teleported, each adept was like shimmers on it, a trembling of power over the land.

She had always seen a few, even though less than one hundred Circle adepts ever became skilled enough to use the advanced spell.

Today, she felt as though she had walked into a big, empty house. Only a few lights shone in Graydon, so steady that they indicated pre-cast spells, and not a person. People were unstable and so was their magic. They flickered.

These lights remained steady and unchanging. They were the remains of some outposts, or some spells, here and there. A few lights shone in the distance that she thought were people. Some in the South, others in the East. But they were untrained. They were the candidates for the next Harvest, not even understanding the potential they had. Perhaps they never would, now.

In the distance of Graydon she could see where the Wall began, shimmering red in the magical world.

Then another light caught her eye. Somewhere further west, at the edge of Rashim or in the wretched Westland land itself, a light shone brightly. Someone had a strong connection with the magic there, and Shirina wondered if another Crimson Circle or perhaps even an Elder had survived. She might find out, one day.

She turned away from it and towards Ravenhold, the keep's signal still the strongest in Graydon, though much weaker than it had once been.

Shirina could feel the staff in her hands and clutched it, her throat aching at what she saw. The keep had slithers of another magic dancing around it, like a snake tightening its grip on its ancient walls.

The snake was as black as the deepest night. The magic of Elihor herself.

Shirina could not tell what the magic was doing, but she doubted it meant good.

She crossed it, her body tingling with the magic, her mind reeling as she knew she would soon re-appear in the middle of a battleground of magic.

Her mind stilled itself as she prepared for the attack.

Sulfur.

As the magical weaves of her teleportation spell began to loosen and crumble around her, Shirina clenched the staff and summoned a defensive spell right away. There was no need to be caught unaware.

She regained sight as the mists vanished. She could sense or see nothing out of the ordinary. The magic which struggled against Ravenhold's defenses had not yet pierced inward, or its threat was so minimal that it didn't trigger any of her defenses.

Yet the smell of sulfur seemed to cling to the whole keep, so thick it left a burning sensation on her skin and made her eyes water.

It smelled of Siabala's Rage itself.

Delora...

Ravenhold had many teleportation circles to allow for its greater traffic, and Shirina had opted for a more concealed one, just in case. The keep was perfectly circular, up to the parapets on top, where resided the largest observatory in all of Graydon. Originally built to keep an eye on all activities along the Wall of Loss, it had also become a center of astral discovery as fears of the Wall failing dwindled with time.

It seemed those old fears had been well-founded, however.

Shirina walked confidently down the corridors of Ravenhold, casting her magic wards before her to ensure no monsters lay in wait. Magic maintained the old keep.

No signs of age marred its stone walls. The walls themselves seemed lit, explaining why no torches lined them. The rare commoner who visited Ravenhold believed magic lit the walls, as soft hues of green or blue danced in magical shimmers through the walls and corridors to light the steps of travelers.

Shirina used to always pause and analyze the keep itself, from its planning to its many secrets, but today she barely glanced at her old home. She walked purposefully through the passageways and down some stairs, crossing the familiar paths of her childhood.

She walked over plants that had once thrived on the energies of Graydon, now decayed and dying as the magic, if not the sunlight, was drained.

Shirina grazed the wall of a stairway with her fingers, feeling only a slight tingle of magic where before there would have been an explosion of light. The keep was losing whatever battle it still fought.

She reached one of the bottom floors and walked out into a vast room, a very large and dead oak tree gracing its center, shriveled leaves littering the floor. The walls shimmered, not with sunlight but with magic here. A weak magic compared to what it used to be. As Shirina stepped forward, the keep tried to follow her, to light her path, sending rays of greens, blues, and golds dancing around the oak tree as though mourning the loss of the majesty it had exuded when alive.

The light cast eerie shadows around her, on the

circular wall surrounding her, doors leading to Elders' studies. Away from the questions of the adepts and the drama of the sproutlings.

Shirina crossed the floor and reached a door.

Tangia's study.

She could sense the magical seals still in place, although others had tried to break them. Shirina smiled. Tangia was the best at wards, and any fool who thought they could break her seals deserved whatever magical punishment Tangia had set for trespassers.

Knowing how her teacher worked, Shirina cast a very small spell and sent it towards the door. The ward shot out and hit the spell, but the color of the counter-spell was her clue. Tangia had taught her spells as colors, and as long as you knew Tangia's system and were a trusted friend, you could easily enter.

Shirina wondered if anyone else knew Tangia's secrets. Her teacher had grown more detached from Circle activities, and one of the many theories Shirina had fostered about being sent after the Grayloft was that Tangia wanted to be alone, away from anyone who knew any of her secrets.

Even Circle Elders needed their personal space, especially after a lifetime of giving.

Shirina cast the correct counter-spell and the wards tumbled to the floor like rose petals, to vanish when they connected with the rays of light cast by the keep.

That was it. Shirina stared at the floor for a long time,

where the last of the strands of light had vanished, feeling as though she had destroyed all that remained of her teacher, in the final spell she had ever cast.

It was then that she noticed that the lights of the keep were spreading under Tangia's door, kept at bay by the ward spell but moments ago. And the light spell would only spread there for one reason.

Someone was in her mentor's room, and had been sealed in there by Tangia herself.

Someone, or something.

Staff at the ready, Shirina collected her magic, ready to cast an attack spell, and she opened the door to her mentor's old study.

The scent of human waste was so strong Shirina had to struggle not to gag.

It was easy to spot where the intruder was, the magic of the keep casting a weak light under them. Shielding her eyes, Shirina cast a strong spell of illumination towards the figure, and the room exploded with light.

A weak moan sounded. After her eyes adjusted, she could see someone huddled on the ground, the face covered by arms. Shirina approached the figure warily.

"Who are you?" she demanded, her staff held before her as she lessened the spell of light, which obviously hurt the person. If she had been trapped in the dark for months, she supposed light would hurt her, too.

"Who are you?" she asked again as she got closer. The figure was obviously male—a wasted old man. His clothes were little more than rags, and his skin paper thin and wrinkled.

"Why are you in Tangia's study?" Shirina asked, and at hearing the name of Tangia, the man moved his arms out of the way a bit.

He croaked something, and Shirina realized he was trying to speak, but hadn't used his voice in so long that it was worn from disuse.

"I promise I won't hurt you," she said, remaining standing and clutching the staff nonetheless. "Now please, try to answer me again."

"Tan…gia?" the man managed to whisper, his face still covered by his hands.

"Yes. She was my mentor and friend. I'm looking for answers into what happened to her."

"Took… her…" the old man managed to croak out.

"The Elders took her, I know."

"To… Siabala… Sulfur…"

Shirina's heart missed a beat as she whispered, "Yes, they sent her to Siabala's Rage, but I need to know why, exactly."

The old man seemed to ponder for a moment, and then he struggled to sit up, removing his arms from his face. But he looked down, as though in great thought, so Shirina could still not see his face. For all she knew, he was someone from the Circle. Perhaps even an Elder.

"Tangia…" His voice regained strength as he spoke. "Tangia was sent to Siabala's lair because of me."

"Why? What would the Circle possibly want with you, and why would she give her life for you?"

The old man looked up then, his cheeks sunken and his skin gray from months in this cell, but it was not that which made Shirina gasp.

What made her gasp were his eyes, without white, and as pure black as the heart of Elihor herself.

2 3

$\mathcal{A}$drenaline coursed through her muscles, each step unhesitating and bold as she approached the bridge that would bring her to Stormhold. The keep spread proudly before her, shimmering in the sunset and the Wall of Loss, a silent witness to stories long forgotten.

She could barely feel her body, worn down by wounds and the fatigue of travel. All that she felt was her pumping heart, thundering evenly and calmly in her chest, like a great war drum. The only one Avarielle needed.

The air was stale here, heavy with the burden of history, and Avarielle hated the smell of it. She would be glad to be gone.

She took the first step on the narrow stone bridge. There were no rails. To miss a step would be to die.

She didn't slow down, not caring about stealth. Knowing they were waiting for her, she had little time to waste on pretending she could sneak up on the keep. Two srocks flew up beside her on the bridge. Avarielle didn't pause as she pulled her last two throwing knives free, throwing them with inhuman accuracy into each of their eyes, the red magic of the creatures exploding from within as they plummeted down, Avarielle's bare arms singed by the fires.

She didn't bother stopping for that either, keeping her stride even, focused on entering the keep. The smell of rotten flesh rose, and Avarielle pulled her short sword free, swinging it as the first Elom charged towards her, screaming a very human scream as she ran him through and killed him.

"Please," one Elom spoke as he charged at her, surprising her for an instant as she parried his blow. "I can't control myself!"

I guess Eloms aren't quite the same while still in Elihor.

"Then consider yourself freed," Avarielle replied as she hacked his head off, not thinking of who it might have been, once.

It didn't matter. They were now monsters and the enemy.

Two more came at her, the same wild look in their eyes as they pleaded. She downed them both, the fatigue just starting to pierce through her anger. A child came towards her, his cheeks drowned in tears, and Avarielle hesitated an instant, which almost cost her an arm as the creature sliced into it.

She turned and made his death quick. Then, they stopped coming.

Avarielle cleaned her sword on one of the bodies and took a moment to rip the bottom part of her shirt and wrap it around her arm.

She kept walking and entered the keep, wondering what else Delora had in store for her, relishing the thought of running her through. For Kryde, and for his people.

She did not have to go far. The keep was dark and musty, but no dust covered its walls and an unnatural glow seemed to permeate everything.

I hate Circle magic. Clutching her sword, she walked forward, longing more than ever for the familiar feel of Graysword. Her family's ancestral blade would alert her of danger, and make quick business of it.

But it hardly mattered now. She had to keep moving, regardless of what she might encounter.

Avarielle entered a room and stopped for a moment, lowering her sword. The room itself seemed to have grown vines, which had snared people in their grasp. The vines had vicious thorns, which bled the imprisoned, a pool of crimson slick on the floor below her. Most of the blood seemed to be collected through holes at the base, and Avarielle was curious where it led, but part of her really didn't want to know.

There was no one left to save here, and they were not the reason she had come, in any case. She crossed the room, her boots sticking to the wet floor, the suction noises drawing even more attention to her presence. Not that it mattered. They already knew she was here.

She reached another door and went through it, glad the stench of blood and rot abated. Her eyes adjusted to the growing darkness and she could see cages lined these walls, of different sizes, all made of the same unbreakable stone as in Siabala's Rage.

A shiver ran down her spine.

She wasn't certain how she'd take down Delora, and Siabala was an even more impressive foe.

I'll figure that out when I have to, Avarielle peered into the cages, eyes looking back at her.

Dark eyes.

They were not quite Eloms, but half human, half monster. They were still changing, the skin baring patches of darkness, the bones crumbling under the weight of magic, the limbs elongating and fingers turning to claws. Avarielle wished she could afford the time and energy to free them. Even then, she couldn't be certain they wouldn't attack her, too.

Then a pair of eyes caught hers, and she recognized Pack Nacker, though he was more beast than man. He stood perfectly still, looking at her with a purpose. Then he pointed down the hall, towards another room.

Avarielle understood. Kryde was down there.

"I'll be back to free you," she said, and she could tell that he understood she didn't mean setting him free from his cage. If she could save Kryde, then she might give peace to his people.

To save its heir was to save the land.

Avarielle slowed as she entered the next room, magic tingling on her skin like a swarm of bugs. The sword felt woefully inadequate in her hands, but she held it loosely nonetheless, relaxing her grip for battle.

There was light here, a red tinge, and it reeked of sulfur. Avarielle knew Siabala lurked near, and she didn't bother crouching or pretending she could hide her presence from him. Although Stormhold might have been a Circle keep at some point, it was now firmly under Siabala's control.

In the center of the room was a deep hole that seemed to lead to Siabala's Rage itself, red embers shooting up from the depths like deep sighs, the heat so great Avarielle felt her sword's pommel slip in her sweat.

She heard a slight moan, and Avarielle turned to see Delora crumpled on the floor, tethered to the wall like a dog. The witch looked up at her, her eyes filled with venom as she opened her mouth to speak, but she only spat out blood. Avarielle realized with disgust that her tongue had been cut out, not too long ago.

The warrior firmed her grip on the blade. "I could let you live, Delora. That would be a worse punishment." She brought up the blade. "But I promised myself you would fall by my sword, and I keep my promises." Avarielle closed the gap between them and struck down, but before her blade could decapitate her, a shield of red magic appeared around the witch. Avarielle struck it hard, sending both her and her weapon flying to the ground.

She quickly stood up again, but two large booted feet stood on her short sword.

"I still have use for her, I fear."

Avarielle's hands turned to trembling fists at her side. Siabala stood before her, black teeth showing under his furled lips, his red eyes a sharp contrast to his gray skin. His muscles seemed to pulsate in the red light.

And then she noticed the man behind Siabala.

Kryde. His head lowered, his shoulders fallen, the pride that used to outline his every movement melted in the shadow of Siabala.

She hissed the words as she glared at Siabala. "What did you do to him?" Siabala grinned, showing crimson teeth.

"I wanted to try something different, and I made him perfect, for you. A soulless man who can only fight and obey."

Pulling her long knife free, Avarielle lunged at Siabala, but just as she came near, he reached out and grabbed her two wrists, which crunched under his hold. She refused to fall to her knees.

"Will you not bow?" Siabala mocked her. "But you are magnificent, as all your family is. See how taking one vow with me has given you so much power and strength?"

"What vow, you deformed lump of flesh?" she demanded as she gritted her teeth. "Let Kryde go!"

"You remember, child of Grayloft, though you may not want to." Siabala's laughter echoed in her mind, lunging into her memories and recalling another time she had heard it, but had not known it was him.

One minute she was standing in front of Siabala, full of rage and revenge, then suddenly she was back at home. She had been alone for over a year, practicing sword with Trevon as the Eloms increased in size and strength. She was getting better, her dancer's training translating into quick and certain footwork. And then came the time to fight Eloms.

One night, they had broken through. Her dance teacher, Eliya, had stood watch that night, an able warrior herself. She had been wounded, and Avarielle had rushed to her side, as had several others. Graysword seemed heavy in her hand back then. The night was cold, and her lungs ached from the run, and the blood rushed to her ears as she swung down on the first Elom, only to strike flesh, without the familiar flash of fire that had always greeted her brother's strikes.

Avarielle had pulled back, barely avoiding getting hit. Eliya tumbled under an Elom, grunting. Avarielle needed her magic. She needed the power to make a difference, remembering her brother's quick smile. And his dead body.

She screamed and struck, but still nothing happened.

And then she had heard the laugh and it had clicked within her like a candle long waiting to be lit suddenly flaring to life.

Blood. Graysword needed blood to lend its powers to a Grayloft. And Avarielle had answered the call, as thirsty as the cursed blade, killing the fighting men and women, and then the Eloms, as Graysword flashed across the night sky, the magic like lightning ripped through her entire body.

Eliya had died by her blow. Not by accident, but by choice. She had *chosen* to take the blood of innocents, to gain the locked powers of Graysword. Avarielle had blocked it from her mind until now, choosing exile over truth.

Avarielle's mind slipped back to the present, back to Siabala, and back to her promise.

"Your family took an oath a long time ago, Grayloft. But it wasn't to save Graydon. It was to have the power to kill Elihor. And you failed, and Graydon died, and history somehow twisted you into believing your sword existed for a greater purpose than to kill."

He brought her forward, her face close to his large mouth, his breath reeking of blood. "But I sent them to wake you, and the others. It's time for this sordid tale to end, and I need you to wake up!" He threw her to the ground and looked towards Kryde.

Kryde looked up, her heart breaking at the sight of two

red eyes filled with Siabala's magic. Their emptiness made her ache and pulse with anger.

"That you would love a descendant of Elihor is such irony it pains me. But don't worry, he now has more of me in him than he does her, so I allow you to have him."

"I can…have him?" Avarielle asked as she stood, trembling with grief and hatred, everything forgotten save Kryde's red eyes. She looked at Siabala and whispered one word.

"Die."

With that word she reached out to her magic with her entire being, calling for Graysword to come to her, to claim blood and avenge her fallen love.

No matter the cost.

Cassara was standing by the fire, enjoying some nearby dancing and politely sipping at the bitter ale. Beside her, Graysword suddenly began to glow. Before she could reach for it, the blade vanished in a streak of light, towards the Wall of Loss, the sky exploding with color.

The dancing stopped and everyone looked first to the Wall, which convulsed madly with red magic. Then they stared at Cassara, and she knew they too could see this magic.

She reached automatically for her amulet, a pit

growing in her stomach as her hand met only her own skin.

Shirina felt the blow like a knife to the gut. Something was terribly wrong.

Leaving the old man where she had found him, she ran up the keep, the lights of Ravenhold following her madly, as though dancing with her worry and echoing her fears.

The Wall of Loss.

Something was happening to the Wall of Loss!

Avarielle felt the blade before it landed in her hand, like a familiar friend greeting her warmly. The pommel appeared in a streak of magic, as red as Siabala's own magic, the jewel on its tip crimson with fury as it solidified in her grasp.

She tightened her hold, the sword like an extension of her as she summoned all of its powers and ran Siabala through, his flesh pliant as though welcoming the blade. Siabala took a step back, towards the pit, and smiled before vanishing, Graysword still in her grasp.

Delora screamed and familiar light blinded Avarielle.

Cassara's magic!

Siabala had activated it, using Delora as the carrier for

the amulet. Delora screamed as she burned, the smell of charred flesh briefly rising before vanishing again, destroyed just as quickly by the consuming magic.

Avarielle fell to her knees, Graysword clanging uselessly to the stone floor, Kryde's motionless feet within eyesight.

Then the light ended and the world above them cracked with energy, thunder ripping the sky as Stormhold shook at its very foundation.

Avarielle closed her eyes and hit the floor with her fist.

By summoning Graysword, she had given Siabala the last piece he had needed to bring down the Wall of Loss.

And she had not even cared.

2 4

Siabala stood on top of the Bloody Mountains, a name he was pleased the children of Graydon had adopted. He took a deep breath of fresh air. Of real fresh air. Around him the Wall crumbled, its magic lashing out at him, but no longer strong enough to contain him.

He threw his head back and laughed so hard tears ran down his cheeks. He had done it. Generations of manipulation and story building and, finally, he was free.

And now only the children of Graydon were left to pay.

He held up his hand and grasped a strand of nearby magic. He could see them both now, the light and darkness, intermingling again, creating the shadows of magic he had so loved.

But that had been so harmful to Graydon and Elihor.

Clutching one of Graydon's strands, he watched it

wriggle under his grasp. He looked out over Graydon, its forests still lush despite his attempts to kill them. But the magic had been terrified by his poisoning the ground, and had risen above it, like a mist over the land.

Just as Elihor's had done.

Like a carefully laid out patch of oil, waiting for the spark to light it. And he no longer had any reason not to, having collected all that had been needed.

Holding the strand, he snapped his fingers and ignited it, sending the same flash fire that had destroyed Elihor to claim Graydon.

He smiled and waited for the world to burn.

The Wall of Loss crumbled in the distance, the strands of magic like the great bricks that had sustained it, collapsing on the Bloody Mountains to vanish in explosions of light. The sky crashed with lightning and thunder, and eerie cries like a thousand wailing spirits pierced the night, the backlash of magic like tiny blades on their skin. And then all was silent, the horizon perfectly clear and free of magic.

Dayshon stepped up beside Cassara. He grabbed her hand. He was scared, too.

They waited. The Westland warriors stood at attention, as though not certain how their skills would be needed, but understanding that battle was afoot.

A few moments passed, the world having stopped breathing while waiting for what would happen next. And then it did.

Graydon caught on fire.

It began on the mountaintops, a string of white flames traveling so fast they would reach them within seconds. They consumed the few trees in their path, even the sand burning in their wake, the light so great it forced them to shield their eyes.

The magic ignited in the air and within Cassara, robbing her of breath as it screamed for her to wield it before the fires destroyed it, heart hammering as its plea increased.

She could feel her mother's warmth upon her chest, hearing the Traveler's Song all around her. The notes washed over her as energy grew within her, threatening to consume her.

The flames from the Bloody Mountains ripped toward them, fanning her own flames to life. She would perish by one or the other, and she made her choice, the music so loud it refused to be ignored, leaving her gasping for air.

She let go of Dayshon's hand and took a step forward.

"Behind me!" she shouted with such authority that everyone quickly obeyed.

Her hand to her empty chest, Cassara looked at the rising fires as they sped towards her, closing her eyes as she summoned the magic, holding out her hand as though it still held the amulet. Tears streamed down her cheeks as the magic finally answered.

Her magic rose as the fires slammed into her, ripping a cry from her and throwing her back.

She dug in her feet and pushed against the flames, knowing that she was all that now stood between the angry magic of Elihor and the people of Graydon. In the white flames before her, unable to distinguish hers from the flash fire, she swore she could see falling blossoms burning, and imagined Edoline burning in the magic's merciless wake.

I will not fail Edoline again! I will not lose!

She fought with all of her strength to maintain her shields, to control the fires, to stop them in any way she could. She was in Rockor again, fighting to protect the villagers, maintaining a wall of magic that could save them all.

Seventy-two souls. She had saved seventy-two then, and now she vowed to save all of Graydon.

She fell to her knees, but she would not lose. She sobbed, pain ripping through her body, leaving her raw. She could not let them down.

And then it was over.

As quickly as it had appeared, the magic was gone. Cassara let the darkness engulf her.

Shirina watched from atop Ravenhold, the keep shuddering with the passing of the Wall, as though sobbing with grief. Graydon's magic waited like a lake of oil to be lit, but then someone had stopped it.

She recognized the magic as Cassara's.

Leaning forward on the edge of the keep, her exposed hands on the cold stone, Shirina looked at the battle still raging for Ravenhold, the great black snake gaining in strength.

She looked up and, while Cassara had managed to stop the flash fire, she had not managed to stop the magic of Elihor. Shirina could see it, with her sorceress' eyes.

Like snakes, the strands of magic infiltrated the land, swallowing the light to turn it into a different strand of magic.

One that would kill us.

Shirina reached for her throat, where the dark patch continued to grow. She knew the magic would consume all of Graydon. And the entire Circle.

She clutched her staff, feeling it draw from the pure magic of Graydon, and watched as the Lisal Gardens were covered far away. She quickly walked to the middle of the roof, where the biggest circle of magic in Graydon slept.

Grasping the staff, she planted it firmly in the center and summoned a teleportation spell. She didn't think she could teleport so many and survive. An Elder had already perished attempting the feat. But Shirina might be able to, hoping the staff would provide her the strength she needed.

It didn't matter now. It didn't matter what happened to her. If this was her last spell, then more witches would survive than just her. She would see to that. And in the keep they would be safe for a time, while their skills grew.

She needed the remaining adepts to survive. The battle for Graydon was only just beginning.

Avarielle got back on her feet, Graysword in her hands. She stood before what remained of Kryde, his shoulders still slumped, as broken as his spirit.

Warm tears coated her cheeks. Without his spirit, there was nothing.

You got me out of Siabala's Rage, Kryde. That's a solid start to our union.

His laughter resonated in her memory. Strong. Alive. Warm.

I know you'd do the same, which heartens me.

She had promised to free him. And Avarielle Grayloft kept her promises, no matter how painful.

She firmly gripped Graysword, its magic coursing through her entire body as she screamed in grief and plunged the blade deep.

She had hit her mark. It had been quick.

She pulled Graysword free as his eyes closed and he

slumped to the ground, half-man and half-monster, his features so twisted she had to look away. She cleaned her blade, the blood black, yet the glimmer of crimson clinging to the metal. She doubted it would ever be clean again, and she didn't care.

Kryde was dead.

There had been no tender farewell. No time to tell him how much she loved him. No flicker of understanding in his red eyes as she had stabbed him through, no hint of what he was thinking or hoping, no final lingering caress on her face.

There had only been an ending.

And the acrid smell of burning flesh and death.

Graysword's magic continued coursing through her arm, reaching deep within her. She glanced down at her own body, numb, seeing Kryde's lifeless arm in her peripheral vision.

She wanted to throw up, to scream, to rip her own hair out, to close her eyes and never open them again.

Instead, she kept looking down, loosely holding her blade, wondering why her magic was still active.

Her heart caught in her throat as she fell to her knees. Graysword was only activated by Elihor's magic.

Maybe Kryde still lived! Maybe she had managed to bring his soul back, and Siabala had been wrong. The blade was not cursed with human blood, and it could save him, not just doom him!

She couldn't bear to look at him as she touched his arm, feeling for a pulse near his wrist. The flesh was clammy and already cold, without life, reminding her of dead fish. She pulled her hand away in disgust.

Yet Graysword's magic continued to dance within her, a dance she was not familiar with, as though it no longer followed her music, but the music of another.

It slithered within her uncomfortably, and a small sweat began to break on her brow. Her body felt like a stranger's, as though no longer her own.

The blade's magic was attacking her. But why would Graysword hurt her? She was not of Elihor!

And yet...slowly her mind retraced her steps, accepting what she had refused to even consider before now. The fatigue, the nausea...*Idiot!* She hit the ground with her fists and stayed on all fours as nausea washed over her, sudden and striking, originating from both her magic and her body.

Idiot! How could she have not seen? Not known!

How could she have not seen that she was pregnant?

Pregnant, with Kryde's child.

With the last heir of Elihor.

And that wielding her magic, created to destroy those of Elihor, could only lead to the child's death, and possibly her own.

Her blood pounding in her ears, she briefly wondered if she would choose life over revenge.

The final battle calls in Heirs of a Broken Land 3:
Sorceress of Shadows.